The Daffodil Case

RUSKIN BOND

The Daffodil Case

RUPA

Published by
Rupa Publications India Pvt. Ltd 2018
7/16, Ansari Road, Daryaganj
New Delhi 110002

Sales centres:
Allahabad Bengaluru Chennai
Hyderabad Jaipur Kathmandu
Kolkata Mumbai

ISBN: 978-81-291-5186-5

First impression 2018

10 9 8 7 6 5 4 3 2 1

Printed at Parksons Graphics Pvt. Ltd., Mumbai

CONTENTS

INTRODUCTION

I have been writing fiction for many years now. Creating those stories have been some of the most joyful moments of my life. But I must confess there has been real inspiration behind my fiction. People, towns, villages, homes, nature—I've been inspired by the whole lot.

This collection though is a thorough mix. A mix of some of the fiction I've written over the years, some anecdotes from my own life, and some stories that are tightly wrapped around history. This anthology has been put together to make you go through a range of emotions. Stories like 'The Skull', 'Toria and the Daughter of the Sun', 'An Evening at the Savoy H.H.', 'Dinner with Foster', 'Who Kissed Me in the Dark', 'Hassan, the Baker' and 'The Walker's Club' will hopefully leave you laughing your head off. 'Topaz', 'Wilson's Bridge' and 'A Fright in the Night' will spook you out. There are those which might make you feel a little sad or nostalgic, like the excerpt from *The Room on the Roof*, 'Gracie', 'Mrs Roberts', 'Death of a Familiar' and 'My Father's Trees in Dehra'. And stories that combine travel, history and my own experiences, such as 'The Lady of Sardhana', 'Ganga Descends' and 'The Road to Badrinath'. There is also a guest appearance by everybody's favourite—Sherlock Holmes.

But my collections are never complete without a few old-time heart-warming stories of leisure like—'Upon an Old World Dreaming', 'A Good Philosophy', 'Voting at Barlowganj', 'Once Upon a Mountain Time' and 'The Thief's Story'.

It is only through these stories that I put down on paper the many characters in my head, the idiosyncratic folks I encounter, my beloved trees, and old memories before they fade away… It is wonderful to have the freedom to write on anything that has taken one's fancy—whether it be daffodils, a skull, a Punjabi household, or a night with a ghost in a boarding school. And here I welcome you to enjoy these twenty-six stories that I hope will continue to display extraordinary vitality for generations of readers to come.

Ruskin Bond

THE THIEF'S STORY

I was still a thief when I met Romi. And though I was only fifteen years old, I was an experienced and fairly successful hand. Romi was watching a wrestling match when I approached him. He was about twenty-five and he looked easy-going, kind and simple enough for my purpose. I was sure I would be able to win the young man's confidence.

'You look a bit of a wrestler yourself,' I said. There's nothing like flattery to break the ice!

'So do you,' he replied, which put me off for a moment because at that time I was rather thin and bony.

'Well,' I said modestly, 'I do wrestle a bit.'

'What's your name?'

'Hari Singh,' I lied. I took a new name every month, which kept me ahead of the police and former employers.

After these formalities Romi confined himself to commenting on the wrestlers, who were grunting, gasping and heaving each other about. When he walked away, I followed him casually.

'Hello again,' he said.

I gave him my most appealing smile. 'I want to work for you,' I said.

'But I can't pay you anything—not for some time, anyway.'

I thought that over for a minute. Perhaps I had misjudged my man. 'Can you feed me?' I asked.

'Can you cook?'

'I can cook,' I lied again.

'If you can cook, then maybe I can feed you.'

He took me to his room over the Delhi Sweet Shop and told me I could sleep on the balcony. But the meal I cooked that night must have been terrible because Romi gave it to a stray dog and told me to be off.

But I just hung around, smiling in my most appealing way, and he couldn't help laughing.

Later, he said never mind, he'd teach me to cook. He also taught me to write my name and said he would soon teach me to write whole sentences and to add figures. I was grateful. I knew that once I could write like an educated person, there would be no limit to what I could achieve.

It was quite pleasant working for Romi. I made tea in the morning and then took my time buying the day's supplies, usually making a profit of two or three rupees. I think he knew I made a little money this way, but he didn't seem to mind.

Romi made money by fits and starts. He would borrow one week, lend the next. He kept worrying about his next cheque, but as soon as it arrived he would go out and celebrate. He wrote for the *Delhi* and *Bombay* magazines: a strange way to make a living.

One evening he came home with a small bundle of notes, saying he had just sold a book to a publisher. That night I saw him put the money in an envelope and tuck it under the mattress.

I had been working for Romi for almost a month and, apart from cheating on the shopping, had not done anything big in my real line of work. I had every opportunity for doing so. I could come and go as I pleased, and Romi was the most trusting person I had ever met.

That was why it was so difficult to rob him. It was easy for me to rob a greedy man. But robbing a nice man could be a problem. And if he doesn't notice he's being robbed, then all the spice goes out of the undertaking!

Well, it's time I got down to some real work, I told myself. If I don't take the money, he'll only waste it on his so-called friends. After all, he doesn't even give me a salary.

Romi was sleeping peacefully. A beam of moonlight reached over the balcony and fell on his bed. I sat on the floor, considering the situation. If I took the money, I could catch the 10.30 express to Lucknow. Slipping out of my blanket, I crept over to the bed.

My hand slid under the mattress, searching for the notes. When I found the packet, I drew it out without a sound. Romi sighed in his sleep and turned on his side. Startled, I moved quickly out of the room.

Once on the road, I began to run. I had the money stuffed into a vest pocket under my shirt. When I'd gotten some distance from Romi's place, I slowed to a walk and, taking the envelope from my pocket, counted the money. Seven hundred rupees in fifties. I could live like a prince for a week or two!

When I reached the station, I did not stop at the ticket office (I had never bought a ticket in my life) but dashed straight on to the platform. The Lucknow Express was just moving out. The train had still to pick up speed and I should have been able to jump into one of the compartments, but I hesitated—for some reason I can't explain—and I lost the chance to get away.

When the train had gone, I found myself standing alone on the deserted platform. I had no idea where to spend the night. I had no friends, believing that friends were more trouble than help. And I did not want to arouse curiosity by staying at one of the small hotels nearby. The only person I knew really well was the man I had robbed. Leaving the station, I walked slowly through the bazaar.

In my short career, I had made a study of people's faces after they had discovered the loss of their valuables. The greedy showed panic; the rich showed anger; the poor, resignation. But I knew that Romi's face when he discovered the theft would show only a touch of sadness—not for the loss of money, but for the loss of trust.

The night was chilly—November nights can be cold in northern India—and a shower of rain added to my discomfort. I sat down in the shelter of the clock tower. A few beggars and vagrants lay beside me, rolled up tight in their blankets. The clock showed midnight. I felt for the notes; they were soaked through.

Romi's money. In the morning, he would probably have given me five rupees to go to the movies, but now I had it all: no more cooking meals, running to the bazaar, or learning to write sentences.

Sentences! I had forgotten about them in the excitement of the theft. Writing complete sentences, I knew, could one day bring me more than a few hundred rupees. It was a simple matter to steal. But to be a really big man, a clever and respected man, was something else. I should go back to Romi, I told myself, if only to learn to read and write.

I hurried back to the room feeling very nervous, for it is much easier to steal something than to return it undetected.

I opened the door quietly, then stood in the doorway in clouded moonlight. Romi was still asleep. I crept to the head of the bed, and my hand came up with the packet of notes. I felt his breath on my hand. I remained still for a few moments. Then my fingers found the edge of the mattress, and I slipped the money beneath it.

I awoke late the next morning to find that Romi had already made the tea. He stretched out a hand to me. There was a fifty-rupee note between his fingers. My heart sank.

'I made some money yesterday,' he said. 'Now I'll be able to pay you regularly.'

My spirits rose. But when I took the note, I noticed that it was still wet from the night's rain.

So he knew what I'd done. But neither his lips nor his eyes revealed anything.

'Today we'll start writing sentences,' he said.

I smiled at Romi in my most appealing way. And the smile came by itself, without any effort.

GRACIE

Show me the way to go home,
I'm tired and I want to go to bed,
I had a little drink but an hour ago,
And it's gone right to my head...

A group of British soldiers, a little drunk, were singing in the middle of the road. It was almost midnight. And yes, it was World War II. But it wasn't a street in Paris or Naples or Rangoon—it was Rajpur Road in Dehradun, then a small town tucked away in the Doon Valley some 200 miles north of New Delhi.

The soldiers were on leave. Not home leave, because they were still far from home—but a break from active duty on the warfront, from the fighting in Burma and the Far East. Dehradun had been designated a 'recreational centre' for Allied troops. Unfortunately, we in Dehra could provide little by way of recreation for these restless young men, who were looking for something more than food and drink.

Coming down the street from the other end of town were a group of American soldiers. They too were engaged in a sing-song. 'Sweet Rosie O'Grady' or something very Irish. They had more money to throw around, as they were better paid than the British soldiers. There was no love lost between these 'allies'. Someone made an insulting gesture and remark, and soon there was a brawl in the middle of the road.

Looking down at them from the balcony of our flat above the road, I asked my mother: 'Has World War III begun?'

'It looks like it,' she said.

'Who's winning?'

A couple of soldiers were already flat on the ground.

'The military police. Here they come!'

A jeep-load of military police, British and American, drove up, and showed their solidarity in the midst of hostilities by rounding up the drunken brigade and carrying them off to barracks.

Silence descended on Rajpur Road, and I went back to bed.

◆

It was the winter of 1944–45, a few months after I'd lost my father, and I was back in Dehra for the winter holidays. My mother and stepfather were always moving from one house or flat to another (usually under pressure from the landlord), and that year we had a flat in Astley Hall, right in the centre of town.

Astley Hall and its environs were having something of a boom during the war years, due mainly to the presence of several thousand Allied troops stationed outside Dehradun. Casinos, cafes and dance halls had sprung up in this otherwise sedate centre of town, and every evening they would be filled to capacity with rowdy roistering soldiers who had survived the fighting but who might well have to return to active duty before long.

To avoid bar fights and street brawls, the Americans were allowed into town three days a week, the British three days a week, and the Italian prisoners of war once a week.

The Italians were the best behaved. They were, after all, war prisoners and confined to a prison camp six days in the week. Nor did they have money to throw around, so they made a little pocket money by selling postage stamps and handmade toys.

The American soldiers had unlimited supplies of chewing gum, and these they distributed freely amongst the children of the locality. Naturally this made them the most popular of the visiting soldiers.

The British did not have much to offer by way of surplus rations, but one young corporal, more educated than his fellows, gave me three well-thumbed paperbacks in the Collins Crime Club Series, and through them I made my first acquaintance with the works of Agatha Christie, Edgar Wallace and Peter Cheyney. As a result I became a lifelong addict of crime novels.

This same young corporal took more than a casual interest in one of our neighbours, a girl called Gracie, who lived in the next flat with her elder sister, a schoolteacher. Gracie was just seventeen or eighteen, a very pretty girl of mixed English, Portuguese, Burmese and Indian descent. A terrific combination of genes and hereditary traits. And physically she had inherited the best of all worlds. No one could have been lovelier. Coffee-coloured, sloe-eyed, with glossy black hair and full inviting lips, she had only to walk down the street for heads to turn in her direction. At ten, I was madly in love with her.

Gracie had a good singing voice—sweet and low and a little husky—and she had been engaged by bandmaster Billy Cotton to sing a few numbers during the late evening dances and cabaret shows at the Casino, Dehra's very own 'night club'. We had never had a night club before the war, and as far as I know there hasn't been one after Independence—not yet, anyway. But in those jolly wartime years, with everyone panting for a little pleasure, the Casino provided music, dance, food and drink, and a 'magic show'.

For the Casino was owned by 'Mustafa Pasha' (real name Roshan Kapoor), one of the country's foremost conjurers and magicians.

Every evening, for an hour, he'd put on a magic show, doing card tricks, taking rabbits out of hats, paper streamers out of his mouth, and egg out of his customers' pockets. He climaxed it by sawing his teenaged daughter in half. She was none the worse for it, naturally.

When the magic show was over, the singing and dancing commenced, and so did the boozing. By midnight the place was in an uproar, chairs flying about, tables overturned, one or two soldiers flat on their backs—knocked out by drink or one of their comrades. The enemy would have loved it.

Gracie would evade the last lurching warrior, slip out from beneath his grasping arms, and leave the Casino by the back entrance. One of the cooks, a local boy, would escort her home.

Gracie received two hundred rupees a month for singing to the troops, which was what her sister got for teaching little children to read and write. Gracie sang at a night club, her sister (I forget her name) taught at a convent. And yet, Gracie was the brighter of the two. She had more conversation, more wit, more joie-de-vivre.

And we had one thing in common—we both enjoyed chaat.

Every evening a chaat-wallah would come around to the Astley Hall shops and flats, preparing chaat on the spot. Served on large green leaves, the chaat and kachalu, flavoured with lemon juice, tamarind juice, chillies and garam masala, was almost an addiction. I did not always have enough pocket money, cheap though it was, but Gracie would call me over and make sure I had as much chaat as I could consume. Corporal Allen did not approve of the chaat, but would occasionally give me a rupee and tell me to run off and buy toffees, so that he could have Gracie to himself for ten or fifteen minutes. I did not care for toffees, but I would keep the rupee and come back after five minutes to find them kissing on the verandah.

The corporal was a little too refined for the Casino, and contented himself with taking Gracie to the pictures. We had three cinemas showing English or American films—the Orient, the Odeon and the Hollywood. Once Gracie took me to the pictures—it was a sentimental drama called *Always in My Heart*— and we held hands throughout the show. I had got the better of Corporal Allen that day.

At the Casino, Gracie sang sentimental ballads such as 'Smoke Gets in Your Eyes' and 'White Christmas', and although Dehra did not get a white Christmas, we got a white New Year on the evening of 31 December.

My mother was in bed, having that week given birth to my baby brother. I was knocking a football around on the parade ground with Bhim and Ranbir and some of the local boys when, to everyone's delight and consternation, it began to snow. As far as we knew it had never snowed in Dehra, so it was a unique, almost freakish event. We ran about, shouting in excitement while it continued snowing, so that by late evening the town was covered with a glistening white mantle. I ran home, breathless with excitement, and told my mother it was snowing outside.

'Don't try to make a fool of me,' she said 'I'm not in the mood for your silly jokes.'

So I went outside and broke off a branch of the litchi tree. The leaves were covered with snow. I took indoors and showed it to my mother, and she said, 'the last time it snowed here was around forty years ago—1905, the year your grandparents were married. It was snowing outside St Thomas Church just as they were taking their marriage vows.'

'They must have seen it as a good sign,' I said.

'Well, they were married for thirty years until your grandfather died.'

'And they had lots of children.'

'Five girls and one spoilt brat of a boy—your Uncle Ken. But I was the youngest and they spoilt me too.'

◆

That night, New Year's Eve, there was a grand dance at the Casino, and Gracie persuaded my mother to allow me to go along with her. I was to sit in a corner of the dance hall and avoid fraternizing with the partying soldiers.

It was an eventful evening. The snowfall had made New Year's Eve even more special, and the dance hall was crowded, mostly with high-spirited soldiers, but there were also a few of the local gentry and their families.

Mustafa Pasha, uttering magical incantations, went through his usual routine, which was always popular—and this was followed by three or four sentimental ballads sung by Gracie to the accompaniment of Billy Cotton's four-piece band. Gracie wasn't a great singer, but her freshness, energy and sensuality always brought the house down—as it did that New Year's Eve.

I had a small table to myself in a corner of the dance hall, and Gracie saw to it that I was well-supplied with my favourite fish fingers, chips, gulab jamuns, and Vimto—the last, a raspberry-flavoured soft drink that was very popular during the war years. Whatever happened to Vimto? Killed off, no doubt, by all the colas and fizzy drinks that came in later.

Between songs, Gracie would come over to see if I was all right. I must have been the only boy in a roomful of adults.

The soldiers whistled and called to Gracie to come over to their table for a change, but she simply smiled good-naturedly and went back to the rostrum to give a fair imitation of Lena Horne. She had the same sultry presence as the famous blues singer.

At midnight the lights went out and everyone began to sing 'Auld Lang Syne'.

> Should old acquaintance be forgot
> And never brought to mind?...
> We'll drink a cup of kindness yet,
> For auld lang syne...

Gracie was standing beside me, singing, and I stood up and took her hand. I loved listening to her singing. My own voice was ragged and tuneless and I thought it best not to inflict it on others.

'Come, Ruskin, give me a kiss,' said Gracie, leaning over me, and I suddenly found my lips pressed against hers in what was, till then, the most magical moment of my life. It was the first time I'd been kissed full on the lips, and I wanted that kiss to go on forever.

But the lights came on, and we drew apart, and everyone shouted 'HAPPY NEW YEAR!' The band struck up again and Gracie sang 'The White Cliffs of Dover', which made the British soldiers very maudlin and homesick.

At two in the morning I accompanied Gracie back to our adjoining flats, but there were no further kisses, as by then we had been joined by Corporal Allen who had missed the party but had turned up to escort us home. I found myself fervently wishing that he'd be sent back to Burma or wherever the fighting was going on.

◆

I have to admit that Gracie did not see me in the same romantic light that I saw her. She looked upon me as a younger brother, and treated me with the openness and light-hearted affection that she would have bestowed on a brother, had there been one.

'Press my back, will you, Ruskin?' she pleaded more than once. 'I can hardly stand straight.'

Most willingly did I oblige, knowing full well that I would not have been assigned this delicious task had I been an adult. I might well have grown up to be a physiotherapist had my holidays not come to an end.

On more than one occasion Gracie changed her dress in front of me, and I saw her lovely breasts and supple waist and thighs as she studied herself in the mirror, almost oblivious of my presence.

I noticed a long scar on her lower abdomen and asked her how she'd got it.

'Oh, when I was in school up in Mussoorie,' she said. 'Dr Butcher removed my appendix.'

'Dr Butcher! Was he a butcher or a doctor?'

'He was the civil surgeon. And he had a thing about appendixes. If you went to him with a tummy ache, he cut you open and took out your appendix. He said it was at the root of all our problems! He had so much difficulty finding mine that he had to make an extra-large cut.'

'Can I touch it?'

'Of course. It doesn't hurt now.'

I ran my finger along her scar. I found it quite thrilling to be touching her like that.

'You don't have to stop at the scar,' said Gracie with a laugh. 'You can touch other places too.'

But I was too shy to be making further explorations. For a ten-year-old, the scar was more fascinating than her hips or her navel. But it put me on terms of close familiarity. Even Corporal Allen hadn't seen her scar, or so she assured me!

◆

My boarding school was in Simla, a day and a night's train journey from Dehra, so when my three-month-long winter holidays were over and I returned to school, I knew it would be nine long months before I came home to Dehra.

In that time a lot could happen, and it generally did. For one thing, the war ended and all the soldiers went home—to England or America or wherever they'd come from. A few war brides went with them. A few illegitimate children were left behind in various countries. Also, everyone knew that India's independence was just around the corner, and the Anglo-Indians and the 'country-born' British were beginning to pack their bags.

When I came home to Dehra in the winter of 1945–46, the Casino, the dance hall and cafes had vanished, and the town was going through something of a slump.

'Where's Gracie?' I asked my mother, as soon as I was home.

'Gracie's in England. She married that baby-faced Corporal who used to hang around her all the time. But her sister's still here, teaching at the convent. Do you want some help with your maths?'

'No.' There was nothing romantic about maths.

Mustafa Pasha was missing too. He had moved to Bombay, where he was making a fortune.

I can't say I missed anyone very much. At eleven, I had my priorities, and they were the four Cs—the cinemas, comics, chaat and Crime Club thrillers, all in that order. With the exception of the chaat, I had, till then, absorbed very little of Indian culture. It was the same with most Anglo-Indian boys of my age. They went to hill schools and came home to railway colonies and

Saturday night dance parties. Some of them excelled at hockey and made it to the Olympics. I played football and occasionally cricket, and the boys I played with were the children of Indian shopkeepers or clerks—boys who, when they grew up, would be the backbone of the prosperous middle class.

Sometimes I accompanied Bhim or Ranbir to a Hindi movie, but most the time I haunted English cinemas which were still running, although to smaller audiences.

Dehra–Simla, Simla–Dehra, and the years slipped by, and before I knew it I was a young man just out of school and without any prospects. I suppose I could have gone to the local college, or joined the army (the truly Indian Army, the British having left three years previously), or possibly got a job on a tea estate; but none of these prospects thrilled me. I wanted to be a happy writer, even though readers were in short supply in 1950s India.

Sensibly, my mother packed me off to the United Kingdom. I had to take a job there, of course. There was no one to see me through a college or university. Even the Regent Street polytechnic was beyond my means. In any case, I was not interested in acquiring a degree. Any kind of work would do, provided I could sit down in my bedsitter over the weekends, sometimes at night, and work on the novel that I had resolved to finish.

For three months I worked in a grocery store, then moved up in the social hierarchy by taking a job as an accounts clerk in a firm making photographic goods and accessories. It was boring work—simple arithmetic, really—but it allowed my mind to wander in various other directions. And the pay packet, a basic wage of five pounds a week, covered my living expenses.

It was a lonely life. Every evening I would return to my cold and silent room, turn on the gas, make myself a marmite sandwich, and sit down to work on my literary opus.

Just occasionally I would go to a cinema or theatre, or take a meal in a cheap restaurant. Sometimes, late at night, I would walk about the city—London's streets were comparatively safe in those days, although occasionally there were gang fights and hold-ups.

The prostitutes would stand, as they always did, every ten yards down the left-hand side of the road, keeping to fixed pitches for the sale of their overripe wares. It was difficult to find one who was under thirty.

Whenever I came out of a cinema in the Piccadilly area, I would walk past them, feigning indifference; but I would steal covert glances at these women, hoping to see someone young and pretty. Late one evening, as I passed a young woman who was a little different from the others—sultry-looking, with Asiatic features—I stopped and looked back, and she smiled and gave me the usual line: 'Come along, darling, I'll give you a good time.' And summoning up a little courage, I went along, hoping for a good time the first time.

She took me down a side street, to a seedy-looking lodging house, and up some stairs to her room.

I tried fondling her, stroking her breasts, but she said there wasn't time for all that. She pulled up her dress. She had varicose veins—probably from too much street-walking. She pulled down her knickers, and that was when I saw the scar.

I could not have mistaken the scar—Dr Butcher's over-eager attempt to locate an appendix.

'Gracie?' I stammered.

She looked hard at me then, and recognition flooded her painted face. Under the heavy make-up, it was Gracie. And I was no longer a ten-year-old. I was an awkward young man trying to prove his manhood.

Desire had died in me the minute I recognized the girl I used to know; all the freshness and romance and youth had vanished, leaving her a well-paid chattel for the gratification of lonely, loveless men.

And all I could say was, 'What happened to Corporal Allen?'

Well, it appeared that Corporal Allen had ditched Gracie soon after they had arrived in Britain. He had been posted in West Berlin, where he had taken up with a fräulein. Gracie had tried to put her talents as a singer to good use, but torch singers were cheaper by the dozen, and she was unable to break into show business. She spent a year working in a garment factory on a basic wage. An engaging young pimp had persuaded her and a couple of other attractive girls to join a West End brothel, and there she was now, still fighting fit although a little battle worn. But she had saved some money.

'In a year or two I'll retire from this racket and start a little boarding house near the sea. Down on the south coast. It's warmer there. I do miss India, though. How's my sister?'

'She's fine. Might start her own school soon. Don't you write to her?'

'Will do, one of these days.'

I got up to leave. I might have had a crush on Gracie when I was a boy, but I couldn't possibly make love to her now. It would be like having sex with a close relative.

'You don't have to go,' she said. 'We can sit and talk.'

'You must have other engagements.'

'No,' she said. 'As soon as you've gone I'll be out on the streets again, trying to hook someone.'

'You're a good hooker. You hooked me all right.'

She laughed then. And her laughter was still the same—unforced, genuine. Some things don't change.

'Is this your first time, then?'

I nodded. 'You were the only girl on the street who had any appeal for me. Perhaps, subconsciously, I recognized you. But it was only when I saw that old scar of yours that I *knew…*'

'And now?'

'No, not now. I couldn't.'

'But you'll come again?'

'We'll meet again.'

There was a loud knocking on the door.

'My landlady,' said Gracie, and went to the door. A formidable-looking madam was waiting outside.

'You've been a long time, dearie.' She looked me up and down. 'Just out of school, too, by the looks of him.'

'He's just leaving.'

'And there's a gentleman in my parlour who's asking for you. Seems he took a fancy to you the last time he was here. Oldish, but well-heeled.'

'I'll be down in a jiffy.'

Gracie gave me a hug and kissed me on the cheek. As I stepped into the street, the strains of an old song floated after me. It came from someone's record-player in one of the apartments. Vera Lynn. But it might have been Gracie…

> We'll meet again,
> Don't know where
> Don't know when,
> But we'll meet again,
> Some sunny day…

We never met again. Life took me in another direction. It usually does. But I hope Gracie saved enough to start a little boarding house in some sunny seaside resort. She deserved something better than a brothel.

THE ROOM ON THE ROOF
(AN EXCERPT)

The afternoon was warm and lazy, unusually so for spring; very quiet, as though resting in the interval between the spring and the coming summer. There was no sign of the missionary's wife or the sweeper boy when Rusty returned, but Mr Harrison's car stood in the driveway of the house.

At sight of the car, Rusty felt a little weak and frightened; he had not expected his guardian to return so soon and had, in fact, almost forgotten his existence. But now he forgot all about the chaat shop and Somi and Ranbir, and ran up the verandah steps in panic.

Mr Harrison was at the top of the verandah steps, standing behind the potted palms.

The boy said, 'Oh, hullo, sir, you're back!' He knew of nothing else to say, but tried to make his little piece sound enthusiastic.

'Where have you been all day?' asked Mr Harrison, without looking once at the startled boy. 'Our neighbours haven't seen much of you lately.'

'I've been for a walk, sir.'

'You have been to the bazaar.'

The boy hesitated before making a denial; the man's eyes were on him now, and to lie Rusty would have had to lower his eyes—and this he could not do...

'Yes, sir, I went to the bazaar.'

'May I ask why?'

'Because I had nothing to do.'

'If you had nothing to do, you could have visited our neighbours. The bazaar is not the place for you. You know that.'

'But nothing happened to me...'

'That is not the point,' said Mr Harrison, and now his normally dry voice took on a faint shrill note of excitement, and he spoke rapidly. 'The point is, I have told you never to visit the bazaar. You belong here, to this house, this road, these people. Don't go where you don't belong.'

Rusty wanted to argue, longed to rebel, but fear of Mr Harrison held him back. He wanted to resist the man's authority, but he was conscious of the supple malacca cane in the glass cupboard.

'I'm sorry, sir...'

But his cowardice did him no good. The guardian went over to the glass cupboard, brought out the cane, flexed it in his hands. He said, 'It is not enough to say you are sorry, you must be made to feel sorry. Bend over the sofa.'

The boy bent over the sofa, clenched his teeth and dug his fingers into the cushions. The cane swished through the air, landing on his bottom with a slap, knocking the dust from his pants. Rusty felt no pain. But his guardian waited, allowing the cut to sink in, then he administered the second stroke, and this time it hurt, it stung into the boy's buttocks, burning up the flesh, conditioning it for the remaining cuts.

At the sixth stroke of the supple malacca cane, which was usually the last, Rusty let out a wild whoop, leapt over the sofa and charged from the room.

He lay groaning on his bed until the pain had eased.

But the flesh was so sore that he could not touch the place where the cane had fallen. Wriggling out of his pants, he examined his backside in the mirror. Mr Harrison had been most accurate: a thick purple welt stretched across both cheeks, and a little blood trickled down the boy's thigh. The blood had a cool, almost soothing effect, but the sight of it made Rusty feel faint.

He lay down and moaned for pleasure. He pitied himself enough to want to cry, but he knew the futility of tears. But the pain and the sense of injustice he felt were both real.

A shadow fell across the bed. Someone was at the window, and Rusty looked up.

The sweeper boy showed his teeth.

'What do you want?' asked Rusty gruffly.

'You hurt, chotta sahib?'

The sweeper boy's sympathies provoked only suspicion in Rusty.

'You told Mr Harrison where I went!' said Rusty.

But the sweeper boy cocked his head to one side, and asked innocently, 'Where you went, chotta sahib?'

'Oh, never mind. Go away.'

'But you hurt?'

'Get out!' shouted Rusty.

The smile vanished, leaving only a sad frightened look in the sweeper boy's eyes.

Rusty hated hurting people's feelings, but he was not accustomed to familiarity with servants; and yet, only a few minutes ago, he had been beaten for visiting the bazaar where there were so many like the sweeper boy.

The sweeper boy turned from the window, leaving wet

fingermarks on the sill; then lifted his buckets from the ground and, with his knees bent to take the weight, walked away. His feet splashed a little in the water he had spilt, and the soft red mud flew up and flecked his legs.

Angry with his guardian and with the servant and most of all with himself, Rusty buried his head in his pillow and tried to shut out reality; he forced a dream, in which he was thrashing Mr Harrison until the guardian begged for mercy.

■

In the early morning, when it was still dark, Ranbir stopped in the jungle behind Mr Harrison's house, and slapped his drum. His thick mass of hair was covered with red dust and his body, naked but for a cloth round his waist, was smeared green; he looked like a painted god, a green god. After a minute he slapped the drum again, then sat down on his heels and waited.

Rusty woke to the sound of the second drum-beat, and lay in bed and listened; it was repeated, travelling over the still air and in through the bedroom window. *Dhum!*... A double-beat now, one deep, one high, insistent, questioning... Rusty remembered his promise, that he would play Holi with Ranbir, meet him in the jungle when he beat the drum. But he had made the promise on the condition that his guardian did not return; he could not possibly keep it now, not after the thrashing he had received.

Dhum-dhum, spoke the drum in the forest; *dhum-dhum*, impatient and getting annoyed...

'Why can't he shut up,' muttered Rusty, 'does he want to wake Mr Harrison...'

Holi, the festival of colours, the arrival of spring, the rebirth of the new year, the awakening of love, what were these things to him, they did not concern his life, he could not start a new life, not for one day...and besides, it all sounded very primitive, this throwing of colour and beating of drums...

Dhum-dhum!

The boy sat up in bed.

The sky had grown lighter.

From the distant bazaar came a new music, many drums and voices, faint but steady, growing in rhythm and excitement. The sound conveyed something to Rusty, something wild and emotional, something that belonged to his dream-world, and on a sudden impulse he sprang out of bed.

He went to the door and listened; the house was quiet, he bolted the door. The colours of Holi, he knew, would stain his clothes, so he did not remove his pyjamas. In an old pair of flattened rubber-soled tennis shoes, he climbed out of the window and ran over the dew-wet grass, down the path behind the house, over the hill and into the jungle.

When Ranbir saw the boy approach, he rose from the ground. The long hand-drum, the dholak, hung at his waist. As he rose, the sun rose. But the sun did not look as fiery as Ranbir who, in Rusty's eyes, appeared as a painted demon, rather than as a god.

'You are late, mister,' said Ranbir, 'I thought you were not coming.'

He had both his fists closed, but when he walked towards Rusty he opened them, smiling widely, a white smile in a green face. In his right hand was the red dust and in his left hand the green dust. And with his right hand he rubbed the red dust on Rusty's left cheek, and then with the other hand he put the green dust on the boy's right cheek; then he stood back and looked at Rusty and laughed. Then, according to the custom, he embraced the bewildered boy. It was a wrestler's hug, and

Rusty winced breathlessly.

'Come,' said Ranbir, 'let us go and make the town a rainbow.'

.

And truly, that day there was an outbreak of spring.

The sun came up, and the bazaar woke up. The walls of the houses were suddenly patched with splashes of colour, and just as suddenly the trees seemed to have burst into flower; for in the forest there were armies of rhododendrons, and by the river the poinsettias danced; the cherry and the plum were in blossom; the snow in the mountains had melted, and the streams were rushing torrents; the new leaves on the trees were full of sweetness, the young grass held both dew and sun, and made an emerald of every dewdrop.

The infection of spring spread simultaneously through the world of man and the world of nature, and made them one.

Ranbir and Rusty moved round the hill, keeping in the fringe of the jungle until they had skirted not only the European community but also the smart shopping centre. They came down dirty little side-streets where the walls of houses, stained with the wear and tear of many years of meagre habitation, were now stained again with the vivid colours of Holi. They came to the Clock Tower.

At the Clock Tower, spring had really been declared open. Clouds of coloured dust rose in the air and spread, and jets of water—green and orange and purple, all rich emotional colours—burst out everywhere.

Children formed groups. They were armed mainly with bicycle pumps, or pumps fashioned from bamboo stems, from which was squirted liquid colour. The children paraded the main road, chanting shrilly and clapping their hands. The men and women preferred the dust to the water. They too sang, but their chanting held a significance, their hands and fingers drummed the rhythms of spring, the same rhythms, the same songs that belonged to this day every year of their lives.

Ranbir was met by some friends and greeted with great hilarity. A bicycle pump was directed at Rusty and a jet of sooty black water squirted into his face.

Blinded for a moment, Rusty blundered about in great confusion. A horde of children bore down on him, and he was subjected to a pumping from all sides. His shirt and pyjamas, drenched through, stuck to his skin; then someone gripped the end of his shirt and tugged at it until it tore and came away. Dust was thrown on the boy, on his face and body, roughly and with full force, and his tender, under-exposed skin smarted beneath the onslaught.

Then his eyes cleared. He blinked and looked wildly round at the group of boys and girls who cheered and danced in front of him. His body was running mostly with sooty black, streaked with red, and his mouth seemed full of it too, and he began to spit.

Then, one by one, Ranbir's friends approached Rusty.

Gently, they rubbed dust on the boy's cheeks, and embraced him; they were like so many flaming demons that Rusty could not distinguish one from the other. But this gentle greeting, coming so soon after the stormy bicycle-pump attack, bewildered Rusty even more.

Ranbir said, 'Now you are one of us, come,' and Rusty went with him and the others.

'Suri is hiding,' cried someone. 'He has locked himself in his house and won't play Holi!'

'Well, he will have to play,' said Ranbir, 'even if we break the house down.'

Suri, who dreaded Holi, had decided to spend the day in

a state of siege; and had set up camp in his mother's kitchen, where there were provisions enough for the whole day. He listened to his playmates calling to him from the courtyard, and ignored their invitations, jeers, and threats; the door was strong and well-barricaded. He settled himself beneath a table, and turned the pages of the English nudists' journal, which he bought every month chiefly for its photographic value.

But the youths outside, intoxicated by the drumming and shouting and high spirits, were not going to be done out of the pleasure of discomfiting Suri. So they acquired a ladder and made their entry into the kitchen by the skylight.

Suri squealed with fright. The door was opened and he was bundled out, and his spectacles were trampled.

'My glasses!' he screamed. 'You've broken them!'

'You can afford a dozen pairs!' jeered one of his antagonists.

'But I can't see, you fools, I can't see!'

'He can't see!' cried someone in scorn. 'For once in his life, Suri can't see what's going on! Now, whenever he spies, we'll smash his glasses!'

Not knowing Suri very well, Rusty could not help pitying the frantic boy.

'Why don't you let him go?' he asked Ranbir. 'Don't force him if he doesn't want to play.'

'But this is the only chance we have of repaying him for all his dirty tricks. It is the only day on which no one is afraid of him!'

Rusty could not imagine how anyone could possibly be afraid of the pale, struggling, spindly-legged boy who was almost being torn apart, and was glad when the others had finished their sport with him.

All day Rusty roamed the town and countryside with Ranbir and his friends, and Suri was soon forgotten. For one day, Ranbir and his friends forgot their homes and their work and the problem of the next meal, and danced down the roads, out of the town and into the forest. And, for one day, Rusty forgot his guardian and the missionary's wife and the supple malacca cane, and ran with the others through the town and into the forest.

The crisp, sunny morning ripened into afternoon.

In the forest, in the cool dark silence of the jungle, they stopped singing and shouting, suddenly exhausted. They lay down in the shade of many trees, and the grass was soft and comfortable, and very soon everyone except Rusty was fast asleep.

Rusty was tired. He was hungry. He had lost his shirt and shoes, his feet were bruised, his body sore. It was only now, resting, that he noticed these things, for he had been caught up in the excitement of the colour game, overcome by an exhilaration he had never known. His fair hair was tousled and streaked with colour, and his eyes were wide with wonder.

He was exhausted now, but he was happy.

He wanted this to go on for ever, this day of feverish emotion, this life in another world. He did not want to leave the forest; it was safe, its earth soothed him, gathered him in so that the pain of his body became a pleasure...

He did not want to go home.

■

Mr Harrison stood at the top of the verandah steps. The house was in darkness, but his cigarette glowed more brightly for it. A road lamp trapped the returning boy as he opened the gate, and Rusty knew he had been seen, but he didn't care much; if he had known that Mr Harrison had not recognized him, he would have turned back instead of walking resignedly up the garden path.

Mr Harrison did not move, nor did he appear to notice the boy's approach. It was only when Rusty climbed the verandah steps that his guardian moved and said, 'Who's that?'

Still he had not recognized the boy; and in that instant Rusty became aware of his own condition, for his body was a patchwork of paint. Wearing only torn pyjamas, he could, in the half-light, have easily been mistaken for the sweeper boy or someone else's servant. It must have been a newly acquired bazaar instinct that made the boy think of escape. He turned about.

But Mr Harrison shouted, 'Come here, you!' and the tone of his voice—the tone reserved for the sweeper boy—made Rusty stop.

'Come up here!' repeated Mr Harrison.

Rusty returned to the verandah, and his guardian switched on a light; but even now there was no recognition.

'Good evening, sir,' said Rusty.

Mr Harrison received a shock. He felt a wave of anger, and then a wave of pain: was this the boy he had trained and educated—this wild, ragged, ungrateful wretch, who did not know the difference between what was proper and what was improper, what was civilized and what was barbaric, what was decent and what was shameful—and had the years of training come to nothing? Mr Harrison came out of the shadows and cursed. He brought his hand down on the back of Rusty's neck, propelled him into the drawing-room, and pushed him across the room so violently that the boy lost his balance, collided with a table and rolled over on to the ground.

Rusty looked up from the floor to find his guardian standing over him, and in the man's right hand was the supple malacca cane and the cane was twitching.

Mr Harrison's face was twitching too, it was full of fire. His lips were stitched together, sealed up with the ginger moustache, and he looked at the boy with narrowed, unblinking eyes.

'Filth!' he said, almost spitting the words in the boy's face. 'My God, what filth!'

Rusty stared fascinated at the deep yellow nicotine stains on the fingers of his guardian's raised hand. Then the wrist moved suddenly and the cane cut across the boy's face like a knife, stabbing and burning into his cheek.

Rusty cried out and cowered back against the wall; he could feel the blood trickling across his mouth. He looked round desperately for a means of escape, but the man was in front of him, over him, and the wall was behind.

Mr Harrison broke into a torrent of words. 'How can you call yourself an Englishman, how can you come back to this house in such a condition? In what gutter, in what brothel have you been! Have you seen yourself? Do you know what you look like?'

'No,' said Rusty, and for the first time he did not address his guardian as 'sir'. 'I don't care what I look like.'

'You don't...well, I'll tell you what you look like! You look like the mongrel that you are!'

'That's a lie!' exclaimed Rusty.

'It's the truth. I've tried to bring you up as an Englishman, as your father would have wished. But, as you won't have it our way, I'm telling you that he was about the only thing English about you. You're no better than the sweeper boy!'

Rusty flared into a temper, showing some spirit for the first time in his life. 'I'm no better than the sweeper boy, but I am as good as him! I'm as good as you! I'm as good as anyone!' And, instead of cringing to take the cut from the cane, he flung himself at his guardian's legs. The cane swished through the air, grazing the boy's back. Rusty wrapped his arms round his guardian's legs and pulled on them with all his strength.

Mr Harrison went over, falling flat on his back.

The suddenness of the fall must have knocked the breath from his body, because for a moment he did not move.

Rusty sprang to his feet. The cut across his face had stung him to madness, to an unreasoning hate, and he did what previously he would only have dreamt of doing. Lifting a vase of the missionary's wife's best sweet peas off the glass cupboard, he flung it at his guardian's face. It hit him on the chest, but the water and flowers flopped out over his face. He tried to get up; but he was speechless.

The look of alarm on Mr Harrison's face gave Rusty greater courage. Before the man could recover his feet and his balance, Rusty gripped him by the collar and pushed him backwards, until they both fell over on to the floor. With one hand still twisting the collar; the boy slapped his guardian's face. Mad with the pain in his own face, Rusty hit the man again and again, wildly and awkwardly, but with the giddy thrill of knowing he could do it: he was a child no longer, he was nearly seventeen, he was a man. He could inflict pain, that was a wonderful discovery; there was a power in his body—a devil or a god—and he gained confidence in his power; and he was a man!

'Stop that, stop it!' The shout of a hysterical woman brought Rusty to his senses. He still held his guardian by the throat, but he stopped hitting him. Mr Harrison's face was very red. The missionary's wife stood in the doorway, her face white with fear. She was under the impression that Mr Harrison was being attacked by a servant or some bazaar hooligan. Rusty did not wait until she found her tongue but, with a new-found speed and agility, darted out of the drawing-room.

He made his escape from the bedroom window. From the

gate he could see the missionary's wife silhouetted against the drawing-room light. He laughed out loud. The woman swivelled round and came forward a few steps. And Rusty laughed again and began running down the road to the bazaar.

■

It was late. The smart shops and restaurants were closed. In the bazaar, oil lamps hung outside each doorway; people were asleep on the steps and platforms of shopfronts, some huddled in blankets, others rolled tight into themselves. The road, which during the day was a busy, noisy crush of people and animals, was quiet and deserted. Only a lean dog still sniffed in the gutter. A woman sang in a room high above the street—a plaintive, tremulous song—and in the far distance a jackal cried to the moon. But the empty, lifeless street was very deceptive; if the roofs could have been removed from but a handful of buildings, it would be seen that life had not really stopped but, beautiful and ugly, persisted through the night.

It was past midnight, though the Clock Tower had no way of saying it. Rusty was in the empty street, and the chaat shop was closed, a sheet of tarpaulin draped across the front. He looked up and down the road, hoping to meet someone he knew; the chaat-walla, he felt sure, would give him a blanket for the night and a place to sleep; and the next day when Somi came to meet him, he would tell his friend of his predicament, that he had run away from his guardian's house and did not intend returning. But he would have to wait till morning: the chaat shop was shuttered, barred and bolted.

He sat down on the steps; but the stone was cold and his thin cotton pyjamas offered no protection. He folded his arms and huddled up in a corner, but still he shivered. His feet were becoming numb, lifeless.

Rusty had not fully realized the hazards of the situation. He was still mad with anger and rebellion and, though the blood on his cheek had dried, his face was still smarting. He could not think clearly: the present was confusing and unreal and he could not see beyond it; what worried him was the cold and the discomfort and the pain.

The singing stopped in the high window. Rusty looked up and saw a beckoning hand. As no one else in the street showed any signs of life, Rusty got up and walked across the road until he was under the window. The woman pointed to a stairway, and he mounted it, glad of the hospitality he was being offered.

The stairway seemed to go to the stars, but it turned suddenly to lead into the woman's room. The door was slightly ajar; he knocked and a voice said, 'Come...'

The room was filled with perfume and burning incense. A musical instrument lay in one corner. The woman reclined on a bed, her hair scattered about the pillow; she had a round, pretty face, but she was losing her youth, and the fat showed in rolls at her exposed waist. She smiled at the boy, and beckoned again.

'Thank you,' said Rusty, closing the door. 'Can I sleep here?'

'Where else?' said the woman.

'Just for tonight.'

She smiled, and waited. Rusty stood in front of her, his hands behind his back.

Sit down,' she said, and patted the bedclothes beside her.

Reverently, and as respectfully as he could, Rusty sat down.

The woman ran little fair fingers over his body, and drew his head to hers; their lips were very close, almost touching, and their breathing sounded terribly loud to Rusty, but he only said, 'I am hungry.'

A poet, thought the woman, and kissed him full on the lips; but the boy drew away in embarrassment, unsure of himself, liking the woman on the bed and yet afraid of her...

'What is wrong?' she asked. 'I'm tired,' he said. The woman's friendly smile turned to a look of scorn; but she saw that he was only a boy whose eyes were full of unhappiness, and she could not help pitying him.

'You can sleep here,' she said, 'until you have lost your tiredness.'

But he shook his head. 'I will come some other time,' he said, not wishing to hurt the woman's feelings. They were both pitying each other, liking each other, but not enough to make them understand each other.

Rusty left the room. Mechanically, he descended the staircase, and walked up the bazaar road, past the silent sleeping forms, until he reached the Clock Tower. To the right of the Clock Tower was a broad stretch of grassland where, during the day, cattle grazed and children played and young men like Ranbir wrestled and kicked footballs. But now, at night, it was a vast empty space.

But the grass was soft, like the grass in the forest, and Rusty walked the length of the maidan. He found a bench and sat down, warmer for the walk. A light breeze was blowing across the maidan, pleasant and refreshing, playing with his hair. Around him everything was dark and silent and lonely. He had got away from the bazaar, which held the misery of beggars and homeless children and starving dogs, and could now concentrate on his own misery; for there was nothing like loneliness for making Rusty conscious of his unhappy state. Madness and freedom and violence were new to him: loneliness was familiar, something he understood.

Rusty was alone. Until tomorrow, he was alone for the rest of his life.

If tomorrow there was no Somi at the chaat shop, no

Ranbir, then what would he do? This question badgered him persistently, making him an unwilling slave to reality. He did not know where his friends lived, he had no money, he could not ask the chaat-walla for credit on the strength of two visits. Perhaps he should return to the amorous lady in the bazaar; perhaps...but no, one thing was certain, he would never return to his guardian...

The moon had been hidden by clouds, and presently there was a drizzle. Rusty did not mind the rain, it refreshed him and made the colour run from his body; but, when it began to fall harder, he started shivering again. He felt sick. He got up, rolled his ragged pyjamas up to the thighs and crawled under the bench.

There was a hollow under the bench, and at first Rusty found it quite comfortable. But there was no grass and gradually the earth began to soften: soon he was on his hands and knees in a pool of muddy water, with the slush oozing up through his fingers and toes. Crouching there, wet and cold and muddy, he was overcome by a feeling of helplessness and self-pity: everyone and everything seemed to have turned against him; not only his people but also the bazaar and the chaat shop and even the elements. He admitted to himself that he had been too impulsive in rebelling and running away from home; perhaps there was still time to return and beg Mr Harrison's forgiveness. But could his behaviour be forgiven? Might he not be clapped into irons for attempted murder? Most certainly he would be given another beating: not six strokes this time, but nine.

His only hope was Somi. If not Somi, then Ranbir. If not Ranbir... Well, it was no use thinking further, there was no one else to think of.

The rain had ceased. Rusty crawled out from under the bench, and stretched his cramped limbs. The moon came out from a cloud and played with his wet, glistening body, and showed him the vast, naked loneliness of the maidan and his own insignificance. He longed now for the presence of people, be they beggars or women, and he broke into a trot, and the trot became a run, a frightened run, and he did not stop until he reached the Clock Tower.

DUST ON THE MOUNTAIN

I

Winter came and went, without so much as a drizzle. The hillside was brown all summer and the fields were bare. The old plough that was dragged over the hard ground by Bisnu's lean oxen made hardly any impression. Still, Bisnu kept his seeds ready for sowing. A good monsoon, and there would be plenty of maize and rice to see the family through the next winter.

Summer went its scorching way, and a few clouds gathered on the south-western horizon.

'The monsoon is coming,' announced Bisnu.

His sister Puja was at the small stream, washing clothes. 'If it doesn't come soon, the stream will dry up,' she said. 'See, it's only a trickle this year. Remember when there were so many different flowers growing here on the banks of the stream? This year there isn't one.'

'The winter was dry. It did not even snow,' said Bisnu. 'I cannot remember another winter when there was no snow,' said his mother. 'The year your father died, there was so much snow the villagers could not light his funeral pyre for hours And now there are fires everywhere.' She pointed to the next mountain, half-hidden by the smoke from a forest fire. At night they sat outside their small house, watching the fire spread. A red line stretched right across the mountain. Thousands of Himalayan trees were perishing in the flames. Oaks, deodars, maples, pines; trees that had taken hundreds of years to grow. And now a fire started carelessly by some campers had been carried up the mountain with the help of the dry grass and strong breeze.

There was no one to put it out. It would take days to die down by itself.

'If the monsoon arrives tomorrow, the fire will go out,' said Bisnu, ever the optimist. He was only twelve, but he was the man in the house; he had to see that there was enough food for the family and for the oxen, for the big black dog and the hens.

There were clouds the next day but they brought only a drizzle. 'It's just the beginning,' said Bisnu as he placed a bucket of muddy water on the steps.

'It usually starts with a heavy downpour,' said his mother. But there were to be no downpours that year. Clouds gathered on the horizon but they were white and puffy and soon disappeared.

True monsoon clouds would have been dark and heavy with moisture. There were other signs—or lack of them— that warned of a long dry summer. The birds were silent, or simply absent. The Himalayan barbet, who usually heralded the approach of the monsoon with strident calls from the top of a spruce tree, hadn't been seen or heard. And the cicadas, who played a deafening overture in the oaks at the first hint of rain, seemed to be missing altogether.

Puja's apricot tree usually gave them a basket full of fruit every summer. This year it produced barely a handful of apricots, lacking juice and flavour. The tree looked ready to die, its leaves curled up in despair. Fortunately there was a store of walnuts, and a binful of wheat grain and another of rice stored from the previous year, so they would not be entirely without food; but it looked as though there would be no fresh fruit or vegetables. And there would be nothing to store away for the following winter.

Money would be needed to buy supplies in Tehri, some thirty miles distant. And there was no money to be earned in the village.

'I will go to Mussoorie and find work,' announced Bisnu.

'But Mussoorie is a two-day journey by bus,' said his mother. 'There is no one there who can help you. And you may not get any work.'

'In Mussoorie there is plenty of work during the summer. Rich people come up from the plains for their holidays. It is full of hotels and shops and places where they can spend their money.'

'But they won't spend any money on you.'

'There is money to be made there. And if not, I will come home. I can walk back over the Nag Tibba mountain. It will take only two and a half days and I will save the bus fare!'

'Don't go, Bhai,' pleaded Puja.

'There will be no one to prepare your food—you will only get sick.'

But Bisnu had made up his mind so he put a few belongings in a cloth shoulder bag, while his mother prised several rupee coins out of a cache in the wall of their living room. Puja prepared a special breakfast of parathas and an egg scrambled with onions, the hen having laid just one for the occasion. Bisnu put some of the parathas in his bag. Then, waving goodbye to his mother and sister, he set off down the road from the village. After walking for a mile, he reached the highway where there was a hamlet with a bus stop. A number of villagers were waiting patiently for a bus. It was an hour late but they were used to that. As long as it arrived safely and got them to their destination, they would be content. They were patient people. And although Bisnu wasn't quite so patient, he too had learnt how to wait—for late buses and late monsoons.

II

Along the valley and over the mountains went the little bus with its load of frail humans. A little misjudgement on the part of the driver, and they would all be dashed to pieces on the rocks far below.

'How tiny we are,' thought Bisnu, looking up at the towering peaks and the immensity of the sky. 'Each of us no more than a raindrop… And I wish we had a few raindrops!'

There were still fires burning to the north but the road went south, where there were no forests anyway, just bare brown hillsides. Down near the river there were small paddy fields but unfortunately rivers ran downhill and not uphill, and there was no inexpensive way in which the water could be brought up the steep slopes to the fields that depended on rainfall.

Bisnu stared out of the bus window at the river running far below. On either bank huge boulders lay exposed, for the level of the water had fallen considerably during the past few months. 'Why are there no trees here?' he asked aloud, and received the attention of a fellow passenger, an old man in the next seat who had been keeping up a relentless dry coughing. Even though it was a warm day, he wore a woollen cap and had an old muffler wrapped about his neck.

'There were trees here once,' he said. 'But the contractors took the deodars for furniture and houses. And the pines were tapped to death for resin. And the oaks were stripped of their leaves to feed the cattle—you can still see a few tree skeletons if you look hard—and the bushes that remained were finished off by the goats!'

'When did all this happen?' asked Bisnu.

'A few years ago. And it's still happening in other areas, although it's forbidden now to cut trees. The only forests that remain are in remote places where there are no roads.' A fit of coughing came over him, but he had found a good listener and was eager to continue. 'The road helps you and me to get about but it also makes it easier for others to do mischief. Rich men from the cities come here and buy up what they want—land, trees, people!'

'What takes you to Mussoorie, Uncle?' asked Bisnu politely. He always addressed elderly people as uncle or aunt. 'I have a cough that won't go away. Perhaps they can do something for it at the hospital in Mussoorie. Doctors don't like coming to villages, you know—there's no money to be made in villages. So we must go to the doctors in the towns. I had a brother who could not be cured in Mussoorie. They told him to go to Delhi. He sold his buffaloes and went to Delhi, but there they told him it was too late to do anything. He died on the way back. I won't go to Delhi. I don't wish to die amongst strangers.'

'You'll get well, Uncle,' said Bisnu.

'Bless you for saying so. And you—what takes you to the big town?'

'Looking for work—we need money at home.'

'It is always the same. There are many like you who must go out in search of work. But don't be led astray. Don't let your friends persuade you to go to Bombay to become a film star! It is better to be hungry in your village than to be hungry on the streets of Bombay. I had a nephew who went to Bombay. The smugglers put him to work selling afeem (opium) and now he is in jail. Keep away from the big cities, boy. Earn your money and go home.' 'I'll do that, Uncle. My mother and sister will expect me to return before the summer season is over.'

The old man nodded vigorously and began coughing again. Presently he dozed off. The interior of the bus smelt of tobacco smoke and petrol fumes and as a result Bisnu had a headache. He kept his face near the open window to get as much fresh air as possible, but the dust kept getting into his mouth and eyes.

Several dusty hours later the bus got into Mussoorie, honking its horn furiously at everything in sight. The passengers, looking dazed, got down and went their different ways. The old man trudged off to the hospital.

Bisnu had to start looking for a job straightaway. He needed a lodging for the night and he could not afford even the cheapest of hotels. So he went from one shop to another, and to all the little restaurants and eating places, asking for work—anything in exchange for a bed, a meal, and a minimum wage. A boy at one of the sweet shops told him there was a job at the Picture Palace, one of the town's three cinemas. The hill station's main road was crowded with people, for the season was just starting. Most of them were tourists who had come up from Delhi and other large towns.

The street lights had come on, and the shops were lighting up, when Bisnu presented himself at the Picture Palace.

III

The man who ran the cinema's tea stall had just sacked the previous helper for his general clumsiness. Whenever he engaged a new boy (which was fairly often) he started him off with the warning: 'I will be keeping a record of all the cups and plates you break, and their cost will be deducted from your salary at the end of the month.'

As Bisnu's salary had been fixed at fifty rupees a month, he would have to be very careful if he was going to receive any of it.

'In my first month,' said Chittru, one of the three tea stall boys, 'I broke six cups and five saucers, and my pay came to three rupees! Better be careful!'

Bisnu's job was to help prepare the tea and samosas, serve these refreshments to the public during intervals in the film, and later wash up the dishes. In addition to his salary, he was allowed to drink as much tea as he wanted or could hold in his stomach. But the sugar supply was kept to a minimum.

Bisnu went to work immediately and it was not long before he was as well-versed in his duties as the other two tea boys, Chittru and Bali. Chittru was an easy-going, lazy boy who always tried to place the brunt of his work on someone else's shoulders. But he was generous and lent Bisnu five rupees during the first week. Bali, besides being a tea boy, had the enviable job of being the poster boy. As the cinema was closed during the mornings, Bali would be busy either pushing the big poster board around Mussoorie, or sticking posters on convenient walls.

'Posters are very useful,' he claimed. 'They prevent old walls from falling down.'

Chittru had relatives in Mussoorie and slept at their house. But both Bisnu and Bali were on their own and had to sleep at the cinema. After the last show the hall was locked up, so they could not settle down in the expensive seats as they would have liked! They had to sleep on a dirty mattress in the foyer, near the ticket office, where they were often at the mercy of icy Himalayan winds.

Bali made things more comfortable by setting his poster board at an angle to the wall, which gave them a little alcove where they could sleep protected from the wind. As they had only one blanket each, they placed their blankets together and rolled themselves into a tight warm ball.

During shows, when Bisnu took the tea around, there was nearly always someone who would be rude and offensive. Once when he spilt some tea on a college student's shoes, he received a hard kick on the shin. He complained to the tea stall owner, but his employer said, 'The customer is always right. You should have got out of the way in time!'

As he began to get used to this life, Bisnu found himself taking an interest in some of the regular customers.

There was, for instance, the large gentleman with the soup-strainer moustache, who drank his tea from the saucer. As he drank, his lips worked like a suction pump, and the tea, after a brief agitation in the saucer, would disappear in a matter of seconds. Bisnu often wondered if there was something lurking in the forests of that gentleman's upper lip, something that would suddenly spring out and fall upon him! The boys took great pleasure in exchanging anecdotes about the peculiarities of some of the customers.

Bisnu had never seen such bright, painted women before. The girls in his village, including his sister Puja, were good-looking and often sturdy; but they did not use perfumes or make-up like these more prosperous women from the towns of the plains. Wearing expensive clothes and jewellery, they never gave Bisnu more than a brief, bored glance. Other women were more inclined to notice him, favouring him with kind words and a small tip when he took away the cups and plates. He found he could make a few rupees a month in tips; and when he received his first month's pay, he was able to send some of it home.

Chittru accompanied him to the post office and helped him to fill in the money order form. Bisnu had been to the village school, but be wasn't used to forms and official paperwork. Chittru, a town boy, knew all about them, even though he could just about read and write.

Walking back to the cinema, Chittru said, 'We can make more money at the limestone quarries.'

'All right, let's try them,' said Bisnu.

'Not now,' said Chittru, who enjoyed the busy season in the hill station. 'After the season—after the monsoon.'

But there was still no monsoon to speak of, just an occasional drizzle which did little to clear the air of the dust that blew up from the plains. Bisnu wondered how his mother and sister were faring at home. A wave of homesickness swept over him. The hill station, with all its glitter, was just a pretty gift box with nothing inside.

One day in the cinema Bisnu saw the old man who had been with him on the bus. He greeted him like a long lost friend. At first the old man did not recognize the boy, but when Bisnu asked him if he had recovered from his illness, the old man remembered and said, 'So you are still in Mussoorie, boy. That is good. I thought you might have gone down to Delhi to make more money.' He added that he was a little better and that he was undergoing a course of treatment at the hospital. Bisnu brought him a cup of tea and refused to take any money for it; it could be included in his own quota of free tea. When the show was over, the old man went his way and Bisnu did not see him again.

In September the town began to get empty. The taps were running dry or giving out just a trickle of muddy water. A thick mist lay over the mountain for days on end, but there was no rain. When the mists cleared, an autumn wind came whispering through the deodars.

At the end of the month the manager of the Picture Palace gave everyone a week's notice, a week's pay, and announced that the cinema would be closing for the winter.

IV

Bali said, 'I'm going to Delhi to find work. I'll come back next summer. What about you, Bisnu, why don't you come with me? It's easier to find work in Delhi.'

'I'm staying with Chittru,' said Bisnu.

'We may work at the quarries.'

'I like the big towns,' said Bali. 'I like shops and people and lots of noise. I will never go back to my village. There is no money there, no fun.'

Bali made a bundle of his things and set out for the bus stand. Bisnu bought himself a pair of cheap shoes, for his old ones had fallen to pieces. With what was left of his money, he sent another money order home. Then he and Chittru set out for the limestone quarries, an eight-mile walk from Mussoorie.

They knew they were nearing the quarries when they saw clouds of limestone dust hanging in the air. The dust hid the next mountain from view. When they did see the mountain, they found that the top of it was missing—blasted away by dynamite to enable the quarries to get at the rich strata of limestone rock below the surface.

The skeletons of a few trees remained on the lower slopes. Almost everything else had gone—grass, flowers, shrubs, birds, butterflies, grasshoppers, ladybirds. A rock lizard popped its head out of a crevice to look at the intruders. Then, like some prehistoric survivor, it scuttled back into its underground shelter. 'I used to come here when I was small,' announced Chittru cheerfully.

'Were the quarries here then?'

'Oh, no. My friends and I—we used to come for the strawberries. They grew all over this mountain. Wild strawberries, but very tasty.'

'Where are they now?' asked Bisnu, looking around at the devastated hillside.

'All gone,' said Chittru. 'Maybe there are some on the next mountain.'

Even as they approached the quarries, a blast shook the hillside. Chittru pulled Bisnu under an overhanging rock to avoid the shower of stones that pelted down on the road. As the dust enveloped them, Bisnu had a fit of coughing. When the air cleared a little, they saw the limestone dump ahead of them.

Chittru, who was older and bigger than Bisnu, was immediately taken on as a labourer; but the quarry foreman took one look at Bisnu and said, 'You're too small. You won't be able to break stones or lift those heavy rocks and load them into the trucks. Be off, boy. Find something else to do.'

He was offered a job in the labourers' canteen, but he'd had enough of making tea and washing dishes. He was about to turn round and walk back to Mussoorie when he felt a heavy hand descend on his shoulder. He looked up to find a grey-bearded, turbanned Sikh looking down at him in some amusement.

'I need a cleaner for my truck,' he said. 'The work is easy, but the hours are long!'

Bisnu responded immediately to the man's gruff but jovial manner.

'What will you pay?' he asked.

'Fifteen rupees a day, and you'll get food and a bed at the depot.'

'As long as I don't have to cook the food,' said Bisnu. The truck driver laughed. 'You might prefer to do so, once you've tasted the depot food. Are you coming on my truck? Make up your mind.'

'I'm your man,' said Bisnu; and waving goodbye to Chittru, he followed the Sikh to his truck.

V

A horn blared, shattering the silence of the mountains, and the truck came round a bend in the road. A herd of goats scattered to left and right.

The goatherds cursed as a cloud of dust enveloped them, and then the truck had left them behind and was rattling along the bumpy, unmetalled road to the quarries.

At the wheel of the truck, stroking his grey moustache with one hand, sat Pritam Singh. It was his own truck. He had never allowed anyone else to drive it. Every day he made two trips to the quarries, carrying truckloads of limestone back to the depot at the bottom of the hill. He was paid by the trip and he was always anxious to get in two trips every day. Sitting beside him was Bisnu, his new cleaner. In less than a month Bisnu had become an experienced hand at looking after trucks, riding in them, and even sleeping in them. He got on well with Pritam, the grizzled, fifty-year-old Sikh, who boasted of two well-off sons—one a farmer in Punjab, the other a wine merchant in far-off London. He could have gone to live with either of them, but his sturdy independence kept him on the road in his battered old truck.

Pritam pressed hard on his horn. Now there was no one on the road—neither beast nor man—but Pritam was fond of the sound of his horn and liked blowing it. He boasted that it was the loudest horn in northern India. Although it struck terror into the hearts of all who heard it—for it was louder than the trumpeting of an elephant—it was music to Pritam's ears.

Pritam treated Bisnu as an equal and a friendly banter had grown between them during their many trips together.

'One more year on this bone-breaking road,' said Pritam, 'and then I'll sell my truck and retire.'

'But who will buy such a shaky old truck?' asked Bisnu. 'It will retire before you do!'

'Now don't be insulting, boy. She's only twenty years old—there are still a few years left in her!' And as though to prove it he blew the horn again. Its strident sound echoed and re-echoed down the mountain gorge. A pair of wildfowl burst from the bushes and fled to more silent regions.

Pritam's thoughts went to his, dinner. 'Haven't had a good meal for days.'

'Haven't had a good meal for weeks,' said Bisnu, although in fact he looked much healthier than when he had worked at the cinema's tea stall.

'Tonight I'll give you a dinner in a good hotel. Tandoori chicken and rice pilaf.'

He sounded his horn again as though to put a seal on his promise. Then he slowed down, because the road had become narrow and precipitous, and trotting ahead of them was a train of mules.

As the horn blared, one mule ran forward, another ran backward. One went uphill, another went downhill. Soon there were mules all over the place. Pritam cursed the mules and the mule drivers cursed Pritam; but he had soon left them far behind.

Along this range, all the hills were bare and dry. Most of the forest had long since disappeared.

'Are your hills as bare as these?' asked Pritam. 'No, we still have some trees,' said. Bisnu. 'Nobody has started blasting the hills as yet. In front of our house there is a walnut tree which gives us two baskets of walnuts every year. And there is an apricot tree. But it was a bad year for fruit. There was no rain. And the stream is too far away.'

'It will rain soon,' said Pritam. 'I can smell rain. It is coming from the north. The winter will be early.'

'It will settle the dust.'

Dust was everywhere. The truck was full of it. The leaves of the shrubs and the few trees were thick with it. Bisnu could feel the dust under his eyelids and in his mouth. And as they approached the quarries, the dust increased. But it was a different kind of dust now—whiter, stinging the eyes, irritating the nostrils.

They had been blasting all morning.

'Let's wait here,' said Pritam, bringing the truck to a halt. They sat in silence, staring through the windscreen at the scarred cliffs a little distance down the road. There was a sharp crack of explosives and the hillside blossomed outwards. Earth and rocks hurtled down the mountain.

Bisnu watched in awe as shrubs and small trees were flung into the air. It always frightened him—not so much the sight of—the rocks bursting asunder, as the trees being flung aside and destroyed. He thought of the trees at home—the walnut, the chestnuts, the pines—and wondered if one day they would suffer the same fate, and whether the mountains would all become a desert like this particular range. No trees, no grass, no water—only the choking dust of mines and quarries.

VI

Pritam pressed hard on his horn again, to let the people at the site know that he was approaching. He parked outside a small shed where the contractor and the foreman were sipping cups of tea. A short distance away, some labourers, Chittru among then, were hammering at chunks of rock, breaking them up into manageable pieces. A pile of stones stood ready for loading; while the rock that had just been blasted lay scattered about the hillside.

'Come and have a cup of tea,' called out the contractor.

'I can't hang about all day,' said Pritam. 'There's another trip to make—and the days are getting shorter. I don't want to be driving by night.'

But he sat down on a bench and ordered two cups of tea from the stall. The foreman strolled over to the group of labourers and told them to start loading. Bisnu let down the grid at the back of the truck. Then, to keep himself warm, he began helping Chittru and the men with the loading.

'Don't expect to be paid for helping,' said Sharma, the contractor, for whom every rupee spent was a rupee off his profits.

'Don't worry,' said Bisnu. 'I don't work for contractors, I work for friends.'

'That's right,' called out Pritam.

'Mind what you say to Bisnu—he's no one's servant!'

Sharma wasn't happy until there was no space left for a single stone. Then Bisnu had his cup of tea and three of the men climbed on the pile of stones in the open truck.

'All right, let's go!' said Pritam. 'I want to finish early today Bisnu and I are having a big dinner!'

Bisnu jumped in beside Pritam, banging the door shut. It never closed properly unless it was slammed really hard. But it opened at a touch.

'This truck is held together with sticking plaster,' joked Pritam.

He was in good spirits. He started the engine, and blew his horn just as he passed the foreman and the contractor.

'They are deaf in one ear from the blasting,' said Pritam. 'I'll make them deaf in the other ear!'

The labourers were singing as the truck swung round the sharp bends of the winding road. The door beside Bisnu rattled on its hinges. He was feeling quite dizzy.

'Not too fast,' he said.

'Oh,' said Pritam. 'About my driving?'

'It's just today,' said Bisnu uneasily.

'You're getting old,' said Pritam. 'And since when did you become nervous?'

'It's a feeling, that's all.'

'That's your trouble.'

'I suppose so,' said Bisnu.

Pritam was feeling young, exhilarated. He drove faster. As they swung round a bend, Bisnu looked out of his window.

All he saw was the sky above and the valley below. They were very near the edge; but it was usually like that on this narrow mountain road.

After a few more hairpin bends, the road descended steeply to the valley. Just then a stray mule ran into the middle of the road. Pritam swung the steering wheel over to the right to avoid the mule, but here the road turned sharply to the left. The truck went over the edge.

As it tipped over, hanging for a few seconds on the edge of the cliff, the labourers leapt from the back of the truck. It pitched forward, and as it struck a rock outcrop, the loose door burst open. Bisnu was thrown out.

The truck hurtled forward, bouncing over the rocks, turning over on its side and rolling over twice before coming to rest against the trunk of a scraggly old oak tree. But for the tree, the truck would have plunged several hundred feet down to the bottom of the gorge.

Two of the labourers sat on the hillside, stunned and badly shaken. The third man had picked himself up and was running back to the quarry for help.

Bisnu had landed in a bed of nettles. He was smarting all over, but he wasn't really hurt; the nettles had broken his fall.

His first impulse was to get up and run back to the road. Then he realized that Pritam was still in the truck.

Bisnu skidded down the steep slope, calling out, 'Pritam Uncle, are you all right?'

There was no answer.

VII

When Bisnu saw Pritam's arm and half his body jutting out of the open door of the truck, he feared the worst. It was a strange position, half in and half out. Bisnu was about to turn away and climb back up the hill, when he noticed that Pritam had opened a bloodied and swollen eye. It looked straight up at Bisnu.

'Are you alive?' whispered Bisnu, terrified.

'What do you think?' muttered Pritam. He closed his eye again. When the contractor and his men arrived, it took them almost an hour to get Pritam Singh out of the wreckage of the truck, and another hour to get him to the hospital in the next big town. He had broken bones, fractured ribs and a dislocated shoulder. But the doctors said he was repairable—which was more than could be said for the truck.

'So the truck's finished,' said Pritam, between groans when Bisnu came to see him after a couple of days. 'Now I'll have to go home and live with my son. And what about you, boy? I can get you a job on a friend's truck.'

'No,' said Bisnu, 'I'll be going home soon.'

'And what will you do at home?'

'I'll work on my land. It's better to grow things on the land, than to blast things out of it.'

They were silent for some time.

'There is something to be said for growing things,' said Pritam. 'But for that tree, the truck would have finished up at the foot of the mountain, and I wouldn't he here, all bandaged up and talking to you. It was the tree that saved me. Remember that, boy.'

'I'll remember, and I won't forget the dinner you promised me, either.'

It snowed during Bisnu's last night at the quarries. He slept on the floor with Chittru, in a large shed meant for the labourers. The wind blew the snowflakes in at the entrance; it whistled down the deserted mountain pass. In the morning Bisnu opened his eyes to a world of dazzling whiteness. The snow was piled high against the walls of the shed, and they had some difficulty getting out. Bisnu joined Chittru at the tea stall, drank a glass of hot sweet tea, and ate two stale buns. He said goodbye to Chittru and set out on the long march home. The road would be closed to traffic because of the heavy snow, and he would have to walk all the way.

He trudged over the hills all day, stopping only at small villages to take refreshment. By nightfall he was still ten miles from home.

But he had fallen in with other travellers, and with them he took shelter at a small inn. They built a fire and crowded round it, and each man spoke of his home and fields and all were of the opinion that the snow and rain had come just in time to save the winter crops. Someone sang, and another told a ghost story. Feeling at home already, Bisnu fell asleep listening to their tales. In the morning they parted and went their different ways. It was almost noon when Bisnu reached his village. The fields were covered with snow and the mountain stream was in spate. As he climbed the terraced fields to his house, he heard the sound of barking, and his mother's big black mastiff came bounding towards him over the snow. The dog jumped on him and licked his arms and then went bounding back to the house to tell the others.

Puja saw him from the courtyard and ran indoors shouting, 'Bisnu has come, my brother has come!'

His mother ran out of the house, calling, 'Bisnu, Bisnu!'

Bisnu came walking through the fields, and he did not hurry, he did not run; he wanted to savour the moment of his return, with his mother and sister smiling, waiting for him in front of the house.

There was no need to hurry now. He would be with them for a long time, and the manager of the Picture Palace would have to find someone else for the summer season... It was his home, and these were his fields! Even the snow was his. When the snow melted he would clear the fields, and nourish them, and make them rich.

He felt very big and very strong as he came striding over the land he loved.

DINNER WITH FOSTER

Straddling a spur of the Mussoorie range as it dips into the Doon valley, Fosterganj came into existence some two hundred years ago and was almost immediately forgotten. And today it is not very different from what it was in 1961, when I lived there briefly.

A quiet corner, where I could live like a recluse and write my stories—that was what I was looking for. And in Fosterganj I thought I'd found my retreat: a cluster of modest cottages, a straggling little bazaar, a post office, a crumbling castle (supposedly haunted), a mountain stream at the bottom of the hill, a winding footpath that took you either uphill or down. What more could one ask for? It reminded me a little of an English village, and indeed that was what it had once been; a tiny settlement on the outskirts of the larger hill station. But the British had long since gone, and the residents were now a fairly mixed lot.

I forget what took me to Fosterganj in the first place. Destiny, perhaps; although I'm not sure why destiny would have bothered to guide an itinerant writer to an obscure hamlet in the hills. Chance would be a better word. For chance plays a great part in all our lives. And it was just by chance that I found myself in the Fosterganj bazaar one fine morning early in May. The oaks and maples were in new leaf; geraniums flourished on sunny balconies; a boy delivering milk whistled a catchy Dev Anand song; a mule train clattered down the street. The chill of winter had gone and there was warmth in the sunshine that played upon old walls.

I sat in a tea shop, tested my teeth on an old bun, and washed it down with milky tea. The bun had been around for some time, but so had I, so we were quits. At the age of forty I could digest almost anything.

The tea shop owner, Melaram, was a friendly sort, as are most tea shop owners. He told me that not many tourists made their way down to Fosterganj. The only attraction was the waterfall, and you had to be fairly fit in order to scramble down the steep and narrow path that led to the ravine where a little stream came tumbling over the rocks. I would visit it one day, I told him.

'Then you should stay here a day or two,' said Melaram. 'Explore the stream. Walk down to Rajpur. You'll need a good walking stick. Look, I have several in my shop. Cherry wood, walnut wood, oak.' He saw me wavering. 'You'll also need one to climb the next hill—it's called Pari Tibba.' I was charmed by the name—Fairy Hill.

I hadn't planned on doing much walking that day—the walk down to Fosterganj from Mussoorie had already taken almost an hour—but I liked the look of a sturdy cherry-wood walking stick, and I bought one for two rupees. Those were the days of simple living. You don't see two-rupee notes anymore. You don't see walking sticks either. Hardly anyone walks.

I strolled down the small bazaar, without having to worry about passing cars and lorries or a crush of people. Two or three schoolchildren were sauntering home, burdened by their school bags bursting with homework. A cow and a couple of stray dogs examined the contents of an overflowing dustbin. A policeman sitting on a stool outside a tiny police outpost yawned, stretched, stood up, looked up and down the street in anticipation of crimes to come, scratched himself in the anal region and sank back upon his stool.

A man in a crumpled shirt and threadbare trousers came up to me, looked me over with his watery grey eyes, and said, 'Sir, would you like to buy some gladioli bulbs?' He held up a basket full of bulbs which might have been onions. His chin was covered with a grey stubble, some of his teeth were missing, the remaining ones yellow with neglect.

'No, thanks,' I said. 'I live in a tiny flat in Delhi. No room for flowers.'

'A world without flowers,' he shook his head. 'That's what it's coming to.'

'And where do you plant your bulbs?'

'I grow gladioli, sir, and sell the bulbs to good people like you. My name's Foster. I own the lands all the way down to the waterfall.'

For a landowner he did not look very prosperous. But his name intrigued me.

'Isn't this area called Fosterganj?' I asked.

'That's right. My grandfather was the first to settle here. He was a grandson of Bonnie Prince Charlie who fought the British at Bannockburn. I'm the last Foster of Fosterganj. Are you sure you won't buy my daffodil bulbs?'

'I thought you said they were gladioli.'

'Some gladioli, some daffodils.'

They looked like onions to me, but to make him happy I parted with two rupees (which seemed the going rate in Fosterganj) and relieved him of his basket of bulbs. Foster shuffled off, looking a bit like Chaplin's tramp but not half as dapper. He clearly needed the two rupees. Which made me feel less foolish about spending money that I should have held on to. Writers were poor in those days. Though I didn't feel poor.

Back at the tea shop I asked Melaram if Foster really owned a lot of land.

'He has a broken-down cottage and the right-of-way. He charges people who pass through his property. Spends all the money on booze. No one owns the hillside, it's government land. Reserved forest. But everyone builds on it.'

Just as well, I thought, as I returned to town with my basket of onions. Who wanted another noisy hill station? One Mall Road was more than enough. Back in my hotel room, I was about to throw the bulbs away, but on second thoughts decided to keep them. After all, even an onion makes a handsome plant.

◆

Keep right on to the end of the road,
Keep right on to the end.
If your way be long
Let your heart be strong,
And keep right on to the end.
If you're tired and weary
Still carry on,
Till you come to your happy abode.
And then all you love
And are dreaming of,
Will be there—
At the end of the road!

The voice of Sir Harry Lauder, Scottish troubadour of the 1930s, singing one of his favourites, came drifting across the hillside as I took the winding path to Foster's cottage.

On one of my morning walks, I had helped him round up some runaway hens, and he had been suitably grateful.

'Ah, it's a fowl subject, trying to run a poultry farm,' he quipped. 'I've already lost a few to jackals and foxes. Hard to keep them in their pens. They jump over the netting and wander all over the place. But thank you for your help. It's good to be young. Once the knees go, you'll never be young again. Why don't you come over in the evening and split a bottle with me? It's a home-made brew, can't hurt you.'

I'd heard of Foster's home-made brew. More than one person had tumbled down the khad after partaking of the stuff. But I did not want to appear standoffish, and besides, I was curious about the man and his history. So towards sunset one summer's evening, I took the path down to his cottage, following the strains of Harry Lauder.

The music grew louder as I approached, and I had to knock on the door several times before it was opened by my bleary-eyed host. He had already been at the stuff he drank, and at first he failed to recognize me.

'Nice old song you have there,' I said. 'My father used to sing it when I was a boy.'

Recognition dawned, and he invited me in. 'Come in, laddie, come in. I've been expecting you. Have a seat!'

The seat he referred to was an old sofa and it was occupied by three cackling hens. With a magnificent sweep of the arm Foster swept them away, and they joined two other hens and a cock-bird on a bookrack at the other end of the room.

I made sure there were no droppings on the sofa before subsiding into it.

'Birds are finding it too hot out in the yard,' he explained. 'Keep wanting to come indoors.'

The gramophone record had run its course, and Foster

switched off the old record player.

'Used to have a real gramophone,' he said, 'but can't get the needles any more. These electric players aren't any good. But I still have all the old records.' He indicated a pile of 78 rpm gramophone records, and I stretched across and sifted through some of them. Gracie Fields, George Formby, The Street Singer...music hall favourites from the 1930s and 40s. Foster hadn't added to his collection for twenty years.

He must have been close to eighty, almost twice my age. Like his stubble (a permanent feature), the few wisps of hair on his sunburnt head were also grey. Mud had dried on his hands. His old patched-up trousers were held up by braces. There were buttons missing from his shirt, laces missing from his shoes.

'What will you have to drink, laddie? Tea, cocoa or whisky?'

'Er—not cocoa. Tea, maybe—oh, anything will do.'

'That's the spirit. Go for what you like. I make my own whisky, of course. Real Scotch from the Himalayas. I get the best barley from yonder village.' He gestured towards the next mountain, then turned to a sagging mantelpiece, fetched a bottle that contained an oily yellow liquid, and poured a generous amount into a cracked china mug. He poured a similar amount into a dirty glass tumbler, handed it to me, and said, 'Cheers! Bottoms up!'

'Bottoms up!' I said, and took a gulp.

It wasn't bad. I drank some more and asked Foster how the poultry farm was doing.

'Well, I had fifty birds to start with. But they keep wandering off, and the boys from the village make off with them. I'm down to forty. Sold a few eggs, though. Gave the bank manager the first lot. He seemed pleased. Would you like a few eggs? There's a couple on that cushion, newly laid.'

The said cushion was on a stool a few feet from me. Two

large hens' eggs were supported upon it.

'Don't sit on 'em,' said Foster, letting out a cackle which was meant to be laughter. 'They might hatch!'

I took another gulp of Foster's whisky and considered the eggs again. They looked much larger now, more like goose eggs.

Everything was looking larger.

I emptied the glass and stood up to leave.

'Don't go yet,' said Foster. 'You haven't had a proper drink. And there's dinner to follow. Sausages and mash! I make my own sausages, did you know? My sausages were famous all over Mussoorie. I supplied the Savoy, Hakman's, the schools.'

'Why did you stop?' I was back on the sofa, holding another glass of Himalayan Scotch.

'Somebody started spreading a nasty rumour that I was using dog's meat. Now why would I do that when pork was cheap? Of course, during the war years a lot of rubbish went into sausages—stuff you'd normally throw away. That's why they were called "sweet mysteries". You remember the old song? "Ah! Sweet Mystery of Life!" Nebon Eddy and Jeanette Macdonald. Well, the troops used to sing it whenever they were given sausages for breakfast. You never knew what went into them—cats, dogs, camels, scorpions. If you survived those sausages, you survived the war!'

'And your sausages, what goes into them?'

'Good, healthy chicken meat. Not crow's meat, as some jealous rivals tried to make out.'

He frowned into his china mug. It was suddenly quieter inside. The hens had joined their sisters in the backyard; they were settling down for the night, sheltering in cardboard cartons and old mango-wood boxes. Quck-quck-quck. Another day nearer to having their sad necks wrung.

I looked around the room. A threadbare carpet. Walls that

hadn't received a coat of paint for many years. A couple of loose rafters letting in a blast of cold air. Some pictures here and there—mostly racing scenes. Foster must have been a betting man. Perhaps that was how he ran out of money.

He noticed my interest in the pictures and said, 'Owned a racehorse once. A beauty, she was. That was in Meerut, just before the war. Meerut had a great racecourse. Races every Saturday. Punters came from Delhi. There was money to be made!'

'Did you win any?' I asked.

'Won a couple of races hands down. Then unexpectedly she came in last, and folks lost a lot of money. I had to leave town in a hurry. All my jockey's fault—he was hand in glove with the bookies. They made a killing, of course! Anyway, I sold the horse to a sporting Parsi gentleman and went into the canteen business with my Uncle Fred in Roorkee. That's Uncle Fred, up there.'

Foster gestured towards the mantelpiece. I expected to see a photograph of his Uncle Fred but instead of a photo I found myself staring at a naked skull. It was a well-polished skull and it glistened in the candlelight.

'That's Uncle Fred,' said Foster proudly.

'That skull? Where's the rest of him?'

'In his grave, back in Roorkee.'

'You mean you kept the skull but not the skeleton?'

'Well, it's a long story,' said Foster, 'but to keep it short, Uncle Fred died suddenly of a mysterious malady—a combination of brain fever, blood-pressure and housemaid's knee.'

'Housemaid's knee!'

'Yes, swollen kneecaps, brought about by being beaten too frequently with police lathis. He wasn't really a criminal, but he'd get into trouble from time to time, harmless little swindles such as printing his own lottery tickets or passing forged banknotes. Spent some time in various district jails until his health broke down. Got a pauper's funeral—but his cadaver was in demand. The students from the local medical college got into the cemetery one night and made off with his cranium! Not that he had much by way of a brain, but he had a handsome, well-formed skull, as you can see.'

I did see. And the skull appeared to be listening to the yarn, because its toothless jaws were extended in a grin; or so I fancied.

'And how did you get it back?' I asked.

'Broke into their demonstration room, naturally. I was younger then, and pretty agile. There it was on a shelf, among a lot of glass containers of alcohol, preserving everything from giant tapeworms to Ghulam Qadir's penis and testicles.'

'Ghulam Qadir?'

'Don't you know your history? He was the fellow who blinded the Emperor Shah Alam. They caught up with him near Saharanpur and cut his balls off. Preserved them for posterity. Waste of alcohol, though. Have another drink, laddie. And then for a sausage. Ah! Sweet Mystery of Life!'

After another drink and several 'mystery' sausages, I made my getaway and stumbled homewards up a narrow path along an open ridge. A jackal slunk ahead of me, and a screech owl screeched, but I got home safely, none the worse for an evening with the descendant of Bonnie Prince Charlie.

THE DAFFODIL CASE

It was a foggy day in March that found me idling along Baker Street, with my hands in my raincoat pockets, a threadbare scarf wound round my neck, and two pairs of socks on my feet. The BBC had commissioned me to give a talk on village life in northern India, and, ambling along Baker Street in the fog, thinking about the talk, I realized that I didn't really know very much about village life in India or anywhere else.

True, I could recall the smell of cowdung smoke and the scent of jasmine and the flood waters lapping at the walls of mud houses, but I didn't know much about village electorates or crop rotation or sugarcane prices. I was on the point of turning back and making my way to India House to get a few facts and figures when I realized I wasn't on Baker Street any more.

Wrapped in thought, I had wandered into Regent's Park. And now I wasn't sure of the way out.

A tall gentleman wearing a long grey cloak was stooping over a flower bed. Going up to him, I asked, 'Excuse me, sir— can you tell me how I get out of here?'

'How did you get in?' he asked in an impatient tone, and when he turned and faced me, I received quite a shock. He wore a peaked hunting cap, and in one hand he held a large magnifying glass. A long curved pipe hung from his sensuous lips. He possessed a strong, steely jaw and his eyes had a fierce expression they were bright with the intoxication of some drug. 'Good heavens!' I exclaimed. 'You're Sherlock Holmes!'

'And you, sir,' he replied, with a flourish of his cloak, 'are just out of India, unemployed, and due to give a lecture on the radio.' 'How did you know all that?' I stammered. 'You've never seen me before. I suppose you know my name, too?'

'Elementary, my dear Bond. The BBC notepaper in your hand, on which you have been scribbling, reveals your intentions. You are unsure of yourself, so you are not a TV personality. But you have a considered and considerate tone of voice. Definitely radio.

Your name is on the envelope which you are holding upside down. It's Bond, but you're definitely not James—you're not the type! You have to he unemployed, otherwise what would you be doing in the Park when the rest of mankind is hard at work in office, field, or factory?'

'And how do you know I'm from India?' I asked, a little resentfully.

'Your accent betrays you,' said Holmes with a knowing smile. I was about to turn away and leave him when he laid a restraining hand on my shoulder.

'Stay a moment,' he said. 'Perhaps you can be of assistance. I'm surprised at Watson. He promised to be here fifteen minutes ago but his wife must have kept him at home. Never marry, Bond. Women sap the intellect.'

'In what way can I help you?' I asked, feeling flattered now that the great man had condescended to take me into his confidence.

'Take a look at this,' said Holmes, going down on his knees near a flower-bed. 'Do you notice anything unusual?'

'Someone's been pulling out daffodils,' I said.

'Excellent, Bond! Your power of observation is as good as Watson's. Now tell me, what else do you see?'

'The ground is a little trampled, that's all.'

'By what?'

'A human foot. In high heels. And...a dog has been here too, it's been helping to dig up the bulbs!'

'You astonish me, Bond. You are quicker than I thought you'd be. Now shall I explain what this is all about? You see, for the past week someone has been stealing daffodils from the park, and the authorities have now asked me to deal with the matter. I think we shall catch our culprit today.'

I was rather disappointed. 'It isn't dangerous work, then?'

'Ah, my dear Bond, the days are past when Ruritanian princes lost their diamonds and maharanis their rubies. There are no longer any Ruritanian princes and maharanis cannot afford rubies unless they've gone into the fast-food business. The more successful criminals now work on the stock exchange, and the East End has been cleaned up. Dr Fu Manchu has a country house in Dorset. And those cretins at Scotland Yard don't even believe in my existence!'

'I'm sorry to hear that,' I said. 'Burt who do you think is stealing the daffodils?'

'Obviously it's someone who owns a dog. Someone who takes a dog out regularly for a morning walk. That points to a woman. A woman in London is likely to keep a small dog—and, judging from the animal's footprints, it was a little Pekinese or a very young Pomeranian. If you observe the damp patch on that lamp post, you will realize that it could not have been very tall. So what I propose, Bond, is that we conceal ourselves behind this herbaceous border and wait for the culprit to return to the scene of the crime. She is sure to come again this morning. She has been stealing daffodils for the past week. And stealing daffodils, like smoking opium, soon becomes a habit.'

Holmes and I concealed ourselves behind the hedge and settled down to a long wait. After half an hour, our patience was rewarded. An elderly but upright woman in a smart green hat, resembling Margaret Thatcher, came walking towards us across the grass, followed by a small white Pom on a lead. Holmes had been right! More than ever did I admire his brilliance. We waited until the woman began pulling daffodil bulbs out of the loose soil, then Holmes leapt from the bushes.

'Ah, we have you, madam!' he cried springing upon her so swiftly that she shrieked and dropped the daffodils. I bent over to gather the evidence, but my efforts were rewarded by a nip on the posterior from the outraged Pomeranian.

Holmes was restraining the woman simply by peering at her heaving bosom through his magnifying glass. I don't know what frightened her more—being caught, or being confronted by that grim-visaged countenance, with its pipe, cloak and hunting-cap.

'Now, madam,' he said firmly, 'why were you stealing Her Majesty's daffodils?'

She had begun to weep—always a woman's best defence— and I thought Holmes would soften. He always did when confronted by weeping women. And this wasn't Mrs Thatcher; she would have gone on the offensive.

'I would be obliged, Bond, if you would call the park attendant,' he said.

I hurried off to a distant greenhouse and after a brief search found a gardener. 'Stealing daffodils, is she?' he said, running up at the double, a wicked-looking rake in one hand.

But when he got to the daffodil bed, we couldn't find the thief anywhere. Nor was Holmes to be seen. Apparently they'd gone off together, leaving me in the lurch. I was overcome by doubt and embarrassment. But then I looked at the ground and saw daffodil bulbs scattered about on the grass.

'Holmes must have taken her to the police,' I said.

'Holmes,' repeated the gardener. 'And who's Holmes?'

'Sherlock Holmes, of course. The celebrated detective. Haven't you heard of him?'

The gardener gave me a suspicious look.

'Sherlock Holmes, eh? And you'll be Dr Watson, I presume?'

'Well, no,' I said apologetically. 'The name is Bond.'

That was enough for the gardener. He'd seen madmen in the park before. He turned and disappeared in the direction of the greenhouse.

Eventually I found my way out of the park, feeling that Holmes had let me down a little. Then, just as I was crossing Baker Street, I thought I saw him on the opposite curb. He was alone, looking up at a lighted room, and his arm was raised as though he was waving to someone. I thought I heard him shout 'Watson!', but I couldn't be sure. I started to cross the road, but a big red bus came out of the fog in front of me and I had to wait for it to pass. When the road was clear, I dashed across. By that time, Mr Holmes was gone, and the rooms above were dark.

TORIA AND THE DAUGHTER OF THE SUN

Once upon a time there was a young shepherd of the Santal tribe named Toria, who grazed his sheep and goats on the bank of a river. Now it happened that the daughters of the Sun would descend from heaven every day by means of a spider's web, to bathe in the river. Finding Toria there, they invited him to bathe with them. After they had bathed and anointed themselves with oils and perfumes, they returned to their heavenly abode, while Toria went to look after his flock.

Having become friendly with the daughters of the Sun, Toria gradually fell in love with one of them. But he was at a loss to know how to obtain such a divine creature. One day, when they met him and said, 'Come along, Toria, and bathe with us,' he suddenly thought of a plan.

While they were bathing, he said, 'Let us see who can stay under water the longest.' At a given signal they all dived, but very soon Toria raised his head above water and, making sure that no one was looking, hurried out of the water, picked up the robe of the girl he loved, and was in the act of carrying it away when the others raised their heads above the water.

The girl ran after him, begging him to return her garment,

but Toria did not stop till he had reached his home. When she arrived, he gave her the robe without a word. Seeing such a beautiful and noble creature before him, for very bashfulness he could not open his mouth to ask her to marry him; so he simply said, 'You can go now.'

But she replied, 'No, I will not return. My sisters by this time will have gone home. I will stay with you, and be your wife.'

All the time this was going on, a parrot, whom Toria had taught to speak, kept on flying about the heavens, calling out to the Sun: 'Oh, great Father, do not look downwards!' As a result, the Sun did not see what was happening on earth to his daughter.

This girl was very different from the women of the country—she was half human, half divine—so that when a beggar came to the house and saw her, his eyes were dazzled just as if he had stared at the Sun.

It happened that this same beggar in the course of his wanderings came to the king's palace, and having seen the queen, who was thought by all to be the most beautiful of women, he told the King: 'The shepherd Toria's wife is far more beautiful than your queen. If you were to see her, you would be enchanted.'

'How can I see her?' asked the King eagerly.

The beggar answered, 'Put on your old clothes and travel in disguise.'

The King did so, and having arrived at the shepherd's house, asked for alms. Toria's wife came out of the house and gave him food and water, but he was so astonished at seeing her great beauty that he was unable to eat or drink. His only thought was, *How can I manage to make her my queen?*

When he got home he thought over many plans and at length decided upon one. He said, 'I will order Toria to dig a large tank with his own hands, and fill it with water, and if he does not perform the task, I will kill him and seize his wife.' He then summoned Toria to the palace, commanded him to dig the tank and threatened him with death if he failed to fill the tank with water the same night.

Toria returned home slowly and sorrowfully.

'What makes you so sad today?' asked his wife.

He replied, 'The King has ordered me to dig a large tank, to fill it with water, and also to make trees grow beside it, all in the course of one night.'

'Don't let it worry you,' said his wife. 'Take your spade and mix a little water with the sand, where the tank is to be, and it will form there by itself.'

Toria did as he was told, and the King was astonished to find the tank completed in time. He had no excuse for killing Toria.

Later, the King planted a great plain with mustard seed. When it was ready for reaping, he commanded Toria to reap and gather the produce into one large heap on a certain day; failing which, he would certainly be put to death.

Toria, hearing this, was again very sad. When he told his wife about it, she said, 'Do not worry, it will be done.' So the daughter of the Sun summoned her children, the doves. They came in large numbers, and in the space of an hour carried the produce away to the King's threshing floor. Again, Toria was saved through the wisdom of his wife. However, the King determined not to be outdone, so he arranged a great hunt. On the day of the hunt he assembled his retainers, and a large number of beaters and provision-carriers, and set out for the jungle. Toria was employed to carry eggs and water. But the object of the hunt was not to kill a tiger, it was to kill Toria, so that the King might seize the daughter of the Sun and make her his wife.

Arriving at a cave, they said that a hare had taken refuge in it. They forced Toria into the cave. Then, rolling large stones against the entrance, they completely blocked it. They gathered large quantities of brushwood at the mouth of the cave, and set fire to it to smother Toria. Having done this, they returned home, boasting that they had finally disposed of the shepherd. But Toria broke the eggs, and all the ashes were scattered. Then he poured the water that he had with him on the remaining embers, and the fire was extinguished. Toria managed to crawl out of the cave. And there, to his great astonishment, he saw that all the white ashes of the fire were becoming cows, whilst the half-burnt wood was turning into buffaloes.

Toria herded the cows and buffaloes together, and drove them home.

When the King saw the herd, he became very envious, and asked Toria where he had found such fine cows and buffaloes. Toria said, 'From that cave into which you pushed me. I did not bring many with me, being on my own. But if you and all your retainers go, you will be able to get as many as you want. But to catch them it will be necessary to close the door of the cave, and light a fire in front, as you did for me.'

'Very well,' said the King. 'I and my people will enter the cave, and, as you have sufficient cows and buffaloes, kindly do not go into the cave with us, but kindle the fire outside.'

The King and his people then entered the cave. Toria blocked up the doorway, and then lit a large fire at the entrance. Before long, all that were in the cave were suffocated.

Some days later the daughter of the Sun said, 'I want to visit my father's house.'

Toria said, 'Very well, I will also go with you.'

'No, it is foolish of you to think of such a thing,' she said. 'You will not be able to get there.'

'If you are able to go, surely I can.' And he insisted on accompanying her.

After travelling a great distance, Toria became so faint from the heat of the sun that he could go no further. His wife said, 'Did I not warn you? As for quenching your thirst, there is no water to be found here. But sit down and rest, I will see if I can find some for you.'

While she was away, driven by his great thirst, Toria sucked a raw egg that he had brought with him. No sooner had he done this than he changed into a fowl. When his wife returned with water, she could not find him anywhere; but, sitting where she had left him, was a solitary fowl. Taking the bird in her arms, she continued her journey.

When she reached her father's house, her sisters asked her, 'Where is Toria, your husband?' She replied, 'I don't know. I left him on the road while I went to fetch water. When I returned, he had disappeared. Perhaps he will turn up later.'

Her sisters, seeing the fowl, thought that it would make a good meal. And so, while Toria's wife was resting, they killed and ate the fowl. Later, when they again inquired of her as to the whereabouts of her husband, she looked thoughtful.

'I can't be sure,' she said. 'But I think you have eaten him.'

MRS ROBERTS

Elsie Roberts had been quite a beauty in her twenties and thirties; one of those fair Anglo-Indians who passed for European until their accents gave them away. Elsie, it was said, did her best to remain fair, staying out of the sun as much as possible. In her later years, she was seldom seen during the day, but by then she had lost her looks and taken to drinking; she slept by day and lived by night.

In her heyday, Elsie (nee MacGowan) was a dancing partner to Roberts, a good-looking French Jew who had made his way to India just before World War II broke out. They danced in the Cabaret at the Imperial and the Swiss in Delhi, and at Hakman's in Mussoorie, and Filetto's in Lahore. They made an elegant pair; they danced beautifully. Inevitably, they were compared to Fred Astaire and Ginger Rogers, the dancing sensation of the silver screen. They married, and continued to partner each other until the war ended. Then, Roberts made a trip to France to claim and collect some compensation due to him as a war refugee. As he stood at the cashier's counter, waiting for the first instalment to be handed over to him, he collapsed and died of a heart attack. Chance gives, and takes away, and sometimes gives again; but human life is equally unpredictable.

However, Elsie, as his widow, was entitled to the proceeds.

She gave up her dancing career and took to breeding dogs. I first saw her when she came to see my mother in New Delhi, sometime in 1958. My mother was breeding Poms, and Elsie, bought a small black Pom. She was still very attractive (Elsie, not the Pom) and was escorted by a gentleman who owned a small restaurant in Mussoorie.

'He's after the money,' said my mother later, and she was right, as the gentleman in question wheedled a large sum of money out of her and then deserted her.

Elsie transferred her affections to her dogs. She rented a house outside Mussoorie and provided board and lodging to a large variety of canines. There was considerable inbreeding. Poms wed dachshunds, Samoyeds wed spaniels, and Labradors wed German shepherds. The resultant mixture was undistinguished, to say the least. Elsie didn't care. She had become devoted to her dogs and had no desire to sell them, with or without pedigree. She fed them well, and the local butcher proclaimed that she was his best customer.

Of course, strays and village dogs also found their way on to the premises. When there are free lunches to be had, dogs and humans are no different. Word soon gets around and everyone drops in for the wedding feast.

They were not a ferocious lot. Like their owner, they were wary of humans, quite paranoid about them. They'd bark furiously but scatter at the approach of anything on two legs.

When I came to live in Mussoorie in the mid-1960s, I thought I'd pay a casual visit to Mrs Roberts; my mother had asked me to look her up. She was then living near Barlowganj, where she had a huge bungalow to herself, most of it occupied by some twenty to thirty dogs.

At first she refused to see me, but when I told her who I was, she let me in. 'So, you're Edie's son,' she said. 'How is your mother?'

'Not too well, I'm afraid.'

'Does she still have her Poms?'

'Several of them.' I refrained from adding that they were a bloody nuisance. Try sharing a Delhi flat with half-a-dozen snapping, yapping, highly strung, hysterical Poms—my least favourite breed!

Mrs Roberts showed me around. The house was filthy. She was equally unkempt; her dress soiled, hands and feet unwashed, hair all over the place. Only traces of her former beauty remained. She was in her late forties, and fading fast.

But she was to live another twenty years.

The next time I saw her, about five years later, she was in considerable distress. Two or three of her dogs were suffering from mange and had to be put down. But the vet's injections hadn't worked properly (it was probably some spurious stuff) and the dogs died slowly and painfully. Mrs Roberts went further into her shell, and moved with her companions to the top of the mountain, near Sister's bazaar. Old timers in that area still remember her.

She would emerge from her house once a month, to collect her money from the local bank. The rest of the time she would remain locked up with her dogs, emerging only to receive the butcher, or the milkman who also brought her the local brew, a potent distillation made from mysterious ingredients. At the time we were going through a period of Prohibition (it was Morarji's government), but Mrs Roberts and the local villagers had beaten the system.

I, too, had come to rely on the local milkman as a source of supply. 'English wines and spirits' having been taken off the market, kacchi-sharab, the special from Kotti, Kanda and other gaons, was the only alternative. My milkman used my hot-water bottle to bring me the stuff. Unfortunately, the hot-water bottle stank for weeks afterwards, and could no longer be used for legitimate purposes. No matter. Those were desperate times.

Mrs Roberts had been on the stuff for years and was apparently none the worse for it. Prohibition came and went, and politicians came and went, and while frail creatures such as I returned to mere whisky and water, tougher souls, such as Elsie Roberts, continued with the local stuff, which was certainly more potent.

Two or three years passed, and I had forgotten Mrs Roberts and her dogs, when one morning the local missionary-doctor, Dr Olsen, dropped in to tell me she had died in the night (of double pneumonia) and did I know if she had any relatives.

'None that I know of,' I had to say, 'Just those dogs.'

She was given a pauper's burial in the little burial ground below Woodstock, where some of the school's Christian servants were laid to rest. No tombstones there. As a beautiful young dancer she'd been the toast of Mussoorie. That had been over forty years ago. Now, friendless, she had been swept away like a dead leaf.

And what of the dogs?

Bereft of their benefactor and bewildered by her absence, they ran wild. Some fled into the forest and perished. A few survived, along with the many street dogs that proliferate around the hill station.

If you see a dog that looks especially weird (bits of terrier, spaniel, Pom and dachshund), you'll know it's descended from one of Mrs Roberts' pets. She did leave us a legacy of sorts.

TOPAZ

It seemed strange to be listening to the strains of 'The Blue Danube' while gazing out at the pine-clad slopes of the Himalayas, worlds apart. And yet the music of the waltz seemed singularly appropriate. A light breeze hummed through the pines, and the branches seemed to move in time to the music. The record player was new, but the records were old, picked up in a junk shop behind the Mall.

Below the pines there were oaks, and one oak tree in particular caught my eye. It was the biggest of the lot and stood by itself on a little knoll below the cottage. The breeze was not strong enough to lift its heavy old branches, but *something* was moving, swinging gently from the tree, keeping time to the music of the waltz, dancing...

It was someone hanging from the tree.

A rope oscillated in the breeze, the body turned slowly, turned this way and that, and I saw the face of a girl, her hair hanging loose, her eyes sightless, hands and feet limp; just turning, turning, while the waltz played on.

I turned off the player and ran downstairs.

Down the path through the trees, and on to the grassy knoll where the big oak stood.

A long-tailed magpie took fright and flew out from the

branches, swooping low across the ravine. In the tree there was no one, nothing. A great branch extended halfway across the knoll, and it was possible for me to reach up and touch it. A girl could not have reached it without climbing the tree.

As I stood there, gazing up into the branches, someone spoke behind me.

'What are you looking at?'

I swung round. A girl stood in the clearing, facing me. A girl of seventeen or eighteen; alive, healthy, with bright eyes and a tantalizing smile. She was lovely to look at. I hadn't seen such a pretty girl in years.

'You startled me,' I said. 'You came up so unexpectedly.'

'Did you see anything—in the tree?' she asked.

'I thought I saw someone from my window. That's why I came down. Did *you* see anything?'

'No.' She shook her head, the smile leaving her face for a moment. 'I don't see anything. But other people do—sometimes.'

'What do they see?'

'My sister.'

'Your *sister*?'

'Yes. She hanged herself from this tree. It was many years ago. But sometimes you can see her hanging there.'

She spoke matter-of-factly: whatever had happened seemed very remote to her.

We both moved some distance away from the tree. Above the knoll, on a disused private tennis court (a relic from the hill station's colonial past) was a small stone bench. She sat down on it: and, after a moment's hesitation, I sat down beside her.

'Do you live close by?' I asked.

'Further up the hill. My father has a small bakery.'

She told me her name—Hameeda. She had two younger brothers.

'You must have been quite small when your sister died.'

'Yes. But I remember her. She was pretty.'

'Like you.'

She laughed in disbelief. 'Oh, I am nothing to her. You should have seen my sister.'

'Why did she kill herself?'

'Because she did not want to live. That's the only reason, no? She was to have been married but she loved someone else, someone who was not of our own community. It's an old story and the end is always sad, isn't it?'

'Not always. But what happened to the boy—the one she loved? Did he kill himself too?'

'No, he took a job in some other place. Jobs are not easy to get, are they?'

'I don't know. I've never tried for one.'

'Then what do you do?'

'I write stories.'

'Do people *buy* stories?'

'Why not? If your father can sell bread, I can sell stories.'

'People must have bread. They can live without stories.'

'No, Hameeda, you're wrong. People can't live without stories.'

Hameeda! I couldn't help loving her. Just loving her. No fierce desire or passion had taken hold of me. It wasn't like that. I was happy just to look at her, watch her while she sat on the grass outside my cottage, her lips stained with the juice of wild bilberries. She chatted away—about her friends, her clothes, her favourite things.

'Won't your parents mind if you come here every day?' I asked.

'I have told them you are teaching me.'

'Teaching you what?'

'They did not ask. You can tell me stories.'

So I told her stories.

It was midsummer.

The sun glinted on the ring she wore on her third finger: a translucent golden topaz, set in silver.

'That's a pretty ring,' I remarked.

'You wear it,' she said, impulsively removing it from her hand. 'It will give you good thoughts. It will help you to write better stories.'

She slipped it on to my little finger.

'I'll wear it for a few days,' I said. 'Then you must let me give it back to you.'

On a day that promised rain I took the path down to the stream at the bottom of the hill. There I found Hameeda gathering ferns from the shady places along the rocky ledges above the water.

'What will you do with them?' I asked.

'This is a special kind of fern. You can cook it as a vegetable.'

'Is it tasty?'

'No, but it is good for rheumatism.'

'Do you suffer from rheumatism?'

'Of course not. They are for my grandmother, she is very old.'

'There are more ferns further upstream,' I said. 'But we'll have to get into the water.'

We removed our shoes and began paddling upstream. The ravine became shadier and narrower, until the sun was almost completely shut out. The ferns grew right down to the water's edge. We bent to pick them but instead found ourselves in each other's arms; and sank slowly, as in a dream, into the soft bed of ferns, while overhead a whistling thrush burst out in a dark sweet song.

'It isn't time that's passing by,' it seemed to say. 'It is you and I. It is you and I...'

I waited for her the following day, but she did not come. Several days passed without my seeing her.

Was she sick? Had she been kept at home? Had she been sent away? I did not even know where she lived, so I could not ask. And if I had been able to ask, what would I have said?

Then one day I saw a boy delivering bread and pastries at the little tea shop about a mile down the road. From the upward slant of his eyes, I caught a slight resemblance to Hameeda. As he left the shop, I followed him up the hill. When I came abreast of him, I asked: 'Do you have your own bakery?'

He nodded cheerfully, 'Yes. Do you want anything—bread, biscuits, cakes? I can bring them to your house.'

'Of course. But don't you have a sister? A girl called Hameeda?'

His expression changed. He was no longer friendly. He looked puzzled and slightly apprehensive.

'Why do you want to know?'

'I haven't seen her for some time.'

'We have not seen her either.'

'Do you mean she has gone away?'

'Didn't you know? You must have been away a long time. It is many years since she died. She killed herself. You did not hear about it?'

'But wasn't that her sister—your other sister?'

'I had only one sister—Hameeda—and she died, when I was very young. It's an old story, ask someone else about it.'

He turned away and quickened his pace, and I was left standing in the middle of the road, my head full of questions that couldn't be answered.

That night there was a thunderstorm. My bedroom window kept banging in the wind. I got up to close it and, as I looked out, there was a flash of lightning and I saw that frail body again, swinging from the oak tree.

I tried to make out the features, but the head hung down and the hair was blowing in the wind.

Was it all a dream?

It was impossible to say. But the topaz on my hand glowed softly in the darkness. And a whisper from the forest seemed to say, 'It isn't time that's passing by, my friend. It is you and I....'

AN EVENING AT THE SAVOY WITH H.H.*

H.H. back in town meant that Signor Montalban was back too, and for the convenience of all concerned it was decided that his family would move into the rented house selected for them. Pablo did not object to the move, as the house was nearer to the town and its cinemas. It meant that I would see less of them as my cottage was almost an hour's walk in the opposite direction.

Montalban's visits to Mussoorie to see his beloved were brief, and he spent more time at the Hollow Oak palace than at his wife's residence. H. H. threw a party whenever he was in town. Mrs Montalban, pleading indisposition, stayed away. I attended only one of them, a lugubrious affair which ended with Neena drinking too much and ending up, quite literally, under the table. In trying to extricate her, I too collapsed on the floor, and we ended up a tangle of arms and legs.

'Just like old times,' said Neena, subsiding into a sofa. 'I wish you had got to grips with me when we were a little younger.'

'I did try,' I said. 'But you were always as elusive as a shark.

---

*From *Maharani*

You were looking for other prey.'

'Well, you were rather dull. Always had your head in a book. But I hear you're quite friendly with that equally dull creature, Signora Montalban.'

'She likes books too,' I said. 'I lend her mine and she lends me hers.'

'How romantic. Like Elizabeth Barrett and Robert Browning, reading their poems to each other.'

'Bet you never read any of their poetry.' 'Yes, I did. At school, remember? "The Pied Piper of Hamelin". And you're a bit of a Pied Piper yourself. That boy follows you around everywhere.'

'Pablo. He needs a father. But his father doesn't need him. Too busy elsewhere. Too busy mixing drinks.'

Montalban was doing just that—standing behind H. H.'s minibar, making drinks for her guests.

'Diplomatic duties,' I said.

'You're just jealous,' said Neena.

'And you're just jealous of Elizabeth Barrett Browning.'

Neena gave a shriek of laughter, got up, and sat down on the floor again. This time I did not help her up, but left her to the attentions of a tall, strikingly handsome foreigner wearing a saffron robe. It turned out that he was an Anglo-German neophyte at an ashram up in the mountains. He was drinking apple juice.

◆

Mrs Montalban moved into her new abode without any fuss or bother, engaged a cook and a maidservant, and directed all her energies into caring for her children. In other words, she was the ideal Indian wife and mother.

So, while H. H. played the femme fatale and Montalban fancied himself a Valentino, Mrs Montalban was simply a homely bread-and-butter woman who busied herself baking cakes and cookies.

And she baked them well, as I discovered one afternoon when I dropped in at Pablo's invitation a week or two after they had moved into their new abode.

Already, the wide verandah looked like no verandah I had ever seen. The walls were festooned with film posters, all assiduously collected over the summer months. Apart from the manager of the Picture Palace, Pablo had made friends with the projectionist at the Rialto, the ticket seller at the Majestic, and the tea stall owner at the Jubilee—all of whom had gone out of their way to save posters for him. Partly it was due to his personal charm and friendly nature; partly due to his generosity with his mother's cakes and cookies.

And now, on my first visit to the rented house, I was taken from one poster to another as though I were the chief guest at a grand art exhibition—which is what it was, in a way. For here were the great stars of the '60s and earlier in some of their most famous roles. And Pablo, in a way, was a pioneer, for he had discovered that the film poster was an art form in itself, and I doubt if anyone, till then, had built up such a collection. He must have had close to a hundred posters. Not all were on the verandah wall. His favourites were in his bedroom. And when I went to the bathroom to ease myself, I found myself staring at a large poster of *It's a Mad Mad Mad Mad World*. And I had to agree with it.

It was little sister Anna's birthday.

A large cake stood on a table in the sunroom—a small sitting room with glazed window. During the day it received the morning sun; at night, the rising moon. It was Anna's favourite room, and she liked to sit there and draw or paint until it grew dark.

I looked at some of her sketches—flower studies, trees, small animals—all quite charming but nothing out of the ordinary—until I came to a sketch of a face, just a line drawing, incomplete but in a way quite compelling; the face of a girl, pretty and vivacious, but a little old-fashioned, judging by the plaited hair and the ribbons.

'Who's this?' I asked.

'Just a girl I saw the other day. She looked at me over the gate and hurried away. It was raining. I saw her again yesterday. She had her face pressed to the window. She looked very sweet, but shy like a gazelle—she had her face against the glass and she kept staring at me. That's how I remember her features so well. But when I got up to open the window, she ran off. Just disappeared! I hope she comes again. I'd like her for a friend.'

I was the only guest at that little birthday party. Mrs Montalban had met a number of people while staying at Hollow Oak, but they had all been Neena's friends; she hadn't hit it off with any of them. Her English was weak and her Hindi non-existent; she spoke to her children in Spanish. But she was aware of Pablo's growing affection for me and she was glad of any overtures of friendship towards her and her family.

Montalban was of course absent—out of town—away on a diplomatic mission to Thailand or Timbuctoo, and this time without H. H. for company.

The cake was splendid, full of good things like walnuts and raisins and cherries, and I have to confess that I consumed the lion's share; but I was always like that, a glutton for the good things in life—birthday cakes, books and a comfortable bed, all in that order. Mrs M and the children were delighted by my appetite, and Mrs M vowed to bake bigger and better cakes if I would come over more often. I promised that I would.

H. H. must have heard that it was Anna's birthday because

presently one of her lackeys arrived with a large gift-wrapped parcel. When opened, it revealed an expensive doll, beautifully dressed, with what appeared to be a real hair—glossy black tresses—done up in a coiffure. Anna stood it up on the table and it immediately broke into a chorus of 'Happy Birthday to you!'

We all clapped and Mrs Montalban sat down to write a thank you note to Neena. She would have sent her some cake too, but for the fact that I had finished it.

Pablo was staring intently at the doll.

'It looks like the maharani,' he said, a glint of the devil in his eyes.

'Even the voice is a bit like hers,' I added.

'It's a beautiful doll,' said Mrs Montalban. 'Especially the dress.'

'And the hair,' said Anna, stroking it gently.

The doll was put aside and Pablo produced a guitar and began strumming on it.

'I didn't know you could play the guitar,' I said.

'Only a little bit,' he said, and played a familiar tune which sounded a bit like 'Jealousy', a tango from an earlier time. The tune was perhaps a fitting prelude to what happened next.

There was a jingle of bells and a rickshaw pulled by two uniformed but barefooted young men pulled up at the gate, and out stepped H. H. in all her finery, looking very regal, albeit a little unsteady on her feet.

'A party without me,' she scolded, genuinely upset. 'Why didn't you invite me?'

'It was just the children,' said Mrs Montalban defensively.

'And I suppose you're Peter Pan,' said Neena, glaring at me.

'I thought I was supposed to be the Pied Piper,' I said. 'But I came accidentally. I didn't know it was Anna's birthday.'

'It's just like the maharani,' said Pablo, straight-faced. 'Even the voice.'

Neena ignored him. She had been conscious of his resentment ever since she had seduced his father. It did not bother her. Spreading a little unhappiness was one of her chief pleasures.

'Well,' she said, hands on hips, a typical pose when she wanted to get her way. 'We're going to celebrate properly. No tea and cakes, just cakes and ale! I'm taking you out for dinner. We'll go to the Savoy! And you can come too, Pied Piper. A pity Ricardo isn't here, but you'll have to do as our escort or whatever.'

'Your friend in need,' I said. 'Always at your service.'

'Good. You can pay for the drinks.'

The rickshaw—the late maharaja's personal rickshaw—was dismissed as it could only seat two. Rickshaws were on their way out and only a few remained in town. But there were now three taxis and we sent for one of them, a large Chevrolet which had seen better days. I sat up front next to the driver and H. H., and Mrs Montalban and the children squeezed in at the back.

It was late July, and a monsoon mist hung over the mountain. There were hardly any tourists in town and the grand old hotel was practically empty; but the bar was functioning, or so it seemed, and Neena headed straight for it.

Like the rickshaw and the taxi and the royal house of Mastipur, the old hotel had also seen better days. A musty odour emanated from the worn carpets. Outside it was raining; but inside, the decorative plants were drooping from lack of water. If you sat on an easy chair in the lounge there was a strong possibility of a loose spring probing your rectum.

H. H. wasn't wasting time in the lounge. She headed straight for the bar. She barged through the swing doors and we were immediately assailed by the combined odour of stale beer, mildew and disintegrating cheese-and-tomato sandwiches.

Neena herded us into this chamber of horrors and called out, 'Barman, barman, beer for all!'

There was no response.

The room was empty and there was no one behind the bar.

'Perhaps it's a dry day,' I said. 'Or someone's death anniversary.'

'Shut up,' said Neena. 'There are no dry days in this town.' She peered over the bar counter, then let out a shriek of laughter. 'Maybe there's a death after all. Our bartender is well and truly pissed!'

True enough, the bartender was stretched out on the floor, snoring away, blissfully unaware of the arrival of customers. It was obvious he'd been helping himself to various liquors and liqueurs, trying each one for taste and aroma.

'He's completely blotto,' said Neena. 'We'll just have to help ourselves.' And she reached for a bottle of Scotch, intoning. 'Don't be vague. Ask for Haig.'

'A glass of wine for me,' interposed Mrs Montalban. 'The children can have soft drinks.'

'No soft drinks here,' said Neena. 'But Pablo can have a beer. My boys started when they were six.'

'No lip from you, Peter Piper. Down your whisky and then go in search of the manager. If you can't find the manager, find the cook. If you can't find the cook, find the masalchi. We want something to eat. It's Anna's birthday, damn and blast!'

Damned and blasted, I went in search of the hotel staff and, after wandering around the empty halls and corridors of this vast mausoleum, finally bumped into someone who looked like a manager.

'We're looking for something to eat,' I said.

'Well, so am I, sir.'

'Are you the manager?'

'No, I'm the pianist.'

'Pianist! But I haven't seen a piano anywhere.'

'There isn't one. They sold it last week to a collector from Bombay. I'm Ivan Lobo,' he said, extending his hand.

We shook hands and I introduced myself.

'The hotel appears to be deserted,' I said. 'And the bartender is fast asleep.'

'Well, the hotel is up for sale, you know. The owner has gone missing—last seen in Bangladesh. And the cook is in hospital with food poisoning.'

'Well, in that case, I don't think we'll want anything to eat. I'd better go back to the bar and tell the others.'

'I'll come with you,' said Mr Lobo. 'Perhaps I can be of help.'

When we got to the bar, Neena was on her second whisky.

'Don't be vague,' she chirruped. 'Ask for Haig!'

'This is Mr Lobo,' I said. 'He's the pianist.'

'How lovely! It's just the sort of evening for some romantic music. "What Do They Do On a Rainy Night in Rio?" I love that one.'

'Well, it's a rainy night in Mussoorie. And there's no piano. And no cook.'

'Well, fetch the owner. Isn't he around?'

'He's gone underground,' I said.

'Oh, it's old Chawla, I am not surprised. Used to play billiards with my husband. Did nothing else. Have a drink, Mr Lobo. I've always had a soft spot for pianists.'

She poured Mr Lobo a Patiala peg and gave herself another. Meanwhile, the bartender had woken from his slumbers. He wiped his face on a tablecloth, burped, and asked us if we'd like something to drink.

'We're doing all right without you,' said Neena. 'But give

yourself a drink, you poor man. You look as though you need one. And you'll probably be out of job next week.'

'Now then, Melaram,' said Mr Lobo, expanding a little under the gentle influence of Haig. 'We have to do something for our guests here. Pull yourself together, run down to the bazaar, and order some food from the Hum Tum Dhaba. What would like madam?'

'Maharani, no madam.'

'A thousand pardons, Your Highness. I didn't know you were you. I've seen your picture in the papers. The Maharani of Ranipur.'

'Mastipur, sir. Mastipur.'

'Coming from Goa, I am unfamiliar with the names of so many of our states.'

'So why aren't you playing the piano in Goa? Everyone there is a musician, I hear.'

'They were, until Jimi Hendrix died in his bathtub and Janis Joplin took an overdose. Singers get nervous when they reach the age of twenty-seven. That's when they succumb to something or the other.'

'Well, you're a pianist, not a singer. And if you're out of a job, you can come and play the piano for me every evening. It needs tuning anyway.'

'Much obliged, ma'am.'

'Maharani ji.'

'Your Highness.'

'That's better.'

Food was brought from the Hum Tum Dhaba (at Savoy prices) and the children and I tucked in. Mrs Montalban never ate much. H. H. concentrated on the whisky. And Mr Lobo, out of politeness, kept pace with us. The taxi having been dismissed, the bartender was sent out in search of another, but failed to return.

The evening had been too much for him.

The clock on the wall hadn't worked since the great earthquake of 1905, but my watch was showing midnight when the party broke up. Mrs Montalban and the children decided to walk home. Neena was by now incapable of walking. Mr Lobo and I got her as far as the front steps, where she subsided into a hydrangea bush.

'There's an old rickshaw kept in a shed near the office,' said Mr Lobo. 'I'll see if I can get someone to pull it for us.'

But at that late hour there was no rickshaw-puller to be found. I was still trying to extricate Neena from the hydrangea— and being roundly abused in the process—when Mr Lobo came round the corner, pulling the decrepit but movable rickshaw.

'If you can get her in,' he gasped, already out of breath, 'we'll take her home ourselves!'

'He's a real man!' shrieked Neena. 'Not a namby-pamby bastard like you!'

'Any more abuse and I'll leave you here with Mr Lobo. You can both occupy the VIP suite. Many famous people have slept in it—Emperor Haile Selassie, the Panchen Lama, Pearl S. Buck, Raj Kapoor, Helen, and Polly Umrigar the cricketer.'

'What—all together?' giggled Neena. 'It must have been quite an orgy!'

'Not all together, Your Highness. Separately, and at different times.'

'Helen of Troy, too.'

'Not Helen of Troy. Helen, the Bollywood dancer.'

'Well then, let's dance,' said H. H., making a great effort to get up. 'Mr Lobo can play the piano while we dance.'

'First we have to get you home. The piano's at your place, remember? The hotel doesn't have one.'

'When We're all out Dancing Cheek to Cheek,' H. H. began singing an old Fred Astaire number.

Mr Lobo and I began singing along with her, at the same time getting her to stand up and stagger towards the rickshaw. We managed to get her on to the seat, where she sat up for a moment, observing, 'These two don't look like my rickshaw boys,' before subsiding again.

'You pull and I'll push,' said Mr Lobo gallantly.

'No, you pull and I'll push,' I countered. 'Pulling is better exercise for piano players. I'm just a pen-pusher.'

That settled, we set off on the long haul to Hollow Oak, and believe me, it was a struggle all the way. The rickshaw was an old one, long out of use. It squeaked and rattled, and the wheels gave every indication of wanting to come off. Nevertheless, we made progress, encouraged by cries of abuse alternating with shouts of merriment from H. H., who was obviously enjoying the ride.

For those few who were out on the Mall that night, it must have been quite a sight—Kipling's phantom rickshaw emerging from the mist on a moonlit night, propelled along by a couple of well-dressed but dishevelled gentlemen who were spurred on by a mad maharani waving in royal fashion to an imaginary crowd—the effect spoilt only by the obscenities that tripped off her tongue.

We got her home eventually and put her to bed. I had the guest room opened for Mr Lobo and told him he'd better stay the night.

'About giving me a job as a pianist,' he said. 'Did she really mean it?'

'You'll know in the morning,' I said. 'Get a good night's sleep. And if she throws you out in the morning, you can come and have breakfast with me.'

WILSON'S BRIDGE

The old wooden bridge has gone, and today an iron suspension bridge straddles the Bhagirathi as it rushes down the gorge below Gangotri. But villagers will tell you that you can still hear the hooves of Wilson's horse as he gallops across the bridge he had built 150 years ago. At the time people were sceptical of its safety, and so, to prove its sturdiness, he rode across it again and again. Parts of the old bridge can still be seen on the far bank of the river. And the legend of Wilson and his pretty hill bride, Gulabi, is still well-known in this region.

I had joined some friends in the old forest rest house near the river. There were the Rays, recently married, and the Duttas, married many years. The younger Rays quarrelled frequently; the older Duttas looked on with more amusement than concern. I was a part of their group and yet something of an outsider. As a single man, I was a person of no importance. And as a marriage counsellor, I wouldn't have been of any use to them.

I spent most of my time wandering along the river banks or exploring the thick deodar and oak forests that covered the slopes. It was these trees that had made a fortune for Wilson and his patron, the Raja of Tehri. They had exploited the great forests to the full, floating huge logs downstream to the timber yards in the plains.

Returning to the rest house late one evening, I was halfway across the bridge when I saw a figure at the other end, emerging from the mist. Presently I made out a woman, wearing the plain dhoti of the hills; her hair fell loose over her shoulders. She appeared not to see me, and reclined against the railing of the bridge, looking down at the rushing waters far below. And then, to my amazement and horror, she climbed over the railing and threw herself into the river.

I ran forward, calling out, but I reached the railing only to see her fall into the foaming waters below, from where she was carried swiftly downstream.

The watchman's cabin stood a little way off. The door was open. The watchman, Ram Singh, was reclining on his bed, smoking a hookah.

'Someone just jumped off the bridge,' I said breathlessly. 'She's been swept down the river!'

The watchman was unperturbed. 'Gulabi again,' he said, almost to himself; and then to me, 'Did you see her clearly?'

'Yes, a woman with long loose hair—but I didn't see her face very clearly.'

'It must have been Gulabi. Only a ghost, my dear sir. Nothing to be alarmed about. Every now and then someone sees her throw herself into the river. Sit down,' he said, gesturing towards a battered old armchair, 'be comfortable and I'll tell you all about it.'

I was far from comfortable, but I listened to Ram Singh tell me the tale of Gulabi's suicide. After making me a glass of hot sweet tea, he launched into a long, rambling account of how Wilson, a British adventurer seeking his fortune, had been hunting musk deer when he encountered Gulabi on the path from her village. The girl's grey-green eyes and peach-blossom complexion enchanted him, and he went out of his way to get to know her people. Was he in love with her, or did he simply find her beautiful and desirable? We shall never really know. In the course of his travels and adventures he had known many women, but Gulabi was different, childlike and ingenuous, and he decided he would marry her. The humble family to which she belonged had no objection. Hunting had its limitations, and Wilson found it more profitable to tap the region's great forest wealth. In a few years he had made a fortune. He built a large timbered house at Harsil, another in Dehradun and a third at Mussoorie. Gulabi had all she could have wanted, including two robust little sons. When he was away on work, she looked after their children and their large apple orchard at Harsil.

And then came the evil day when Wilson met the Englishwoman, Ruth, on the Mussoorie Mall, and decided that she should have a share of his affections and his wealth. A fine house was provided for her, too. The time he spent at Harsil with Gulabi and his children dwindled. 'Business affairs'—he was now one of the owners of a bank—kept him in the fashionable hill resort. He was a popular host and took his friends and associates on shikar parties in the Doon.

Gulabi brought up her children in village style. She heard stories of Wilson's dalliance with the Mussoorie woman and, on one of his rare visits, she confronted him and voiced her resentment, demanding that he leave the other woman. He brushed her aside and told her not to listen to idle gossip. When he turned away from her, she picked up the flintlock pistol that lay on the gun table and fired one shot at him. The bullet missed him and shattered her looking glass. Gulabi ran out of the house, through the orchard and into the forest, then down the steep path to the bridge built by Wilson only two or three years before. When he had recovered his composure, he mounted his horse and came looking for her. It was too late. She had already thrown herself off the bridge into the swirling waters far below. Her body was found a mile or two downstream, caught between some rocks.

This was the tale that Ram Singh told me, with various flourishes and interpolations of his own. I thought it would make a good story to tell my friends that evening, before the fireside in the rest house. They found the story fascinating, but when I told them I had seen Gulabi's ghost, they thought I was doing a little embroidering of my own. Mrs Dutta thought it was a tragic tale. Young Mrs Ray thought Gulabi had been very silly. 'She was a simple girl,' opined Mr Dutta. 'She responded in the only way she knew...'; 'Money can't buy happiness,' said Mr Ray. 'No,' said Mrs Dutta, 'but it can buy you a great many comforts.' Mrs Ray wanted to talk of other things, so I changed the subject. It can get a little confusing for a bachelor who must spend the evening with two married couples. There are undercurrents which he is aware of but not equipped to deal with.

I would walk across the bridge quite often after that. It was busy with traffic during the day, but after dusk there were only a few vehicles on the road and seldom any pedestrians. A mist rose from the gorge below and obscured the far end of the bridge. I preferred walking there in the evening, half-expecting, half-hoping to see Gulabi's ghost again. It was her face that I really wanted to see. Would she still be as beautiful as she was fabled to be?

It was on the evening before our departure that something happened that would haunt me for a long time afterwards.

There was a feeling of restiveness as our days there drew to a close. The Rays had apparently made up their differences, although they weren't talking very much. Mr Dutta was anxious to get back to his office in Delhi and Mrs Dutta's rheumatism was playing up. I was restless too, wanting to return to my writing desk in Mussoorie.

That evening I decided to take one last stroll across the bridge to enjoy the cool breeze of a summer's night in the mountains. The moon hadn't come up, and it was really quite dark, although there were lamps at either end of the bridge providing sufficient light for those who wished to cross over.

I was standing in the middle of the bridge, in the darkest part, listening to the river thundering down the gorge, when I saw the sari-draped figure emerging from the lamplight and making towards the railings.

Instinctively I called out, 'Gulabi!'

She half-turned towards me, but I could not see her clearly. The wind had blown her hair across her face and all I saw was wildly staring eyes. She raised herself over the railing and threw herself off the bridge. I heard the splash as her body struck the water far below.

Once again I found myself running towards the part of the railing where she had jumped. And then someone was running towards the same spot, from the direction of the rest house. It was young Mr Ray.

'My wife!' he cried out. 'Did you see my wife?'

He rushed to the railing and stared down at the swirling waters of the river.

'Look! There she is!' He pointed at a helpless figure bobbing about in the water.

We ran down the steep bank to the river but the current had swept her on. Scrambling over rocks and bushes, we made frantic efforts to catch up with the drowning woman. But the river in that defile is a roaring torrent, and it was over an hour before we were able to retrieve poor Mrs Ray's body, caught in driftwood about a mile downstream.

She was cremated not far from where we found her and we returned to our various homes in gloom and grief, chastened but none the wiser for the experience.

If you happen to be in that area and decide to cross the bridge late in the evening, you might see Gulabi's ghost or hear the hoofbeats of Wilson's horse as he canters across the old wooden bridge looking for her. Or you might see the ghost of Mrs Ray and hear her husband's anguished cry. Or there might be others. Who knows?

DEATH OF A FAMILIAR

When I learnt from a mutual acquaintance that my friend Sunil had been killed, I could not help feeling a little surprised, even shocked. Had Sunil killed somebody, it would not have surprised me in the least; he did not greatly value the lives of others. But for him to have been the victim was a sad reflection of his rapid decline.

He was twenty-one at the time of his death. Two friends of his had killed him, stabbing him several times with their knives. Their motive was said to have been revenge. Apparently he had seduced their wives. They had invited him to a bar in Meerut, had plied him with country liquor, and had then accompanied him out into the cold air of a December night. It was drizzling a little. Near the bridge over the canal, one of his companions seized him from behind, while the other plunged a knife first into his stomach and then into his chest. When Sunil slumped forward, the other friend stabbed him in the back. A passing cyclist saw the little group, heard a cry and a groan, saw a blade flash in the light from his lamp. He pedalled furiously into town, burst into the kotwali and roused the sergeant on duty. Accompanied by two constables, they ran to the bridge but found the area deserted. It was only as the rising sun drew an open wound across the sky that they found Sunil's body on the canal bank, his head and shoulders on the sand, his legs in running water.

The bar keeper was able to describe Sunil's companions, and they were arrested that same morning in their homes. They had not found time to get rid of their blood-soaked clothes. As they were not known to me, I took very little interest in the proceedings against them; but I understand that they have appealed against their sentences of life imprisonment.

I was in Delhi at the time of the murder, and it was almost a year since I had last seen Sunil. We had both lived in Shahganj and had left the place for jobs; I to work in a newspaper office, he in a paper factory owned by an uncle. It had been hoped that he would in time acquire a sense of responsibility and some stability of character. But I had known Sunil for over two years, and in that time it had been made abundantly clear that he had not been born to fit in with the conventions. And as for character, his had the stability of a grasshopper. He was forever in search of new adventures and sensations, and this appetite of his for every novelty led him into some awkward situations.

He was a product of Partition, of the frontier provinces, of Anglo-Indian public schools, of films Indian and American, of medieval India, knights in armour, hippies, drugs, sex magazines and the subtropical Terai. Had he lived in the time of the Moguls, he might have governed a province with saturnine and spectacular success. Being born into the twentieth century, he was but a juvenile delinquent.

It must be said to his credit that he was a delinquent of charm and originality. I realized this when I first saw him, sitting on the wall of the football stadium, his long legs—looking even longer and thinner because of the tight trousers he wore— dangling over the wall, his chappals trailing in the dust of the road, while his white bush-shirt lay open, unbuttoned, showing his smooth brown chest. He had a smile on his long face, which, with its high cheekbones, gave his cheeks a cavernous look, an impression of unrequited hunger.

We were both watching the wrestling. Two practice bouts were in progress—one between two thin, undernourished boys, and the other between the master of the *akhara* and a bearded Sikh who drove trucks for a living. They struggled in the soft mud of the wrestling pit, their well-oiled bodies glistening in the sunlight that filtered through a massive banyan tree. I had been standing near the akhara for a few minutes when I became conscious of the young man's gaze. When I turned round to look at him, he smiled satanically.

'Are you a wrestler, too?' he asked.

'Do I look like one?' I countered.

'No, you look more like an athlete,' he said. 'I mean a long-distance runner. Very thin.'

'I'm a writer. Like long-distance runners most writers are very thin.'

'You're an Anglo-Indian, aren't you?'

'My family history is very complicated, otherwise I'd be delighted to give you all the details.'

'You could pass for a European, you know. You're quite fair. But you have an Indian accent.'

'An Indian accent is very similar to a Welsh accent,' I observed. 'I might pass for Welsh, but not many people in India have met Welshmen!'

He chuckled at my answer, then stared at me speculatively. 'I say,' he said at length, as though an idea of great weight and importance had occurred to him. 'Do you have any magazines with pictures of dames?'

'Well, I may have some old *Playboys*. You can have them if you like.'

'Thanks,' he said, getting down from the wall. 'I'll come and fetch them. This wresting is boring, anyway.'

He slipped his hand into mine (a custom of no special significance), and began whistling snatches of Hindi film tunes and the latest American hits.

I was living at the time in a small flat above the town's main shopping centre. Below me there were shops, restaurants and a cinema. Behind the building lay a junkyard littered with the framework of vintage cars and broken-down tongas. I was paying thirty rupees a month for my two rooms, and sixty to the Punjabi restaurant where I took my meals. My earnings as a freelance writer were something like a hundred and fifty rupees a month, sufficient to enable me to make both ends meet, provided I remained in the backwater that was Shahganj.

Sunil (I had learnt his name during our walk from the stadium) made himself at home in my flat as soon as he entered it. He went through all my magazines, books and photographs with the thoroughness of an executor of a will. In India, it is customary for people to try and find out all there is to know about you, and Sunil went through the formalities with considerable thoroughness. While he spoke, his roving eyes made a mental inventory of all my belongings. These were few—a typewriter, a small radio and a cupboard full of books and clothes, besides the furniture that went with the flat. I had no valuables. Was he disappointed? I could not be sure. He wore good clothes and spoke fluent English, but good clothes and good English are no criteria for honesty. He was a little too glib to inspire confidence. Apparently, he was still at college. His father owned a cloth shop—a strict man who did not give his son much spending money.

But Sunil was not seriously interested in money, as I was shortly to discover. He was interested in experience, and searched for it in various directions.

'You have a nice view,' he said, leaning over my balcony and looking up and down the street. 'You can see everyone on parade. Girls! They're becoming quite modern now. Short hair and small blouses. Tight salwars. Maxis, minis. Falsies. Do you like girls?'

'Well...' I began, but he did not really expect an answer to his question.

'What are little girls made of? That's an English poem, isn't it? "Sugar and spice and everything nice..." And I don't remember the rest.' He lowered his voice to a confidential undertone. 'Have you had any girls?'

'Well...'

'I had fun with a girl, you know, my cousin. She came to stay with us last summer. Then there's a girl in college who's stuck on me. But this is such a backward country. We can't be seen together in public and I can't invite her to my house. Can I bring her here some day?'

'Well, I don't know...' I hadn't lived in a small town like Shahganj for some time, and wasn't sure if morals had changed along with the fashions.

'Oh, not now,' he said. 'There's no hurry. I'll give you plenty of warning, don't worry.' He put an arm around my shoulders and looked at me with undisguised affection. 'We are going to be great friends, you and I.'

After that I began to receive almost daily visits from Sunil. His college classes got over at three in the afternoon, and though it was seldom that he attended them, he would stop at my place after putting in a brief appearance at the study hall. I could hardly blame him for neglecting his books: Shakespeare and Chaucer were prescribed for students who had but a rudimentary knowledge of modern English usage. Vast numbers of graduates were produced every year, and most of them became clerks or bus conductors or, perhaps, schoolteachers. But Sunil's father wanted the best for his son. And in Shahganj that meant as many degrees as possible.

Sunil would come stamping into my rooms, waking me from the siesta which had become a habit during summer afternoons. When he found that I did not relish being woken up, he would leave me to sleep while he took a bath under the tap. After making liberal use of my hair cream and aftershave lotion (he had just begun shaving, but used the lotion on his body), he would want to go to a picture or restaurant, and would sprinkle me with cold water so that I leapt off the bed.

One afternoon he felt more than usually ebullient, and poured a whole bucket of water over me, soaking the sheets and mattress. I retaliated by flinging the water jug at his head. It missed him and shattered itself against the wall. Sunil then went berserk and started splashing water all over the room, while I threatened and shouted. When I tried restraining him by force, we rolled over on the ground, and I banged my head against the bedstead and almost lost consciousness. He was then full of contrition and massaged the lump on my head with hair cream and refused to borrow any money from me that day.

Sunil's 'borrowing' consisted of extracting a few rupees from my wallet, saying he needed the money for books or a tailor's bill or a shopkeeper who was threatening him with violence, and then spending it on something quite different. Before long I gave up asking him to return anything, just as I had given up asking him to stop seeing me.

Sunil was one of those people best loved from a distance. He was born with a special talent for trouble. I think it pleased his vanity when he was pursued by irate creditors, shopkeepers, brothers whose sisters he had insulted and husbands whose wives he had molested. My association with him did nothing to improve my own reputation in Shahganj.

My landlady, a protective motherly Punjabi widow said: 'Son, you are in bad company. Do you know that Sunil has already been expelled from one school for stealing, and from another for sexual offences?'

'He's only a boy,' I said. 'And he's taking longer than most boys to grow up. He doesn't realize the seriousness of what he does. He will learn as he grows older.'

'If he grows older,' said my landlady darkly. 'Do you know that he nearly killed a man last year? When a fruit seller who had been cheated threatened to report Sunil to the police, he threw a brick at the man's head. The poor man was in hospital for three weeks. If Sunil's father did not have political influence, the boy would be in jail now, instead of climbing your stairs every afternoon.'

Once again I suggested to Sunil that he come to see me less often.

He looked hurt and offended. 'Don't you like me any more?'

'I like you immensely. But I have work to do...'

'I know. You think I am a crook. Well, I am a crook.' He spoke with all the confidence of a young man who has never been hurt or disillusioned; he had romantic notions about swindlers and gangsters. 'I'll be a big crook one day, and people will be scared of me. But don't worry, old boy, you're my friend. I wouldn't harm you in any way. In fact, I'll protect you.'

'Thank you, but I don't require protection, I want to be left alone. I have work, and you are a worry and a distraction.'

'Well, I'm not going to leave you alone,' he said, assuming the posture of a spoilt child. 'Why should you be left alone? Who do you think you are? If we're friends now, it's your fault. I'm not going to buzz off just to suit your convenience.'

'Come less often, that's all.'

'I'll come more often, you old snob! I know, you're thinking of your reputation—as if you had any. Well, you don't have to worry, *mon ami*—as they say in Hollywood. I'll be very discreet, Daddyji!'

Whenever I complained or became querulous, Sunil would call me daddy or uncle or sometimes mum, and make me feel more ridiculous. If he was in a good mood, he would use the Hindi word chacha (uncle). All it did was to make me feel much older than my twenty-five years.

Sunil turned up one afternoon with blood streaming from his nose and from a gash across his forehead. He sat down at the foot of the bed and began dabbing his face with the bedsheet.

'What have you done to yourself?' I asked in some alarm.

'Some fellows beat me up. There were three of them. They followed me on their cycles.'

'Who were they?' I asked, looking for iodine on the dressing table.

'Just some fellows...'

'They must have had a reason.'

'Well, a sister of one of them had been talking to me.'

'Well, that isn't a reason, even in Shahganj. You must have said or done something to offend her.'

'No, she likes me,' he said, wincing as I dabbed iodine on his forehead. 'We went to the guava orchard near my uncle's farm.'

'She went out there alone with you?'

'Sure. I took her on my bike. They must have followed us. Anyway, we weren't doing much except kissing and fooling around. But some people seem to think that's worse than...'

Both he and the other boys of Shahganj had grown up to look upon girls as strange, exotic animals, who must be seized at the first opportunity. Experimenting in sex was like playing a surreptitious game of marbles.

Sunil produced a clasp knife from his pocket, opened it and held the blade against the flat of his hand.

'Don't worry, Uncle, I can look after myself. The next fellow who tries to interfere with me will get this in his guts.'

'Don't be silly,' I said. 'You will go to prison for ten years. Listen, I'm going up to Simla for a couple of weeks, just for a change. Why don't you come with me? It will be a pleasant change from Shahganj, and in the meantime all this fuss will die down.'

It was one of those invitations which I make so readily and instantly regret. As soon as I had made the suggestion, I realized that Sunil in Simla might be even more of a problem than Sunil in Shahganj. But it was too late for me to back out.

'Simla! Why not? The college is closing for the summer holidays, and my father won't mind my going with you. He believes you're the only respectable friend I've got. Boy! We'll have a good time in Simla.'

'You'll have to behave yourself there, if you want to come with me. No girls, Sunil.'

'No girls, sir. I'll be very good, Chachaji. Please take me to Simla.'

'I think two hundred rupees should be enough for a fortnight for both of us,' I said.

'Oh, too much,' said Sunil modestly.

'And a week later we were actually in Simla, putting up at a moderately priced, middle-class hotel.

Our first few days in the hill station were pleasant enough. We went for long walks, tired ourselves out and acquired enormous appetites. Sunil, in the hills for the first time in his life, declared that they were wonderful, and thanked me a score of times for bringing him along. He took a genuine interest in exploring remote valleys, forests and waterfalls, and seemed to be losing some of his self-centredness. I believe that mountains do affect one's personality, if one can remain among them long enough; and if Sunil had grown up in the hills instead of in a refugee township, I have no doubt he would have been a completely different person.

There was one small waterfall I rather liked. It was down a ravine, in a rather inaccessible spot, where very few people ever went. The water fell about thirty feet into a small pool. We bathed here on two occasions, and Sunil quite forgot the attractions of the town. And we would have visited the spot again had I not slipped and sprained my ankle. This accident confined me to the hotel balcony for several days, and I was afraid that Sunil, for want of companionship, would go in search of more mundane distractions. But though he went out often enough, he came back dusty and sunburnt; and the fact that he asked me for very little money was evidence enough of his fondness for the outdoors. Striding through forests of oak and pine, with all the world stretched out far below, was no doubt a new and exhilarating experience for him. But how long would it be before the spell was broken?

'Don't you need any money?' I asked him uneasily, on the third day of his Thoreau-like activities.

'What for, Uncle? Fresh air costs nothing. And besides, I don't owe money to anyone in Simla. We haven't been here long enough.'

'Then perhaps we should be going,' I said.

'Shahganj is a miserable little dump.'

'I know, but it's your home. And for the time being, it's mine.'

'Listen, Uncle,' he said, after a moment of reflection, 'yesterday, on one of my walks, I met a schoolteacher. She's over thirty, so don't get nervous. She doesn't have any brothers or relatives who will come chasing after me. And she's nuch fairer than you, Uncle. Is it all right if I'm friendly with her?'

'I suppose so,' I said uncertainly. Schoolteachers can usually take care of themselves (if they want to), and, besides, an older woman might have a sobering influence on Sunil.

He brought her over to see me that same evening, and seemed quite proud of his new acquisition. She was indeed fair, perhaps insipidly so, with blonde hair and light blue eyes. She had a young face and a healthy body, but her voice was peculiarly toneless and flat, giving an impression of boredom, of lassitude. I wondered what she found attractive in Sunil apart from his obvious animal charm. They had hardly anything in common, but perhaps the absence of similar interests was an attraction in itself. In six or seven years of teaching, Maureen must have been tired of the usual scholastic types. Sunil was refreshingly free from all classroom associations.

Maureen let her hair down at the first opportunity. She switched on the bedroom radio and found Ceylon. Soon she was teaching Sunil to dance. This was amusing, because Sunil, with his long legs, had great difficulty in taking small steps; nor could Maureen cope with his great strides. But he was very earnest about it all, and inserting an unlighted cigarette between his lips, did his best to move rhythmically around the bedroom. I think he was convinced that by learning to dance he would reach the high watermark of Western culture. Maureen stood for all that was remote and romantic, and for all the films that he had seen, to conquer her would, for Sunil, be a voyage of discovery, not a mere gratification of his senses. And for Maureen, this new unconventional friendship must have been a refreshing diversion from the dreariness of her school routine. She was old enough to realize that it was only a diversion. The intensity of emotional attachments had faded with her early youth and love could wound her heart no more. But for Sunil, it was only the beginning of something that stirred him deeply, moved him inexorably towards manhood.

It was unfortunate that I did not then notice this subtle change in my friend. I had known him only as a shallow creature, and was certain that this new infatuation would disappear as soon as the novelty of it wore off. As Maureen had no encumbrances, no relations that she would speak of, I saw no harm in encouraging the friendship and seeing how it would develop.

'I think we'd better have something to drink,' I said, and ringing the bell for the room bearer, ordered several bottles of beer.

Sunil gave me an odd, whimsical look. I had never before encouraged him to drink. But he did not hesitate to open the bottles, and, before long, Maureen and he were drinking from the same glass.

'Let's make love,' said Sunil, putting his arm around Maureen's shoulders and gazing adoringly into her dreamy blue eyes.

They seemed unconcerned by my presence; but I was embarrassed, and, getting up, said I would be going for a walk.

'Enjoy yourself,' said Sunil, winking at me over Maureen's shoulder.

'You ought to get yourself a girlfriend,' said the young woman in a conciliatory tone.

'True,' I said, and moved guiltily out of the room I was paying for.

Our stay in Simla lasted several days longer than we had planned. I saw little of Sunil and Maureen during this time. As Sunil had no desire to return to Shahganj any earlier than was absolutely necessary, he avoided me during the day but I managed to stay awake late enough one night to confront him when he crept quietly into the room.

'Dear friend and familiar,' I said. 'I hate to spoil your beautiful romance, but I have absolutely no money left, and unless you have resources of your own—or if Maureen can support you—I suggest that you accompany me back to Shahganj the day after tomorrow.'

'How mean you are, Chachaji. This is something serious. I mean Maureen and me. Do you think we should get married?'

'No.'

'But why not?'

'Because she cannot support you on a teacher's salary. And she probably isn't interested in a permanent relationship—like ours.'

'Very funny. And you think I'd let my wife slave for me?'

'I do. And besides...'

'And besides,' he interrupted, grinning, 'she's old enough to be my mother.'

'Are you really in love with her?' I asked him. 'I've never

known you to be serious about anything.'

'Honestly, Uncle.'

'And what about her?'

'Oh, she loves me terribly, really she does. She's ready to come down with us if it's possible. Only I've told her that I'll first have to break the news to my father, otherwise he might kick me out of the house.'

'Well, then,' I said shrewdly, 'the sooner we return to Shahganj and get your father's blessings, the sooner you and Maureen can get married, if that's what both of you really want.'

Early next morning Sunil disappeared, and I knew he would be gone all day. My foot was better, and I decided to take a walk on my own to the waterfall I had liked so much. It was almost noon when I reached the spot and began descending the steep path to the ravine. The stream was hidden by dense foliage, giant ferns and dahlias, but the water made a tremendous noise as it tumbled over the rocks. When I reached a sharp promontory, I was able to look down on the pool. Two people were lying on the grass.

I did not recognize them at first. They looked very beautiful together, and I had not expected Sunil and Maureen to look so beautiful. Sunil, on whom no surplus flesh had as yet gathered, possessed all the sinuous grace and power of a young god; and the woman, her white flesh pressed against young grass, reminded me of a painting by Titian that I had seen in a gallery in Florence. Her full, mature body was touched with a tranquil intoxication, her breasts rose and fell slowly, and waves of muscle merged into the shadows of her broad thighs. It was as though I had stumbled into another age, and had found two lovers in a forest glade. Only a fool would have wished to disturb them. Sunil had for once in his life risen above mediocrity, and I hurried away before the magic was lost.

The human voice often shatters the beauty of the most tender passions; and when we left Simla the next day, and Maureen and Sunil used all the stock cliches to express their love, I was a little disappointed. But the poetry of life was in their bodies, not in their tongues.

Back in Shahganj, Sunil actually plucked up the courage to speak to his father. This, to me, was a sign that he took the affair very seriously, for he seldom approached his father for anything. But all the sympathy that he received was a box on the ears. I received a curt note suggesting that I was having a corrupting influence on the boy and that I should stop seeing him. There was little I could do in the matter, because it had always been Sunil who had insisted on seeing me.

He continued to visit me, bring me Maureen's letters (strange, how lovers cannot bear that the world should not know their love), and his own to her, so that I could correct his English!

It was at about this time that Sunil began speaking to me about his uncle's paper factory and the possibility of working in it. Once he was getting a salary, he pointed out, Maureen would be able to leave her job and join him.

Unfortunately, Sunil's decision to join the paper factory took months to crystallize into a definite course of action, and in the meantime he was finding a panacea for lovesickness in rum and sometimes cheap country spirit. The money that he now borrowed was used not to pay his debts, or to incur new ones, but to drink himself silly. I regretted having been the first person to have offered him a drink. I should have known that Sunil was a person who could do nothing in moderation.

He pestered me less often now, but the purpose of his

occasional visits became all too obvious. I was having a little success, and thoughtlessly gave Sunil the few rupees he usually demanded. At the same time I was beginning to find other friends, and I no longer found myself worrying about Sunil, as I had so often done in the past. Perhaps this was treachery on my part...

When finally I decided to leave Shahganj for Delhi, I went in search of Sunil to say goodbye. I found him in a small bar, alone at a table with a bottle of rum. Though barely twenty, he no longer looked a boy. He was a completely different person from the handsome, cocksure youth I had met at the wrestling pit a year previously. His cheeks were hollow and he had not shaved for days. I knew that when I first met him he had been without scruples, a shallow youth, the product of many circumstances. He was no longer so shallow and he had stumbled upon love, but his character was too weak to sustain the weight of disillusionment. Perhaps I should have left him severely alone from the beginning. Before me sat a ruin, and I had helped to undermine the foundations. None of us can really avoid seeing the outcome of our smallest actions...

'I'm off to Delhi, Sunil.'

He did not look up from the table.

'Have a good time,' he said.

'Have you heard from Maureen?' I asked, certain that he had not.

He nodded, but for once did not offer to show me the letter.

'What's wrong?' I asked.

'Oh, nothing,' he said, looking up and forcing a smile. 'These dames are all the same, Uncle. We shouldn't take them too seriously, you know.'

'Why, what has she done, got married to someone else?'

'Yes,' he said scornfully. 'To a bloody teacher.'

'Well, she wasn't young,' I said. 'She couldn't wait for you for ever, I suppose.'

'She could if she had really loved me. But there's no such thing as love, is there, Uncle?'

I made no reply. Had he really broken his heart over a woman? Were there, within him, unsuspected depths of feeling and passion? You find love when you least expect to and lose it when you are sure that it is in your grasp.

'You're a lucky beggar,' he said. 'You're a philosopher. You find a reason for every stupid thing and so you are able to ignore all stupidity.'

I laughed. 'You're becoming a philosopher yourself. But don't think too hard, Sunil, you might find it painful.'

'Not I, Chachaji,' he said, emptying his glass. 'I'm not going to think. I'm going to work in a paper factory. I shall become respectable. What an adventure that will be!'

And that was the last time I saw Sunil.

He did not become respectable. He was still searching like a great discoverer for something new, someone different, when he met his pitiful end in the cold rain of a December night.

Though murder cases usually get reported in the papers, Sunil was a person of such little importance that his violent end was not considered newsworthy. It went unnoticed, and Maureen could not have known about it. The case has already been forgotten, for in the great human mass that is India, hundreds of people disappear every day and are never heard of again. Sunil will be quickly forgotten by all except those to whom he owed money.

HASSAN, THE BAKER[*]

I needed somewhere to stay, if I was going to spend some time in Fosterganj.

Melaram directed me to the local bakery. Hassan, the baker, had a room above his shop that had lain vacant since he built it a few years ago. An affable man, Hassan was the proud father of a dozen children; I say dozen at random, because I never did get to ascertain the exact number as they were never in one place at the same time. They did not live in the room above the bakery, which was much too small, but in a rambling old building below the bazaar, which housed a number of large families—the baker's, the tailor's, the postman's, among others.

I was shown the room. It was scantily furnished, the bed taking up almost half the space. A small table and chair stood near the window. Windows are important. I find it impossible to live in a room without a window. This one provided a view of the street and the buildings on the other side. Nothing very inspiring, but at least it wouldn't be dull.

A narrow bathroom was attached to the room. Hassan was very proud of it, because he had recently installed a flush tank and western-style potty. I complimented him on the potty

---

[*]From *Tales of Fosterganj*

and said it looked very comfortable. But what really took my fancy was the bathroom window. It hadn't been opened for some time, and the glass panes were caked with dirt. But when finally we got it open, the view was remarkable. Below the window was a sheer drop of two or three hundred feet. Ahead, an open vista, a wide valley, and then the mountains striding away towards the horizon. I don't think any hotel in town had such a splendid view. I could see myself sitting for hours on that potty, enraptured, enchanted, having the valley and the mountains all to myself. Almost certain constipation of course, but I would take that risk.

'Forty rupees a month,' said Hassan, and I gave him two months' rent on the spot.

'I'll move in next week,' I said. 'First I have to bring my books from Delhi.'

On my way back to the town I took a short cut through the forest. A swarm of yellow butterflies drifted across the path. A woodpecker pecked industriously on the bark of a tree, searching for young cicadas. Overhead, wild duck flew north, on their way across Central Asia, all travelling without passports. Birds and butterflies recognize no borders.

I hadn't been this way before, and I was soon lost. Two village boys returning from town with their milk cans gave me the wrong directions. I was put on the right path by a girl who was guiding a cow home. There was something about her fresh face and bright smile that I found tremendously appealing. She was less than beautiful but more than pretty, if you know what I mean. A face to remember.

A little later I found myself in an open clearing, with a large pool in the middle. Its still waters looked very deep. At one end there were steps, apparently for bathers. But the water did not look very inviting. It was a sunless place, several old oaks shutting out the light. Fallen off leaves floated on the surface. No birds sang. It was a strange, haunted sort of place. I hurried on...

It did not take me long to settle down in my little room above the bakery. Recent showers had brought out the sheen on new leaves, transformed the grass on the hillside from a faded yellow to an emerald green. A barbet atop a spruce tree was in full cry. It would keep up its monotonous chant all summer. And early morning, a whistling-thrush would render its interrupted melody, never quite finishing what it had to say.

It was good to hear the birds and laughing schoolchildren through my open window. But I soon learnt to shut it whenever I went out. Late one morning, on returning from my walk, I found a large rhesus monkey sitting on my bed, tearing up a loaf of bread that Hassan had baked for me. I tried to drive the fellow away, but he seemed reluctant to leave. He bared his teeth and swore at me in monkey language. Then he stuffed a piece of bread into his mouth and glared at me, daring me to do my worst. I recalled that monkeys carry rabies, and not wanting to join those who had recently been bitten by rabid dogs, I backed out of the room and called for help. One of Hassan's brood came running up the steps with a hockey stick, and chased the invader away.

'Always keep a mug of water handy,' he told me. 'Throw the water on him and he'll be off. They hate cold water.'

'You may be right,' I said. 'I've never seen a monkey taking a bath.'

'See how miserable they are when it rains,' said my rescuer. 'They huddle together as though it's the end of the world.'

'Strange, isn't it? Birds like bathing in the rain.'

'So do I. Wait till the monsoon comes. You can join me then.'

'Perhaps I will.'

On this friendly note we parted, and I cleaned up the mess made by my simian visitor, and then settled down to do some writing.

But there was something about the atmosphere of Fosterganj that discouraged any kind of serious work or effort. Tucked away in a fold of the hills, its inhabitants had begun to resemble their surroundings: one old man resembled a willow bent by rain and wind; an elderly lady with her umbrella reminded me of a colourful mushroom, quite possibly poisonous; my good baker-cum-landlord looked like a bit of the hillside, scarred and uneven but stable. The children were like young grass, coming up all over the place; but the adolescents were like nettles, you never knew if they would sting when touched. There was a young Tibetan lady whose smile was like the blue sky opening up. And there was no brighter blue than the sky as seen from Fosterganj on a clear day.

It took me some time to get to know all the inhabitants. But one of the first was Professor Lulla, recently retired, who came hurrying down the road like the White Rabbit in *Alice's Adventures in Wonderland*, glancing at his watch and muttering to himself. If, like the White Rabbit, he was saying 'I'm late, I'm late!' I wouldn't have been at all surprised. I was standing outside the bakery, chatting to one of the children, when he came up to me, adjusted his spectacles, peered at me through murky lenses, and said, 'Welcome to Fosterganj, sir. I believe you've come to stay for the season.'

'I'm not sure how long I'll stay,' I said. 'But thank you for your welcome.'

'We must get together and have a cultural and cultured exchange,' he said, rather pompously. 'Not many intellectuals in Fosterganj, you know.'

'I was hoping there wouldn't be.'

'But we'll talk, we'll talk. Only can't stop now. I have a funeral to attend. Eleven o'clock at the Camel's Back cemetery. Poor woman. Dead. Quite dead. Would you care to join me?'

'Er—I'm not in the party mood,' I said. 'And I don't think I knew the deceased.'

'Old Miss Gamleh. Your landlord thought she was a flowerpot—would have been ninety next month. Wonderful woman. Hated chokra-boys.' He looked distastefully at the boy grinning up at him. 'Stole all her plums, if the monkeys didn't get them first. Spent all her life in the hill station. Never married. Jilted by a weedy British colonel, awful fellow, even made off with her savings. But she managed on her own. Kept poultry, sold eggs to the hotels.'

'What happens to the poultry?' I asked.

'Oh, hens can look after themselves,' he said airily. 'But I can't linger or I'll be late. It's a long walk to the cemetery.'

And he set off in determined fashion, like Scott of the Antarctic about to brave a blizzard.

'Must have been a close friend, the old lady who passed away,' I remarked.

'Not at all,' said Hassan, who had been standing in his doorway listening to the conversation. 'I doubt if she ever spoke to him. But Professor Lulla never misses a funeral. He goes to all of them—cremations, burials—funerals of any well-known person, even strangers. It's a hobby with him.'

'Extraordinary,' I said. 'I thought collecting match-box labels was sad enough as a hobby. Doesn't it depress him?'

'It seems to cheer him up, actually. But I must go too, sir. If you don't mind keeping an eye on the bakery for an hour or two, I'll hurry along to the funeral and see if I can get her poultry cheap. Miss Gamla's hens give good eggs, I'm told. Little Ali will look after the customers, sir. All you have to do is see that they don't make off with the buns and cream-rolls.'

I don't know if Hassan attended the funeral, but he came back with two baskets filled with cackling hens, and a rooster to keep them company.

THE SKULL

I am not normally bothered by skeletons and old bones—they are, after all, just the chalky remains of the long dead—so that, when my nephew Anil came back from medical college with a well-preserved skull, it was no cause for alarm. He was a second-year student, at times a bit of a prankster.

'I hope you didn't take it without permission,' I said, taking the skull in my hands and admiring its symmetry but without philosophizing upon it like Hamlet.

'Oh, the college is full of them,' said Anil. 'I just borrowed it for the vacation.' He placed it on the mantelpiece, among some of the awards and mementos (cheap brassware mostly) that had accumulated over the years, and I must say it livened up the shelf a little.

Anil had placed the skull at one end of the mantelpiece, and there it stood until we'd had our dinner. He settled down with a book, while I poured myself a small glass of cognac before settling into an easy chair with a notebook on my knee. It was midsummer, and the window was open, so that we could hear the crickets singing in the oak trees. My cottage was on the outskirts of Mussoorie, surrounded by Himalayan oak and maple.

I had been making some notes for an article on wild flowers.

When I had finished my notes and cognac, I looked up and noticed that the skull now stood in the centre of the mantelpiece.

'Did you move the skull?' I asked.

'No,' said Anil, looking up. 'I placed it at the end of the shelf.'

'Well, it's now in the middle. How did it get there?'

'You must have moved it yourself, without noticing. That was a stiff cognac you drank, uncle.'

I let it pass, it did not seem important.

◆

People often dropped in to see me. Schoolteachers, visitors to the hill station, students, other writers, neighbours. During that week I had a number of visitors, and of course everyone noticed the skull on the mantelpiece. Some were intrigued, and wanted to know whose skull it was. One or two lady teachers were frightened by it. A fellow writer thought it was in bad taste, displaying human remains in my sitting room. One visitor offered to buy it.

I would gladly have sold the wretched thing, but it belonged to Anil and he intended taking it back to Meerut. But when the time came to leave he forgot about the skull, his mind no doubt taken up with other matters—such as the daily phone calls he received from a girl student in Delhi. After seeing him off at the bus stop, I came home to find that the skull was still occupying pride of place on the mantelpiece.

I ignored it for a few days, and the skull didn't seem to mind that. It was receiving plenty of attention from visitors during the day.

But it was beginning to get on my nerves. Every evening, when I sat down to enjoy a whisky or a cognac, I would feel its empty eye sockets staring at me. And on one occasion, when I tried to change its position, my hand got caught in its jawbone and it was with some difficulty that I withdrew it.

Getting fed up of its presence, I decided to lock the thing away where it wouldn't be seen. There was a wall cupboard in the room, where I kept my manuscripts, notebooks, and writing materials, and there was plenty of room there for the skull. So I shifted it to the cupboard, and made sure the doors were locked.

That evening I enjoyed my drink without being watched by that remnant of a human head. The crickets were singing, a nightjar was calling, and a zephyr of a wind moved softly through the trees. I finished my article and went to bed in a happy frame of mind.

In the middle of the night I woke to a loud rattling sound. At first I thought it was a loose door latch or a wobbly drainpipe; then realized the noise was coming from the wall cupboard. A rat, perhaps? But no. As soon as I opened the cupboard door, out popped the skull, landing near my feet and bouncing away right across the drawing room.

For the sake of peace and quiet, I returned it to the mantelpiece. If a skull could smile, it would probably have done so. I went back to my bed and slept like a baby. It takes more than a dancing skull to keep me from enjoying a good night's sleep.

But next morning I got to work making up a parcel. Normally, I hate making parcels, they usually fall apart. But for once I took pleasure in making a parcel. I wrapped the skull in a plastic bag, then placed it in a strong cardboard box, wrapped this in brown parcel paper, used a liberal amount of Sellotape, and addressed the package to Dr Anil at his medical college. Then I walked into town and handed it over to the registration clerk at the post office.

Rubbing my hands with satisfaction, I treated myself to

fish and chips and an ice cream before setting out on the walk down the hill to my cottage.

How did the skull get out of that parcel? I shall never know. Perhaps a nosy postal clerk had opened it to check the contents. I hope he got the fright of his life.

Anyway, I was about halfway down the steep path that leads to one of our famous schools when I heard something rattling down the slope behind me. At first I thought it was an empty tin, but then I recognized my boon companion, that wretched skull, embellished with bits of wrapping paper and Sellotape, bouncing down the hill towards me. I broke into a run, making a dash for the cottage door. But it was there before me, grinning up at me from a pot full of flowering petunias.

So back it went to its favourite place on the mantelpiece. And there it remained for several weeks.

◆

The school's playing field was situated just above the path to the cottage, and during the football season I could hear the boys kicking a football around.

One day a football escaped from the field and came bouncing down the hillside, landing on a flower bed. The match was over and no one bothered to come down to retrieve the ball. But it gave me an idea. I removed the bladder, stuffed the skull into the leather interior, and tied it up firmly. Then I had the football delivered to the school's games master, with my compliments.

Nothing happened for a couple of days. There was no shortage of footballs. Then in the middle of the game against St George's College, a ball went out of the grounds and a spare one was required.

The replacement did not bounce quite as well as the previous one, and it was inclined to spin around a lot and take off in directions opposite to those intended. Also, it squeaked whenever it received a kick, and sometimes those squeaks sounded a bit like screams of protest. The goalkeepers at either end found the ball difficult to hold, it did its best to elude their grasp. And more goals were scored by accident rather than design. Finally this eccentric ball was kicked out of play and was replaced by another.

What happens to old footballs? I expect they finally fall apart and end up in a dustbin.

In this case, the football found a new owner, for the sports-master was a kind man who gave away old bats, balls and other worn-out stuff to the poor children of the locality. A boy from a village near Rajpur was the recipient of the battered football, and he and his friends carried it away with a cheer, kicking it all the way down the steep path, making so much noise that they did not hear the groans of protest that issued from the battered old football.

Well, weeks passed, months passed, without the skull making a reappearance. But then something strange began to happen. I found myself missing that troublesome skull!

It had, after all, been company of a sort for a lonely writer living on his own on the edge of the forest. And when you have lived with someone for a long time, then, no matter how much you may quarrel or get on each other's nerves, a bond is formed, and the strength of that bond can only be known when it is broken.

The skull had been sharing my life for over a year, and now that it was gone, seemingly forever, my life seemed rather empty.

So I began searching for the skull. I enquired amongst the children down in Rajpur; but they had long since lost the football. I made a round of all the junk shops in Dehradun, without any luck. There were lots of old footballs lying around, but not the one I wanted. And no, they didn't buy or sell human skulls.

Young Anil, the doctor, paid me a brief visit and found me looking depressed.

'What's the trouble?' he asked. 'You look as though you've just lost a friend.'

'I have, indeed,' I said. 'I miss that skull you gave me. It was company of a sort.'

'Well, I'll get you another. No shortage of skulls in my college.'

'No, I don't want another. I want the same skull. It had a personality of its own.'

Anil looked at me as though he thought I was going off my rocker. And perhaps I was.

And then one day, as I was walking down a busy street in neighbouring Saharanpur, I noticed a fortune teller plying his trade on the pavement. I don't believe in fortune telling, but everyone has to make a living, and telling fortunes seems to me a harmless way of doing it. And then I noticed that he had a skull beside him, and that he would consult it before handing his customer a slip of paper with words of advice or encouragement written on it. It looked a bit like my skull, but I couldn't be sure. All the kicking and manhandling it had received had possibly altered its appearance.

But anyway, I gave the fortune teller some money and asked him for a prediction. He chanted something, then extracted a slip of paper from beneath the skull and handed it to me with a flourish.

I read the words printed neatly on the paper.

'*Ullu ka patha*' went the message, followed by '*Gadhe ka baccha!*'

It was definitely my skull! Only an old friend could abuse me like that.

So I pleaded and haggled with the fortune teller, paid him a hundred rupees for the skull, and carried it home in triumph.

And there it is today, decorating my mantelpiece, a little the worse for wear, and with a silly grin on its skeletal face. To improve its looks I have placed an old cricket cap on its head.

Sometimes we don't value our friends until we lose them.

UPON AN OLD WORLD DREAMING

It is time to confess that at least half of my life has been spent in idleness. My old school would not be proud of me. Nor would my Aunt Muriel.

'You spend most of your time sitting on that wall, doing nothing,' scolded Aunt Muriel, when I was seven or eight. 'Are you *thinking* about something?'

'No, Aunt Muriel.'

'Are you *dreaming*?'

'I'm awake!'

'Then what on earth are you doing there?'

'Nothing, Aunt Muriel.'

'He'll come to no good,' she warned the world at large. 'He'll spend all his life sitting on walls, doing nothing.'

And how right she proved to be! Sometimes I bestir myself, and bang out a few sentences on my old typewriter, but most of the time I'm still sitting on the wall, preferably in the winter sunshine. Thinking? Not very deeply. Dreaming? But I've grown too old to dream. Meditation, perhaps. That's been fashionable for some time. But it isn't that either. Contemplation might come closer to the mark.

Was I born with a silver spoon in my mouth that I could afford to sit in the sun for hours, doing nothing? Far from it; I was born poor and remained poor, as far as worldly riches went. But one has to eat and pay the rent. And there have been others to feed too. So I have to admit that between long bouts of idleness there have been short bursts of creativity. My typewriter after more than thirty years of loyal service, has finally collapsed, proof enough that it has not lain idle all this time.

Sitting on walls, apparently doing nothing, has always been my favourite form of inactivity. But for these walls, and the many idle hours I have spent upon them, I would not have written even a fraction of the hundreds of stories, essays and other diversions that have been banged out on the typewriter over the years. It is not the walls themselves that set me off or give me ideas, but a personal view of the world that I receive from sitting there.

Creative idleness, you could call it. A receptivity to the world around me—the breeze, the warmth of the old stone, the lizard on the rock, a raindrop on a blade of grass—these and other impressions impinge upon me as I sit in that passive, benign condition that makes people smile tolerantly at me as they pass. 'Eccentric writer' they remark to each other, as they drive on, hurrying in a heat of hope, towards the pot of gold at the end of their personal rainbows.

It's true that I am eccentric in many ways, and old walls bring out the essence of my eccentricity.

I do not have a garden wall. This shaky, tumbledown house in the hills is perched directly above a motorable road, making me both accessible and vulnerable to casual callers of all kinds—inquisitive tourists, local busybodies, schoolgirls with their poems, hawkers selling candyfloss, itinerant sadhus, scrap merchants, potential Nobel Prize winners...

To escape them, and to set my thoughts in order, I walk a little way up the road, cross it, and sit down on a parapet wall overlooking the Woodstock spur. Here, partially shaded by an overhanging oak, I am usually left alone. I look suitably down and out, shabbily dressed, a complete nonentity—not the sort of person you would want to be seen talking to!

Stray dogs sometimes join me here. Having been a stray dog myself at various periods of my life, I can empathize with these friendly vagabonds of the road. Far more intelligent than your inbred Pom or peke, they let me know by their silent companionship that they are on the same wavelength. They sport about on the road, but they do not yap at all and sundry.

Left to myself on the wall, I am soon in the throes of composing a story or poem. I do not write it down—that can be done later—I just work it out in my mind, memorize my words, so to speak, and keep them stored up for my next writing session.

Occasionally a car will stop, and someone I know will stick his head out and say, 'No work today, Mr Bond? How I envy you! Not a care in the world!'

I travel back in time some fifty years ago to Aunt Muriel asking me the same question. The years melt away, and I am a child again, sitting on the garden wall, doing nothing.

'Don't you get bored sitting there?' asks the latest passing motorist, who has one of those half-beards which are in vogue with TV news readers. 'What are you doing?'

'Nothing, Aunty,' I reply.

He gives me a long hard stare.

'You must be dreaming. Don't you recognize me?'

'Yes, Aunt Muriel.'

He shakes his head sadly, steps on the gas, and goes roaring up the hill in a cloud of dust.

'Poor old Bond,' he tells his friends over evening cocktails. 'Must be going round the bend. This morning he called me Aunty.'

A GOOD PHILOSOPHY

The other day, when I was with a group of students, a bright young thing asked me, 'Sir, what is your philosophy of life?' She had me stumped.

There I was, a seventy-five-year-old, still writing, and still functioning physically and mentally (or so I believed), but quite helpless when it came to formulating a 'philosophy of life'.

How dare I reach the venerable age of seventy-five without a philosophy; without anything resembling a religious outlook; without arming myself with a battery of great thoughts with which to impress my young interlocutor, who is obviously in need of a little practical if not spiritual guidance to help her navigate the shoals of life.

This morning I was pondering on this absence of a philosophy or religious outlook in my make-up, and feeling a little low because it was cloudy and dark outside, and gloomy weather always seems to dampen my spirits. Then the clouds broke up and the sun came out, large, yellow splashes of sunshine in my room and upon my desk, and almost immediately I felt an uplift of spirit. And at the same time I realized that no philosophy would be of any use to a person so susceptible to changes in light and shade, sunshine and shadow. I was a pagan, pure and simple; a sensualist; sensitive to touch and colour and fragrance and odour and sounds of every description; a creature of instinct, of spontaneous attractions, given to illogical fancies and attachments. As a guide, philosopher and friend I am of no use to anyone, least of all myself.

I think the best advice I ever had was contained in these lines from Shakespeare which my father had copied into one of my notebooks when I was nine years old:

> This above all, to thine own self be true,
> And it must follow as the night of the day,
> Thou canst not then be false to any man.

Each one of us is a mass of imperfections, and to be able to recognize and live with our imperfections, our basic nature, defects of genes and birth—hereditary flaws—makes for an easier transit on life's journey.

I am always a little weary of saints and godmen, preachers and teachers, who are ready with solutions for all our problems. For one thing, they talk too much. When I was at school, I mastered the art of sleeping (without appearing to sleep) through a long speech or lecture by the principal or visiting dignitary, and I must confess to doing the same thing today. The trick is to sleep with your eyes half-closed; this gives the impression of concentrating very hard on what is being said, even though you might well be roaming happily in dreamland.

In our imperfect world there is far too much talk and not enough thought.

The TV channels are awash with TV gurus telling us how to live, and they do so at great length. This verbal diarrhoea is infectious and appears to affect newspersons and TV anchors who are prone to lecturing and bullying the guests on their show. Too many know-alls. A philosophy for living? You won't find it on your TV sets. You will learn more from a cab driver or street vendor.

'And what's your philosophy?' I asked my sabziwala, as he weighed out a kilo of onions.

'Philosophy? What's that?' He turned to his assistant. 'Is this gentleman trying to abuse me?'

'No sir,' I said. 'It's not a term of abuse. I was just asking—are you a happy man?'

'Why do you want to know? Are you from the income tax department?'

'No, I'm just a storyteller. So tell me—what makes you happy?'

'A good customer,' he said. 'So tell me what makes *you* happy?'

'The same thing, I suppose,' I had to confess. 'A good publisher!'

I did not tell him about the sunshine, the birdsong, the bedside book, the potted geranium, and all the other little things that make life worth living. It's better that he finds out for himself.

THE LADY OF SARDHANA

The bus that took us to Sardhana was prehistoric. I do believe it was kept from falling apart by a liberal use of sellotape. The noise and rattle made by its nuts and bolts and shaky chassis reminded me of Kipling's story 'The Ship that Found Herself'. Every part seemed alive and complaining. The bus conductor found the crank handle under somebody's seat, and, panting and sweating in the sun, kept turning it until, reluctantly, the engine spluttered into life. The bus moved off of its own volition, and the conductor just had time to get on and collect our tickets. Most of the passengers were rural folk, descendants of those Jats and Rohillas who made this fertile Doab region (the Doab is the area between the Ganges and the Jumna) one of the richest granaries of India, only to have it plundered by marauding Marathas, Sikhs and Afghans. They smoked bidis or chewed paan, shooting the coloured spittle out of the open windows; and, seeing my watch, asked me the time every few minutes.

The Sardhana bus stop, when we got to it, was the usual unexciting swamp of churned-up mud, with a tea stall, and several stray dogs and pigs nosing about in a garbage heap. We hailed a cycle rickshaw and told the man to take us to the church.

The Sardhana church was built at the expense of Begum

Samru by an Italian architect. Upon her husband's death she had become a devout Catholic, and earned from the Pope the title of 'Joanna Nobilis'. The Emperor at Delhi, grateful to her for services rendered in the battlefield, gave her another title: Zeb-un-Nissa, the 'Ornament of Her Sex'. Her life, until she reached old age, was a succession of love affairs, intrigue and petty warfare. It was never a dull life. She had certain admirable qualities which made her attractive to men. As a young girl, she was beautiful; in middle age, rather plump. She was a courageous woman, and rode into battle at the head of her troops, something which few women have done before or since. But we must begin at the beginning, and in the beginning was Sombre, alias Samru, alias Walter Reinhardt...

Sombre's real name was Walter Reinhardt, but due to a dusky complexion he acquired the name of Sombre, which in Hindustani was soon corrupted to Samru. He was perhaps the most notorious of foreign adventurers, and this notoriety was acquired when he was in the service of the Nawab of Bengal, Kassim Ali, who, warring with the English, had attacked and captured a large number of English residents at Patna, and ordered them to be executed.

None of Kassim's own native officers came forward to undertake this, but Sombre, wishing to ingratiate himself with his new employer, agreed to carry out the execution. Details of the murders are given in the Annual Register:

'Somers invited about forty officers and other gentlemen, who were amongst these unfortunate prisoners, to sup with him on the day he had fixed for the execution, and when his guests were in full security, protected as they imagined by the laws of hospitality, as well as by the right of prisoners, he ordered the Indians under his command to fall upon them and cut their throats. Even these barbarous soldiers revolted at the orders of this savage European. They refused to obey, and desired that arms should be given to the English, and that they would then engage them. Somers, fixed in his villainy, compelled them with blows and threats to the accomplishment of that odious service. The unfortunate victims, though thus suddenly attacked and wholly unarmed, made a long and brave defence, and with their plates and bottles even killed some of their assailants, but in the end they were all slaughtered... Proceeding then, with a file of sepoys, to the prison where a number of prisoners then remained, he directed the massacre, and with his own hands assisted in the inhuman slaughter of 148 defenceless Europeans confined within its walls—an appalling act of atrocity that has stamped his name with infamy for ever.'

Sombre left Kassim Ali's service before an avenging British army could catch up with him, and by the end of his subsequent career he had served twelve to fourteen masters. He finally tendered his services to Shah Alam, the Emperor of Delhi, who agreed to pay him ₹65,000 for his services and those of his two battalions. He remained in the service of the Delhi Court and was assigned a rich jagir, or estate, at Sardhana, a district forty miles north of the capital, where he built and fortified his headquarters and settled down. He had adopted native dress, and the custom of keeping a harem.

At Sardhana he fell in love with a very beautiful woman. One historian asserts that she was the daughter of a decadent Moghul nobleman, another that she was a Kashmiri dancing girl, and a third that she was a lineal descendant of the Prophet. In due course she became Sombre's Begum. He died at Agra on the fourth of May 1778, aged fifty-eight years; infamous, unloved even by his own followers, but successful to the end.

After his death the command of his troops, their pay and the jagir of Sardhana became the property of his Begum, who, on being baptized and received into the Roman Catholic faith, was christened 'Joanna Nobilis'. By means of rare ability and force of character, she proved equal to her responsibilities; but she was unfortunate in her officers. Only the most dissolute had cared to join Sombre, and their conduct often incited the troops to mutiny. She gave the command to a German named Pauly 'perhaps because he was a countryman of her husband, but, it has been suggested, for more tender reasons'; Pauly was murdered 'by a bloody process' in 1783; and those who succeeded him did not remain long in command.

It was at this time that George Thomas, the Irish freelance, rose to a position of some importance in the army of Begum Samru.

When the Begum saw Thomas, it did not take her long to decide to give him a command. He had the pleasing, honeyed speech of the Irishman; he was tall, handsome, virile; far more attractive physically than most of the Europeans in her service. How could the Begum resist him? For months he would remain her most trusted officer, her lover, and then, seeking some other novelty, she would transfer her affections to another, only appealing to Thomas for help in time of distress.

This arrangement suited Thomas. He was willing to make love to the Begum without making the mistake of falling in love with her. He used her as she used him; but he never betrayed her, as she was often to betray him.

Several years after Thomas had left her service and had established himself at Panipat and Karnal, Begum Samru, faced with a mutiny, appealed to him for help. She must have known Thomas's character well, for she had only recently raided his territory; any other person would have shown retaliation instead of succour; but when beauty was in distress Thomas always forsook his own interests to become the gallant knight-errant.

The Begum was now forty-five, inclined to plumpness, but her skin was still very smooth and fair, and her eyes 'black, large and animated'. The trouble at Sardhana had arisen from her having taken a new husband, a Frenchman named Le Vassoult.

Le Vassoult was no friend of Thomas's and had in fact proposed marriage to the Begum earlier, in order to gain an advantage over the Irishman who was then in her service. He was well-educated and from an aristocratic family, but aloof by nature and unpopular with his men. A free and easy roisterer like Thomas got more from his troops than the conventional disciplinarian. Both officers and troops resented the fact that Le Vassoult, after his marriage to the Begum, refused to eat with them or treat them as equals; they planned on deposing the Begum and transferring their allegiance to Balthazar Sombre, a debauched son of Sombre by his first wife. This first wife was still alive, and when she died in 1838 she must have been over a hundred years old. (The Sardhana cemetery contains the remains of many centenarians.)

Another officer named Legois, a friend of George Thomas, had tried to dissuade the Begum from raiding Thomas's territory in Haryana, and for this had been badly treated by Le Vassoult. The troops, who had served Legois for a long time, and obviously liked him, broke into mutiny, and the Begum and her husband had no alternative but to try and reach Anupshahr, then the last outpost of British territory in northern India.

The troops had sent for Balthazar Sombre from Delhi. Le Vassoult and the Begum slipped away, but were soon pursued and overtaken. The lovers had agreed that rather than fall into the hands of the mutineers they would first kill themselves. While Le Vassoult, an unimaginative man of honour, was quite serious about this pact, the Begum treated it lightly. On being surrounded, she drew a dagger and made a half-hearted attempt at stabbing herself; but all she did was nick her breast and bespatter her blouse with blood. Le Vassoult was more thorough. On hearing that the Begum was bleeding to death, he drew his pistol, put the muzzle to his mouth, and pulled the trigger.

'The ball passed through his brain, and he sprang from the saddle a full foot in the air, before he fell dead to the ground. His corpse was subjected to every indignity and insult that the gross and bestial imagination of his officers and men could conceive, and left to rot, unburied, on the ground.'

However, the Begum did not get off too lightly. She was taken back to Sardhana and chained between two guns, occasionally being placed astride one of them at midday, when it was nearly red hot. The only food she received was smuggled to her by her maidservants. This was the Begum's plight when Thomas, by forced marches, reached Sardhana and quelled the mutiny.

The command of the Begum's force was now given to Colonel Saleur (the only European who could write) and he and the others signed or affixed their seals to a document in which they swore allegiance to their mistress. This was drawn up by a Mohammedan scribe in Persian, and as his religion prevented him from acknowledging Christ as God, the document was superscribed: 'In the name of God, and of His Majesty Christ!'

In 1803, after the British had defeated the Marathas, and established themselves in Hindustan (then the name for most of northern India) the Begum submitted to General Lake near Agra. James Skinner, the famous Eurasian adventurer, left a description of her meeting with the General: 'When the Begum came in person to pay her respects to General Lake, an incident occurred of a curious and characteristic description. She arrived at headquarters just after dinner, and being carried in her palanquin at once to the reception tent, the General came out to meet and receive her. As the adhesion of every petty chieftain was, in those days, of consequence, Lord Lake was not a little pleased at the early demonstration of the Begum's loyalty, and being a little elevated by the wine which had just been drunk, he forgot the novel circumstance of its being a native female, instead of some well-bearded chief, so he gallantly advanced, and, to the utter dismay of her attendants, took her in his arms and kissed her. The mistake might have been awkward, but the lady's presence of mind put all right. Receiving courteously the proferred attention, she turned calmly around to her astonished attendants and observed, 'It is the salute of a priest to his daughter.'

When the Begum accepted British protection, her income increased, and she disbanded most of her troops. Bishop Heber saw her in 1825 and described her as a 'very queer-looking old woman, with brilliant but wicked eyes, and the remains of beauty in her features'.

She became very rich and philanthropic. She sent the Pope at Rome `150,000, the Archbishop of Canterbury `50,000. She built a church at Meerut—less pretentious but more handsome than the one at Sardhana—where the Roman Catholic bishop was an Italian named Julius Caesar. At Meerut she often entertained Governors-General and Commanders-in-Chief, and when she died in 1836, at the age of ninety, she left behind a fortune of £700,000 and an immense army of pensioners.

The Sardhana church hasn't changed much over the years. The dome is nobly proportioned, but the twin spires on either side somehow spoil the effect. They are not spires actually, but pyramidal structures that serve no purpose, aesthetic or practical. The interior of the church is handsome, and has several new additions; but the centre of interest are the eleven life-size statues and three panels in bas-relief. This marble monument is the work of an Italian sculptor, Adamo Tadolini of Bologna. The Begum in her rich dress is seated on a chair of state holding in her right hand a folded scroll, the Emperor's firman conferring on her the jagir of Sardhana. On her right stands Dyce Sombre, her stepson, and on her left Dewan Rae Singh, her minister. Immediately behind are Bishop Julius Caesar and Innayat Ullah, her commandant of cavalry.

Of the three panels one represents an incident in the consecration of the church when she presented rich vestments to the Bishop (these are still in existence). The other panel shows the Begum holding a durbar, surrounded by European officers; and the third shows the Begum mounted on an elephant in triumphant procession.

We felt like intruders, our footsteps resounding in the silent church, and we did not stay long. There was nothing else to see except the Begum's palace, now a school, and a few old houses and graves. The spirit of the Begum's time has left Sardhana, and it is just another district town, hot and dusty and malarious. It is difficult to believe that there was drama here once, intrigue, battle and romance. The place is a backwater, cut off somehow from the mainstream of life. A few nuns pass through the church cloisters, and a bullock cart trundles along the road. The fields are waterlogged.

We went away before sunset, afraid that if we stayed too long we might meet the ghost of a queer-looking old woman with brilliant and wicked eyes, lurking in the mango grove near the church.

BHABIJI'S HOUSE

(My neighbours in Rajouri Garden back in the 1960s were the Kamal family. This entry from my journal, which I wrote on one of my later visits, describes a typical day in that household.)

At first light there is a tremendous burst of birdsong from the guava tree in the little garden. Over a hundred sparrows wake up all at once and give tongue to whatever it is that sparrows have to say to each other at five o'clock on a foggy winter's morning in Delhi.

In the small house, people sleep on; that is, everyone except 'Bhabiji'—Granny—the head of the lively Punjabi middle-class family with whom I nearly always stay when I am in Delhi.

She coughs, stirs, groans, grumbles and gets out of bed. The fire has to be lit, and food prepared for two of her sons to take to work. There is her daughter-in-law, Shobha, to help her; but the girl is not very bright at getting up in the morning. Actually, it is this way: Bhabiji wants to show up her daughter-in-law; so, no matter how hard Shobha tries to be up first, Bhabiji forestalls her. The old lady does not sleep well, anyway; her eyes are open long before the first sparrow chirps, and as soon as she sees her daughter-in-law stirring, she scrambles out of bed and hurries to the kitchen. This gives her the opportunity to say: 'What good is a daughter-in-law when I have to get up to prepare her husband's food?'

The truth is that Bhabiji does not like anyone else preparing her sons' food. She looks no older than when I first saw her ten years ago. She still has complete control over a large family and, with tremendous confidence and enthusiasm, presides over the lives of three sons, a daughter, two daughters-in-law and fourteen grandchildren. This is a joint family (there are not many left in a big city like Delhi), in which the sons and their families all live together as one unit under their mother's benevolent (and sometimes slightly malevolent) autocracy. Even when her husband was alive, Bhabiji dominated the household.

The eldest son, Shiv, has a separate kitchen, but his wife and children participate in all the family celebrations and quarrels. It is a small miracle how everyone (including myself when I visit) manages to fit into the house; and a stranger might be forgiven for wondering where everyone sleeps, for no beds are visible during the day. That is because the beds—light wooden frames with rough string across—are brought in only at night, and are taken out first thing in the morning and kept in the garden shed.

As Bhabiji lights the kitchen fire, the household begins to stir, and Shobha joins her mother-in-law in the kitchen. As a guest I am privileged and may get up last. But my bed soon becomes an island battered by waves of scurrying, shouting children, eager to bathe, dress, eat and find their school books. Before I can get up, someone brings me a tumbler of hot sweet tea. It is a brass tumbler and burns my fingers; I have yet to learn how to hold one properly. Punjabis like their tea with lots of milk and sugar—so much so that I often wonder why they bother to add any tea.

Ten years ago, 'bed tea' was unheard of in Bhabiji's house. Then, the first time I came to stay, Kamal, the youngest son, told Bhabiji: 'My friend is Angrez. He must have tea in bed.' He forgot to mention that I usually took my morning cup at seven; they gave it to me at five. I gulped it down and went to sleep again. Then, slowly, others in the household began indulging in morning cups of tea. Now everyone, including the older children, has 'bed tea'. They bless my English forebears for instituting the custom; I bless the Punjabis for perpetuating it.

Breakfast is by rota, in the kitchen. It is a tiny room and accommodates only four adults at a time. The children have eaten first; but the smallest children, Shobha's toddlers, keep coming in and climbing over us. Says Bhabiji of the youngest and most mischievous: 'He lives only because God keeps a special eye on him.'

Kamal, his elder brother Arun and I sit cross-legged and barefooted on the floor while Bhabiji serves us hot parathas stuffed with potatoes and onions, along with omelettes, an excellent dish. Arun then goes to work on his scooter, while Kamal catches a bus for the city, where he attends an art college. After they have gone, Bhabiji and Shobha have their breakfast.

By nine o'clock everyone who is still in the house is busy doing something. Shobha is washing clothes. Bhabiji has settled down on a cot with a huge pile of spinach, which she methodically cleans and chops up. Madhu, her fourteen-year-old granddaughter, who attends school only in the afternoons, is washing down the sitting room floor. Madhu's mother is a teacher in a primary school in Delhi, and earns a pittance of Rs 150 a month. Her husband went to England ten years ago, and never returned; he does not send any money home.

Madhu is made attractive by the gravity of her countenance. She is always thoughtful, reflective; seldom speaks, smiles rarely (but looks very pretty when she does). I wonder what she thinks about as she scrubs floors, prepares meals with Bhabiji, washes dishes and even finds a few hard-pressed moments for her schoolwork. She is the Cinderella of the house. Not that she has to put up with anything like a cruel stepmother. Madhu is Bhabiji's favourite. She has made herself so useful that she is above all reproach. Apart from that, there is a certain measure of aloofness about her—she does not get involved in domestic squabbles—and this is foreign to a household in which everyone has something to say for himself or herself. Her two young brothers are constantly being reprimanded; but no one says anything to Madhu. Only yesterday morning, when clothes were being washed and Madhu was scrubbing the floor, the following dialogue took place.

Madhu's mother (picking up a school book left in the courtyard): 'Where's that boy Popat? See how careless he is with his books! Popat! He's run off. Just wait till he gets back. I'll give him a good beating.'

Vinod's mother: 'It's not Popat's book. It's Vinod's. Where's Vinod?'

Vinod (grumpily): 'It's Madhu's book.'

Silence for a minute or two. Madhu continues scrubbing the floor; she does not bother to look up. Vinod picks up the book and takes it indoors. The women return to their chores.

Manju, daughter of Shiv and sister of Vinod, is averse to housework and, as a result, is always being scolded—by her parents, grandmother, uncles and aunts.

Now, she is engaged in the unwelcomed chore of sweeping the front yard. She does this with a sulky look, ignoring my cheerful remarks. I have been sitting under the guava tree, but Manju soon sweeps me away from this spot. She creates a drifting cloud of dust, and seems satisfied only when the dust settles on the clothes that have just been hung up to dry. Manju is a sensuous creature and, like most sensuous people, is lazy by nature. She does not like sweeping because the boy next door can see her at it, and she wants to appear before him in a more glamorous light. Her first action every morning is to turn to the cinema advertisements in the newspaper. Bombay's movie moguls cater for girls like Manju who long to be tragic heroines. Life is so very dull for middle-class teenagers in Delhi that it is only natural that they should lean so heavily on escapist entertainment. Every residential area has a cinema. But there is not a single bookshop in this particular suburb, although it has a population of over twenty thousand literate people. Few children read books; but they are adept at swotting up examination 'guides'; and students of, say, Hardy or Dickens read the guides and not the novels.

Bhabiji is now grinding onions and chillies in a mortar. Her eyes are watering but she is in a good mood. Shobha sits quietly in the kitchen. A little while ago she was complaining to me of a backache. I am the only one who lends a sympathetic ear to complaints of aches and pains. But since last night, my sympathies have been under severe strain. When I got into bed at about ten o'clock, I found the sheets wet. Apparently Shobha had put her baby to sleep in my bed during the afternoon.

While the housework is still in progress, cousin Kishore arrives. He is an itinerant musician who makes a living by arranging performances at weddings. He visits Bhabiji's house frequently and at odd hours, often a little tipsy, always brimming over with goodwill and grandiose plans for the future. It was once his ambition to be a film producer, and some years back he lost a lot of Bhabiji's money in producing a film that was never completed. He still talks of finishing it.

'Brother,' he says, taking me into his confidence for the

hundredth time, 'do you know anyone who has a movie camera?'

'No,' I say, knowing only too well how these admissions can lead me into a morass of complicated manoeuvres. But Kishore is not easily put off, especially when he has been fortified with country liquor.

'But you *knew* someone with a movie camera?' He asks.

'That was long ago.'

'How long ago?' (I have got him going now.)

'About five years back.'

'Only five years? Find him, find him!'

'It's no use. He doesn't have the movie camera any more. He sold it.'

'Sold it!' Kishore looks at me as though I have done him an injury. 'But why didn't you buy it? All we need is a movie camera, and our fortune is made. I will produce the film, I will direct it, I will write the music. Two in one, Charlie Chaplin and Raj Kapoor. Why didn't you buy the camera?'

'Because I didn't have the money.'

'But we could have borrowed the money.'

'If you are in a position to borrow money, you can go out and buy another movie camera.'

'We could have borrowed the camera. Do you know anyone else who has one?'

'Not a soul.' I am firm this time; I will not be led into another maze.

'Very sad, very sad,' mutters Kishore. And with a dejected, hangdog expression designed to make me feel that I am responsible for all his failures, he moves off.

Bhabiji had expressed some annoyance at his arrival, but he softens her up by leaving behind an invitation to a wedding party this evening. No one in the house knows the bride's or bridegroom's family, but that does not matter; knowing one of the musicians is just as good. Almost everyone will go.

While Bhabiji, Shobha and Madhu are preparing lunch, Bhabiji engages in one of her favourite subjects of conversation, Kamal's marriage, which she hopes she will be able to arrange in the near future. She freely acknowledges that she made grave blunders in selecting wives for her other sons—this is meant to be heard by Shobha—and promises not to repeat her mistakes. According to Bhabiji, Kamal's bride should be both educated and domesticated; and of course she must be fair.

'What if he likes a dark girl?' I ask teasingly.

Bhabiji looks horrified. 'He cannot marry a dark girl,' she declares.

'But dark girls are beautiful,' I tell her.

'Impossible!'

'Do you want him to marry a European girl?'

'No foreigners! I know them, they'll take my son away. He shall have a good Punjabi girl, with a complexion the colour of wheat.'

Noon. The shadows shift and cross the road. I sit beneath the guava tree and watch the women at work. They will not let me do anything, but they like talking to me and they love to hear my broken Punjabi. Sparrows flit about at their feet, snapping up the grain that runs away from their busy fingers. A crow looks speculatively at the empty kitchen, sidles towards the open door; but Bhabiji has only to glance up and the experienced crow flies away. He knows he will not be able to make off with anything from this house.

One by one the children come home, demanding food. Now it is Madhu's turn to go to school. Her younger brother Popat, an intelligent but undersized boy of thirteen, appears in the doorway and asks for lunch.

'Be off!' says Bhabiji. 'It isn't ready yet.'

Actually the food is ready and only the chapatis remain to be made. Shobha will attend to them. Bhabiji lies down on her cot in the sun, complaining of a pain in her back and ringing noises in her ears.

'I'll press your back,' says Popat. He has been out of Bhabiji's favour lately, and is looking for an opportunity to be rehabilitated.

Barefooted he stands on Bhabiji's back and treads her weary flesh and bones with a gentle walking-in-one-spot movement. Bhabiji grunts with relief. Every day she has new pains in new places. Her age, and the daily business of feeding the family and running everyone's affairs, are beginning to tell on her. But she would sooner die than give up her position of dominance in the house. Her working sons still hand over their pay to her, and she dispenses the money as she sees fit.

The pummelling she gets from Popat puts her in a better mood, and she holds forth on another favourite subject, the respective merits of various dowries. Shiv's wife (according to Bhabiji) brought nothing with her but a string cot; Kishore's wife brought only a sharp and clever tongue; Shobha brought a wonderful steel cupboard, fully expecting that it would do all the housework for her.

This last observation upsets Shobha, and a little later I find her under the guava tree, weeping profusely. I give her the comforting words she obviously expects; but it is her husband Arun who will have to bear the brunt of her outraged feelings when he comes home this evening. He is rather nervous of his wife. Last night he wanted to eat out, at a restaurant, but did not want to be accused of wasting money; so he stuffed fifteen rupees into my pocket and asked me to invite both him and Shobha to dinner, which I did.

We had a good dinner. Such unexpected hospitality on my

part has further improved my standing with Shobha. Now, in spite of other chores, she sees that I get cups of tea and coffee at odd hours of the day.

Bhabiji knows Arun is soft with his wife, and taunts him about it. She was saying this morning that whenever there is any work to be done Shobha retires to bed with a headache (partly true). She says even Manju does more housework (not true). Bhabiji has certain talents as an actress, and does a good take-off of Shobha sulking and grumbling at having too much to do.

While Bhabiji talks, Popat sneaks off and goes for a ride on the bicycle. It is a very old bicycle and is constantly undergoing repairs. 'The soul has gone out of it,' says Vinod philosophically and makes his way on to the roof, where he keeps a store of pornographic literature. Up there, he cannot be seen and cannot be remembered, and so avoids being sent out on errands.

One of the boys is bathing at the handpump. Manju, who should have gone to school with Madhu, is stretched out on a cot, complaining of fever. But she will be up in time to attend the wedding party...

Towards evening, as the birds return to roost in the guava tree, their chatter is challenged by the tumult of people in the house getting ready for the wedding party.

Manju presses her tight pyjamas but neglects to darn them. She wears a loose-fitting, diaphanous shirt. She keeps flitting in and out of the front room so that I can admire the way she glitters. Shobha has used too much powder and lipstick in an effort to look like the femme fatale which she indubitably is not. Shiv's more conservative wife floats around in loose, old-fashioned pyjamas. Bhabiji is sober and austere in a white sari. Madhu looks neat. The men wear their suits.

Popat is holding up a mirror for his Uncle Kishore, who is combing his long hair. (Kishore kept his hair long, like a court musician at the time of Akbar, before the hippies had been heard of.) He is nodding benevolently, having fortified himself from a bottle labelled 'Som Ras' ('Nectar of the Gods'), obtained cheaply from an illicit still.

Kishore: 'Don't shake the mirror, boy!'

Popat: 'Uncle, it's your head that's shaking.'

Shobha is happy. She loves going out, especially to weddings, and she always takes her two small boys with her, although they invariably spoil the carpets.

Only Kamal, Popat and I remain behind. I have had more than my share of wedding parties.

The house is strangely quiet. It does not seem so small now, with only three people left in it. The kitchen has been locked (Bhabiji will not leave it open while Popat is still in the house), so we visit the dhaba, the wayside restaurant near the main road, and this time I pay the bill with my own money. We have kababs and chicken curry.

Yesterday Kamal and I took our lunch on the grass of the Buddha Jayanti Gardens (Buddha's Birthday Gardens). There was no college for Kamal, as the majority of Delhi's students had hijacked a number of corporation buses and headed for the Pakistan High Commission, with every intention of levelling it to the ground if possible, as a protest against the hijacking of an Indian plane from Srinagar to Lahore. The students were met by the Delhi police in full strength, and a pitched battle took place, in which stones from the students and tear gas shells from the police were the favoured missiles. There were two shells fired every minute, according to a newspaper report. And this went on all day. A number of students and policemen were injured, but by some miracle no one was killed. The police held their ground, and the Pakistan High Commission remained inviolate. But the Australian High Commission, situated to the rear of the student brigade, received most of the tear gas shells, and had to close down for the day.

Kamal and I attended the siege for about an hour, before retiring to the Gardens with our ham sandwiches. A couple of friendly squirrels came up to investigate, and were soon taking bread from our hands. We could hear the chanting of the students in the distance. I lay back on the grass and opened my copy of *Barchester Towers*. Whenever life in Delhi, or in Bhabiji's house (or anywhere, for that matter), becomes too tumultuous, I turn to Trollope. Nothing could be further removed from the turmoil of our times than an English cathedral town in the nineteenth century. But I think Jane Austen would have appreciated life in Bhabiji's house.

By ten o'clock, everyone is back from the wedding. (They had gone for the feast, and not for the ceremonies, which continue into the early hours of the morning.) Shobha is full of praise for the bridegroom's good looks and fair complexion. She describes him as being 'gora-chitta'—very white! She does not have a high opinion of the bride.

Shiv, in a happy and reflective mood, extols the qualities of his own wife, referring to her as the Barrel. He tells us how, shortly after their marriage, she had threatened to throw a brick at the next-door girl. This little incident remains fresh in Shiv's mind, after eighteen years of marriage.

He says: 'When the neighbours came and complained, I told them, "It is quite possible that my wife will throw a brick at your daughter. She is in the habit of throwing bricks." The neighbours held their peace.'

I think Shiv is rather proud of his wife's militancy when it comes to taking on neighbours; recently she vanquished the woman next door (a formidable Sikh lady) after a verbal battle that lasted three hours. But in arguments or quarrels with Bhabiji, Shiv's wife always loses, because Shiv takes his mother's side. Arun, on the other hand, is afraid of both wife and mother, and simply makes himself scarce when a quarrel develops. Or he tells his mother she is right, and then, to placate Shobha, takes her to the pictures.

Kishore turns up just as everyone is about to go to bed. Bhabiji is annoyed at first, because he has been drinking too much; but when he produces a bunch of cinema tickets, she is mollified and asks him to stay the night. Not even Bhabiji likes missing a new picture.

Kishore is urging me to write his life story.

'Your life would make a most interesting story,' I tell him. 'But it will be interesting only if I put in everything—your successes *and* your failures.'

'No, no, only successes,' exhorts Kishore. 'I want you to describe me as a popular music director.'

'But you have yet to become popular.'

'I will be popular if you write about me.'

Fortunately we are interrupted by the cots being brought in. Then Bhabiji and Shiv go into a huddle, discussing plans for building an extra room. After all, Kamal may be married soon.

One by one, the children get under their quilts. Popat starts massaging Bhabiji's back. She gives him her favourite blessing: 'God protect you and give you lots of children.' If God listens to all of Bhabiji's prayers and blessings, there will never be a fall in the population.

The lights are off and Bhabiji settles down for the night. She is almost asleep when a small voice pipes up: 'Bhabiji, tell us a story.'

At first Bhabiji pretends not to hear; then, when the request is repeated, she says: 'You'll keep Aunty Shobha awake, and then she'll have an excuse for getting up late in the morning.'

But the children know Bhabiji's one great weakness, and they renew their demand.

'Your grandmother is tired,' says Arun. 'Let her sleep.'

But Bhabiji's eyes are open. Her mind is going back over the crowded years, and she remembers something very interesting that happened when her younger brother's wife's sister married the eldest son of her third cousin...

Before long, the children are asleep, and I am wondering if I will ever sleep, for Bhabiji's voice drones on, into the darker reaches of the night.

Voting at Barlowganj

I am standing under the deodars, waiting for a taxi. Devilal, one of the candidates in the civic election, is offering free rides to all his supporters, to ensure that they get to the polls in time. I have assured him that I prefer walking but he does not believe me; he fears that I will settle down with a bottle of beer rather than walk the two miles to the Barlowganj polling station to cast my vote. He has gone to the expense of engaging a taxi for the day just to make certain of lingerers like me. He assures me that he is not using unfair means—most of the other candidates are doing the same thing.

It is a cloudy day, promising rain, so I decide I will wait for the taxi. It has been plying since 6 a.m., and now it is ten o'clock. It will continue plying up and down the hill till 4 p.m. and by that time it will have cost Devilal over a hundred rupees.

Here it comes. The driver—like most of our taxi drivers, a Sikh—sees me standing at the gate, screeches to a sudden stop, and opens the door. I am about to get in when I notice that the windscreen carries a sticker displaying the Congress symbol of the cow and calf. Devilal is an Independent, and has adopted a cock bird as his symbol.

'Is this Devilal's taxi?' I ask.

'No, it's the Congress taxi,' says the driver.

'I'm sorry,' I say. 'I don't know the Congress candidate.'

'That's all right,' he says agreeably; he isn't a local man and has no interest in the outcome of the election. 'Devilal's taxi will be along any minute now.'

He moves off, looking for the Congress voters on whose behalf he has been engaged. I am glad that the candidates have had to adopt different symbols; it has saved me the embarrassment of turning up in a Congress taxi, only to vote for an Independent. But the real reason for using symbols is to help illiterate voters know whom they are voting for when it comes to putting their papers in the ballot box. All through the hill station's mini-election campaign, posters have been displaying candidates' symbols—a car, a radio, a cock bird, a tiger, a lamp—and the narrow, winding roads resound to the cries of children who are paid to shout, 'Vote for the Radio!' or 'Vote for the Cock!'

Presently my taxi arrives. It is already full, having picked up others on the way, and I have to squeeze in at the back with a stout lalain and her bony husband, the local ration-shop owner. Sitting up front, near the driver, is Vinod, a poor, ragged, quite happy-go-lucky youth, who contrives to turn up wherever I happen to be, and frequently involves himself in my activities. He gives me a namaste and a wide grin.

'What are you doing here?' I ask him.

'Same as you, Bond sahib. Voting. Maybe Devilal will give me a job if he wins.'

'But you already have a job. I thought you were the games-boy at the school.'

'That was last month, Bond sahib.'

'They kicked you out?'

'They asked me to leave.'

The taxi gathers speed as it moves smoothly down the

winding hill road. The driver is in a hurry; the more trips he makes, the more money he collects. We swerve round sharp corners, and every time the lalain's chubby hands, covered with heavy bangles and rings, clutch at me for support. She and her husband are voting for Devilal because they belong to the same caste; Vinod is voting for him in the hope of getting a job; I am voting for him because I like the man. I find him simple, courteous and ready to listen to complaints about drains, street lighting and wrongly assessed taxes. He even tries to do something about these things. He is a tall, cadaverous man, with paan-stained teeth; no Nixon, Heath or Indira Gandhi; but he knows that Barlowganj folk care little for appearances.

Barlowganj is a small ward (one of four in the hill station of Mussoorie); it has about 1,000 voters. An election campaign has, therefore, to be conducted on a person-to-person basis. There is no point in haranguing a crowd at a street corner; it would be a very small crowd. The only way to canvass support is to visit each voter's house and plead one's cause personally. This means making a lot of promises with a perfectly straight face.

The bazaar and village of Barlowganj crouch in a vale on the way down the mountain to Dehra. The houses on either side of the road are nearly all English-looking, most of them built before the turn of the century. The bazaar is Indian, charming and quite prosperous: tailors sit cross-legged before their sewing machines, turning out blazers and tight trousers for the well-to-do students who attend the many public schools that still thrive here; halwais—potbellied sweet vendors—spend all day sitting on their haunches in front of giant frying pans; and coolies carry huge loads of timber or cement or grain up the steep hill paths.

Who was Barlow, and how did the village get his name? A search through old guides and gazetteers has given me no clue. Perhaps he was a revenue superintendent or a surveyor, who came striding up from the plains in the 1830s to build a hunting lodge in this pleasantly wooded vale. That was how most hill stations began. The police station, the little Church of the Resurrection, and the ruined brewery were among the earliest buildings in Barlowganj.

The brewery is a mound of rubble, but the road that came into existence to serve the needs of the old Crown Brewery is the one that now serves our taxi. Buckle and Co.'s 'Bullock Train' was the chief means of transport in the old days. Mr Bohle, one of the pioneers of brewing in India, started the 'Old Brewery' at Mussoorie in 1830. Two years later he got into trouble with the authorities for supplying beer to soldiers without permission; he had to move elsewhere.

But the great days of the brewery business really began in 1876, when everyone suddenly acclaimed a much-improved brew. The source was traced to Vat 42 in Whymper's Crown Brewery (the one whose ruins we are now passing), and the beer was retasted and retested until the diminishing level of the barrel revealed the perfectly brewed remains of a soldier who had been reported missing some months previously. He had evidently fallen into the vat and been drowned and, unknown to himself, had given the Barlowganj beer trade a real fillip. Apocryphal though this story may sound, I have it on the authority of the owner of the now defunct *Mafasalite Press* who, in a short account of Mussoorie, wrote that 'meat was thereafter recognized as the missing component and was scrupulously added till more modern, and less cannibalistic, means were discovered to satiate the froth-blower'.

Recently, confirmation came from an old India hand now living in London. He wrote to me reminiscing of early days in the hill station and had this to say:

Uncle Georgie Forster was working for the Crown Brewery when a coolie fell in. Coolies were employed to remove scum etc. from the vats. They walked along planks suspended over the vats. Poor devil must have slipped and fallen in. Uncle often told us about the incident and there was no doubt that the beer tasted very good.

What with soldiers and coolies falling into the vats with seeming regularity, one wonders whether there may have been more to these accidents than met the eye. I have a nagging suspicion that Whymper and Buckle may have been the Burke and Hare of Mussoorie's beer industry.

But no beer is made in Mussoorie today, and Devilal probably regrets the passing of the breweries as much as I do. Only the walls of the breweries remain, and these are several feet thick. The roofs and girders must have been removed for use in other buildings. Moss and sorrel grow in the old walls, and wildcats live in dark corners protected from rain and wind.

We have taken the sharpest curves and steepest gradients, and now our taxi moves smoothly along a fairly level road which might pass for a country lane in England were it not for the clumps of bamboo on either side.

A mist has come up the valley to settle over Barlowganj, and out of the mist looms an imposing mansion, Sikander Hall, which is still owned and occupied by the Skinners, descendants of Colonel James Skinner who raised a body of Irregular Horse for the Marathas. This was absorbed by the East India Company's forces in 1803. The cavalry regiment is still known as Skinner's Horse, but of course it is a tank regiment now. Skinner's troops called him 'Sikander' (a corruption of both Skinner and Alexander), and that is the name his property bears. The Skinners who live here now have, quite sensibly, gone in for keeping pigs and poultry.

The next house belongs to the Raja of K but he is unable to maintain it on his diminishing privy purse, and it has been rented out as an ashram for members of a saffron-robed sect who would rather meditate in the hills than in the plains. There was a time when it was only the sahibs and rajas who could afford to spend the entire 'season' in Mussoorie. The new rich are the industrialists and maharishis. The coolies and rickshaw pullers are no better off than when I was a boy in Mussoorie. They still carry or pull the same heavy loads, for the same pittance, and seldom attain the age of forty. Only their clientele has changed.

One more gate, and here is Colonel Powell in his khaki bush shirt and trousers, a uniform that never varies with the seasons. He is an old shikari; once wrote a book called *The Call of the Tiger.* He is too old for hunting now, but likes to yarn with me when we meet on the road. His wife has gone home to England, but he does not want to leave India.

'It's the mountains,' he was telling me the other day. 'Once the mountains are in your blood, there is no escape. You have to come back again and again. I don't think I'd like to die anywhere else.'

Today there is no time to stop and chat. The taxi driver, with a vigorous blowing of his horn, takes the car round the last bend, and then through the village and narrow bazaar of Barlowganj, stopping about a hundred yards from the polling stations.

There is a festive air about Barlowganj today, I have never seen so many people in the bazaar. Bunting, in the form of rival posters and leaflets, is strung across the street. The tea shops are doing a roaring trade. There is much last-minute canvassing, and I have to run the gamut of various candidates and their agents. For the first time I learn the names of some of the candidates. In all, seven men are competing for this seat.

A schoolboy, smartly dressed and speaking English, is the first to accost me. He says: 'Don't vote for Devilal, sir. He's a big crook. Vote for Jatinder! See, sir, that's his symbol—the bow and arrow.'

'I shall certainly think about the bow and arrow,' I tell him politely.

Another agent, a man, approaches, and says, 'I hope you are going to vote for the Congress candidate.'

'I don't know anything about him,' I say.

'That doesn't matter. It's the party you are voting for. Don't forget it's Mrs Gandhi's party.'

Meanwhile, one of Devilal's lieutenants has been keeping a close watch on both Vinod and me, to make sure that we are not seduced by rival propaganda. I give the man a reassuring smile and stride purposefully towards the polling station, which has been set up in the municipal schoolhouse. Policemen stand at the entrance, to make sure that no one approaches the voters once they have entered the precincts.

I join the patient queue of voters. Everyone is in good humour, and there is no breaking of the line; these are not film stars we have come to see. Vinod is in another line, and grins proudly at me across the passageway. This is the one day in his life on which he has been made to feel really important. And he *is*. In a small constituency like Barlowganj, every vote counts.

Most of my fellow voters are poor people. Local issues mean something to them, affect their daily living. The more affluent can buy their way out of trouble, can pay for small conveniences; few of them bother to come to the polls. But for the 'common man'—the shopkeeper, clerk, teacher, domestic servant, milkman, mule driver—this is a big day. The man he is voting for has promised him something, and the voter means to take the successful candidate up on his promise. Not for another five years will the same fuss be made over the local cobblers, tailors and laundrymen. Their votes are indeed precious.

And now it is my turn to vote. I confirm my name, address and roll number. I am down on the list as 'Rusking Bound', but I let it pass: I might forfeit my right to vote if I raise any objection at this stage! A dab of marking-ink is placed on my forefinger—this is so that I do not come round a second time— and I am given a paper displaying the names and symbols of all the candidates. I am then directed to the privacy of a small booth, where I place the official rubber stamp against Devilal's name. This done, I fold the paper in four and slip it into the ballot box.

All has gone smoothly. Vinod is waiting for me outside. So is Devilal.

'Did you vote for me?' asks Devilal.

It is my eyes that he is looking at, not my lips, when I reply in the affirmative. He is a shrewd man, with many years' experience in seeing through bluff. He is pleased with my reply, beams at me, and directs me to the waiting taxi.

Vinod and I get in together, and soon we are on the road again, being driven swiftly homewards up the winding hill road.

Vinod is looking pleased with himself; rather smug, in fact. 'You did vote for Devilal?' I ask him. 'The symbol of the cock bird?'

He shakes his head, keeping his eyes on the road. 'No, the cow,' he says.

'You ass!' I exclaim. 'Devilal's symbol was the cock, not the cow!'

'I know,' he says, 'but I like the cow better.'*

I subside into silence. It is a good thing no one else in the taxi has been paying any attention to our conversation. It would be a pity to see Vinod turned out of Devilal's taxi and made to walk the remaining mile to the top of the hill. After all, it will be another five years before he gets another free taxi ride.

---

*In spite of Vinod's defection, Devilal won 1974

A FRIGHT IN THE NIGHT

Our elderly school nurse, Miss Babcock, passed away quite suddenly one autumn evening, apparently of a heart attack. She was laid out on her camp bed in the little room adjoining our four-bed hospital ward. The funeral would be held next day.

Tata and I were school prefects that year, and we both knew Miss Babcock quite well, having often feigned stomach aches or sore throats in order to escape morning PT (physical training) or extra maths periods. It wasn't really a hospital, just a sick bay for the usual cases of measles or mumps. Anyone who went down with something really serious would be sent to Simla's Ripon Hospital.

Mr Fisher, our headmaster, summoned Tata and me to his office.

'Bond,' he said. 'You liked Miss Babcock, didn't you?'

'Yes, sir.'

'And you, Tata?'

'She was a good sport, sir.'

'Good. And since you are both familiar with the hospital, having got yourselves admitted whenever possible, I think it only right that you should be given the duty of keeping a vigil for Miss Babcock. It's not good to leave the dead alone all night.

All you have to do is spend the night beside her bed. Keep the rats away! You can take turns. From nine to midnight, Bond will be on duty. After that, Tata will take over. There's a spare bed in the ward, and an easy chair in the bedroom. Now have your supper, and then go down to the hospital and relieve Mr Jones, who has been there all evening.'

Mr Jones was happy to be able to return to arranging his stamp collection, and wished us a comfortable night in the company of Miss Babcock.

The old lady looked peaceful enough stretched out on her camp bed. She was covered in a bedsheet and only her face and hands were visible. Someone had tried to close her eyes but they remained only half shut.

'Don't try anything funny,' said Tata. 'I think she's watching us.'

'She's been dead for hours,' I said. 'You go and lie down. I'll wake you up at twelve.'

Tata returned to the ward, and I sat down in the easy chair near Miss Babcock's bed. It was a still, silent night, the only sound being the ticking of a wall clock in a corner of the room. A small light bulb glowed over the dressing table. But in those days we were subject to power failures just as we are today, and presently the bulb went out and we were plunged into darkness.

But not for long.

Presently, a full moon came up over the mountains, flooding the garden with moonlight. A moonbeam crept in at the window and moved slowly across the room. Outside, a nightjar honked.

I had been watching Miss Babcock's peaceful countenance for some time, wondering if her spirit was hovering around the room, keeping a watch over me even as I kept a watch over her. In the dark I could only make out the outline of her face, but as the moonlight crept across her bed, I began to make out her features.

Presently the moonlight rested on her face. I could see all her features quite distinctly.

And then, to my horror, she began to smile at me.

A corpse smiling at you in the middle of the night is not the most pleasant of experiences. It is calculated to give you goosebumps. And when the smile becomes an evil grimace, it is time to say your prayers.

But there was no time for prayer. The smile widened even further, and then, with a loud bang—somewhat like a firecracker going off—Miss Babcock's set of false teeth shot out of her mouth and landed on the bedsheet.

At the same time I shot out of my chair and fled from the room, calling to Tata for help.

'She's alive!' I cried. 'Miss Babcock's after me!'

Tata leapt out of bed, peeked into Miss Babcock's room, saw her grinning face, and came back shouting, 'Let's get Fishy!' ('Fishy' being short for our headmaster, Mr Fisher.) 'Before she starts screaming at us!'

Together we rushed up the hospital steps and down the path to the headmaster's house. The headmaster dragged Mr Jones away from his stamp collection, and the four of us tramped down to the hospital, fully expecting to find Miss Babcock walking about.

But she was still laid out, and still very much dead—according to Mr Jones, who'd been in the army and seen many dead people.

'We forgot to take her teeth out,' he explained, indicating Miss Babcock's false teeth which had popped out during my vigil. 'When rigor mortis set in, and her jaw stiffened, the teeth were forced out.'

'They came out with a lot of noise, sir,' I said, still shaken up. 'And she was grinning at me all the time.'

'Well, we know you're a funny fellow, Bond,' said Mr Fisher, giving me one of his own sarcastic smiles. 'Even a corpse can't help grinning at you!'

Tata and I were excused from further 'invigilation', and sent back to our dormitories, where we regaled everyone with a hair-raising account of our experience.

This is a perfectly true story; but it is not really a ghost story.

I think I would prefer seeing a ghost to sitting up with a corpse late into the night.

GANGA DESCENDS

There has ALWAYS been a mild sort of controversy as to whether the true Ganga (in its upper reaches) is the Alaknanda or the Bhagirathi. Of course the two rivers meet at Deoprayag and then both are Ganga. But there are some who assert that geographically the Alaknanda is the true Ganga, while others say that tradition should be the criterion, and traditionally the Bhagirathi is the Ganga.

I put the question to my friend Dr Sudhakar Misra, from whom words of wisdom sometimes flow; and true to form, he answered: 'The Alaknanda is Ganga, but the Bhagirathi is Ganga-ji.'

One sees what he means. The Bhagirathi is beautiful, almost caressingly so, and people have responded to it with love and respect, ever since Lord Shiva released the waters of the goddess from his locks and she sped plainswards in the tracks of Prince Bhagirath's chariot.

> He held the river on his head,
> And kept her wandering, where,
> Dense as Himalayas' woods were spread,
> The tangles of his hair.

Revered by Hindus, and loved by all, the Goddess Ganga weaves her spell over all who come to her. Moreover, she issues from the very heart of the Himalayas. Visiting Gangotri in 1820, the writer and traveller Baillie Fraser noted: 'We are now in the centre of the Himalayas, the loftiest and perhaps the most rugged range of mountains in the world.'

Perhaps it is his realization that one is at the very centre and heart of things that gives one an almost primeval sense of belonging to these mountains, and to this river valley in particular. For me, and for many who have been in the mountains, the Bhagirathi is the most beautiful of the four main river valleys of Garhwal. It will remain so provided we do not pollute its waters and strip it of its virgin forests.

The Bhagirathi seems to have everything—a gentle disposition, deep glens and forests, the ultravision of an open valley graced with tiers of cultivation leading up by degrees to the peaks and glaciers as its head.

From some twenty miles above Tehri, as far as Bhatwari, a distance of fifty-five miles along the valley, there are extensive forests of pine. It covers the mountains on both sides of the rivers and its affluents, filling the ravines and plateaus up to a height of about 5,000 feet. Above Bhatwari, forests of box, yew and cypress commence, and if we leave the valley and take the roads to Nachiketa Tal or Dodi Tal—little lakes at around 9,000 feet above sea level—we pass through dense forests of oak and chestnut. From Gangnani to Gangotri, the deodar is the principal tree. The *Sp. excelsia* pine also extends eight miles up the valley above Gangotri, and birch is found in patches to within half a mile of the glacier.

On the right bank of the river, above Sukni, the forest is nearly pure deodar, but on the left bank, with a northern aspect, there is a mixture of silver fir, spruce, and birch. The valley of the Jadganga is also full of deodar, and towards its head the valuable pencil cedar is found. The only other area of Garhwal where the deodar is equally extensive is the Jaunsar Bawar tract to the west.

It was the valuable timber of the deodar that attracted the adventurer Frederic 'Pahari' Wilson to the valley in the 1850s. He leased the forests from the Raja of Tehri in 1859 for a period of five years. In that short span of time he made a fortune.

The old forest rest houses at Dharasu, Bhatwari and Harsil were all built by Wilson as staging posts, for the only roads were narrow tracks linking one village to another. Wilson married a local girl, Gulabi, from the village of Mukhba, and the portraits of the Wilsons (early examples of the photographer's art) still hang in these sturdy little bungalows. At any rate, I found their pictures at Bhatwari. Harsil is now out of bounds to civilians, and I believe part of the old house was destroyed in a fire a few years ago. This sturdy building withstood the earthquake which devastated the area in 1991.

Amongst other things, Wilson introduced the apple into this area, 'Wilson apples'—large, red and juicy—sold to travellers and pilgrims on their way to Gangotri. This fascinating man also acquired an encyclopaedic knowledge of the wildlife of the region, and his articles, which appeared in *Indian Sporting Life* in the 1860s, were later plundered by so-called wildlife writers for their own works.

Bridge-building was another of Wilson's ventures. These bridges were meant to facilitate travel to Harsil and the shrine at Gangotri. The most famous of them was a suspension bridge spanning 350 feet over the Jatganga at Bhaironghat, over 1,200 feet above the young Bhagirathi, where it thunders through a deep defile. This rippling contraption of a bridge was at first a source of terror to travellers, and only a few ventured across it. To reassure people, Wilson would often mount his horse and gallop to and fro across the bridge. It has since collapsed, but local people will tell you that the hoofbeats of Wilson's horse can still be heard on full-moon nights. The supports of the old bridge were complete tree trunks, and they can still be seen to one side of the new motor-bridge built by engineers of the Northern Railway.

Wilson's life is fit subject for a romance; but even if one were never written, his legend would live on, as it has done for over a hundred years. There has never been any attempt to commemorate him, but people in the valley still speak of him in awe and admiration, as though he had lived only yesterday. Some men leave a trail of legend behind them because they give their spirit to the place where they have lived, and remain forever a part of the rocks and mountain streams.

In the old days, only the staunchest of pilgrims visited the shrines at Gangotri and Jamnotri. The roads were rocky and dangerous, winding along in some places, ascending and descending the faces of deep precipices and ravines, at times leading along banks of loose earth where landslides had swept the original path away. There are still no large towns above Uttarkashi, and this absence of large centres of population may be the reason why the forests are better preserved than those in the Alaknanda valley, or further downstream.

Gangotri is situated at just a little over 10,300 feet. On the right bank of the river is the Gangotri temple, a small neat building without too much ornamentation, built by Amar Singh Thapa, a Nepali general, early in the nineteenth century. It was renovated by the Maharaja of Jaipur in the 1920s. The rock on which it stands is called Bhagirath Shila and is said to be the place where Prince Bhagirath did penance in order that Ganga be brought down from her abode of eternal snow.

Here the rocks are carved and polished by ice and water,

so smooth that in places they look like rolls of silk. The fast flowing waters of this mountain torrent look very different from the huge sluggish river that finally empties its waters into the Bay of Bengal 1,500 miles away.

The river emerges from beneath a great glacier, thickly studded with enormous loose rocks and earth. The glacier is about a mile in width and extends upwards for many miles. The chasm in the glacier through which the stream rushed forth into the light of day is named Gaumukh, the cow's mouth, and is held in deepest reverence by Hindus. The regions of eternal frost in the vicinity were the scene of many of their most sacred mysteries.

The Ganga enters the world no puny stream, but bursts from its icy womb a river thirty or forty yards in breadth. At Gauri Kund (below the Gangotri temple) it falls over a rock of considerable height and continues tumbling over a succession of small cascades until it enters the Bhaironghati gorge.

A night spent beside the river, within the sound of the fall, is an eerie experience. After some time it begins to sound, not like one fall but a hundred, and this sound permeates both one's dreams and waking hours. Rising early to greet the dawn proved rather pointless at Gangotri, for the surrounding peaks did not let the sun in till after 9 a.m. Everyone rushed about to keep warm, exclaiming delightedly at what they call 'gulabi thand', literally, 'rosy cold'. Guaranteed to turn the cheeks a rosy pink! A charming expression, but I prefer a rosy sunburn, and remained beneath a heavy quilt until the sun came up to throw its golden shafts across the river.

This is mid-October, and after Diwali the shrine and the small township will close for winter, the pandits retreating to the relative warmth of Mukbha. Soon snow will cover everything, and even the hardy purple-plumaged whistling thrushes, lovers of deep shade, will move further down the valley. And down below the forest line, the Garhwali farmers go about harvesting their terraced fields which form patterns of yellow, green and gold above the deep green of the river.

Yes, the Bhagirathi is a green river. Although deep and swift, it does not lose its serenity. At no place does it look hurried or confused—unlike the turbulent Alaknanda, fretting and frothing as it goes crashing down its boulder-strewn bed. The Alaknanda gives one a feeling of being trapped, because the river itself is trapped. The Bhagirathi is free-flowing, easy. At all times and places it seems to find its true level.

Uttarkashi, though a large and growing town, is as yet uncrowded. The seediness of towns like Rishikesh and parts of Dehradun is not yet evident here. One can take a leisurely walk through its long (and well-supplied) bazaar, without being jostled by crowds or knocked over by three-wheelers. Here, too, the river is always with you, and you must live in harmony with its sound as it goes rushing and humming along its shingly bed.

Uttarkashi is not without its own religious and historical importance, although all traces of its ancient town of Barahat appear to have vanished. There are four important temples here, and on the occasion of Makar Sankranti, early in January, a week-long fair is held when thousands from the surrounding areas throng the roads to the town. To the beating of drums and blowing of trumpets, the gods and goddesses are brought to the fair in gaily decorated palanquins. The surrounding villages wear a deserted look that day as everyone flocks to the temples and bathing ghats and to the entertainments of the fair itself.

We have to move far downstream to reach another large centre of population, the town of Tehri, and this is a very different place from Uttarkashi. Tehri has all the characteristics of a small town in the plains—crowds, noise, traffic congestion, dust and refuse, scruffy dhabas—with this difference that here it is all ephemeral, for Tehri is destined to be submerged by the water of the Bhagirathi when the Tehri dam is finally completed.

The rulers of Garhwal were often changing their capitals, and when, after the Gurkha War (of 1811–15), the former capital of Srinagar became part of British Garhwal, Raja Sudershan Shah established his new capital at Tehri. It is said that when he reached this spot, his horse refused to go any further. This was enough for the king, it seems; or so the story goes.

Perhaps Prince Bhagirath's chariot will come to a halt here too, when the dam is built. The two 246 metre-high earthen dam, with forty-two square miles of reservoir capacity, will submerge the town and about thirty villages.

But as we leave the town and cross the narrow bridge over the river, a mighty blast from above sends rocks hurtling down the defile, just to remind us that work is indeed in progress.

Unlike the Raja's horse, I have no wish to be stopped in my tracks at Tehri. There are livelier places upstream. And as for the Ganga herself, that deceptively gentle river, I wonder if she will take kindly to our efforts to contain her.

MY FATHER'S TREES IN DEHRA

Our trees still grow in Dehra. This is one part of the world where trees are a match for man. An old peepul may be cut down to make way for a new building; two peepul trees will sprout from the walls of the building. In Dehra the air is moist, the soil hospitable to seeds and probing roots. The valley of Dehra Dun lies between the first range of the Himalayas and the smaller but older Siwalik range. Dehra is an old town, but it was not in the reign of Rajput princes or Mogul kings that it really grew and flourished; it acquired a certain size and importance with the coming of British and Anglo-Indian settlers. The English have an affinity with trees, and in the rolling hills of Dehra they discovered a retreat which, in spite of snakes and mosquitoes, reminded them, just a little bit, of England's green and pleasant land.

The mountains to the north are austere and inhospitable; the plains to the south are flat, dry and dusty. But Dehra is green. I look out of the train window at daybreak to see the sal and shisham trees sweep by majestically, while trailing vines and great clumps of bamboo give the forest a darkness and density which add to its mystery. There are still a few tigers in these forests; only a few, and perhaps they will survive, to stalk the spotted deer and drink at forest pools.

I grew up in Dehra. My grandfather built a bungalow on the outskirts of the town at the turn of the century. The house was sold a few years after Independence. No one knows me now in Dehra, for it is over twenty years since I left the place, and my boyhood friends are scattered and lost. And although the India of Kim is no more, and the Grand Trunk Road is now a procession of trucks instead of a slow-moving caravan of horses and camels, India is still a country in which people are easily lost and quickly forgotten.

From the station I can take either a taxi or a snappy little scooter rickshaw (Dehra had neither before 1950), but, because I am on an unashamedly sentimental pilgrimage, I take a tonga, drawn by a lean, listless pony, and driven by a tubercular old Muslim in a shabby green waistcoat. Only two or three tongas stand outside the station. There were always twenty or thirty here in the 1940s when I came home from boarding school to be met at the station by my grandfather; but the days of the tonga are nearly over, and in many ways this is a good thing, because most tonga ponies are overworked and underfed. Its wheels squeaking from lack of oil and its seat slipping out from under me, the tonga drags me through the bazaars of Dehra. A couple of miles of this slow, funereal pace makes me impatient to use my own legs, and I dismiss the tonga when we get to the small Dilaram Bazaar.

It is a good place from which to start walking.

The Dilaram Bazaar has not changed very much. The shops are run by a new generation of bakers, barbers and banias, but professions have not changed. The cobblers belong to the lower castes, the bakers are Muslims, the tailors are Sikhs. Boys still fly kites from the flat rooftops, and women wash clothes on the canal steps. The canal comes down from Rajpur and goes underground here, to emerge about a mile away.

I have to walk only a furlong to reach my grandfather's house. The road is lined with eucalyptus, jacaranda and laburnum trees. In the compounds there are small groves of mangoes, litchis and papayas. The poinsettia thrusts its scarlet leaves over garden walls. Every verandah has its bougainvillea creeper, every garden its bed of marigolds. Potted palms, those symbols of Victorian snobbery, are popular with Indian housewives. There are a few houses, but most of the bungalows were built by 'old India hands' on their retirement from the army, the police or the railways. Most of the present owners are Indian businessmen or government officials.

I am standing outside my grandfather's house. The wall has been raised, and the wicket gate has disappeared; I cannot get a clear view of the house and garden. The nameplate identifies the owner as Major General Saigal; the house has had more than one owner since my grandparents sold it in 1949.

On the other side of the road there is an orchard of litchi trees. This is not the season for fruit, and there is no one looking after the garden. By taking a little path that goes through the orchard, I reach higher ground and gain a better view of our old house.

Grandfather built the house with granite rocks taken from the foothills. It shows no sign of age. The lawn has disappeared; but the big jackfruit tree, giving shade to the side verandah, is still there. In this tree I spent my afternoons, absorbed in my Magnets, Champions and Hotspurs, while sticky mango juice trickled down my chin. (One could not eat the jackfruit unless it was cooked into a vegetable curry.) There was a hole in the bole of the tree in which I kept my pocket knife, top, catapult and any badges or buttons that could be saved from my father's RAF tunics when he came home on leave. There was also an Iron Cross, a relic of the First World War, given to me by my grandfather. I have managed to keep the Iron Cross; but what did I do with my top and catapult? Memory fails me. Possibly they are still in the hole in the jackfruit tree; I must have forgotten to collect them when we went away after my father's death. I am seized by a whimsical urge to walk in at the gate, climb into the branches of the jackfruit tree and recover my lost possessions. What would the present owner, the major general (retired), have to say if I politely asked permission to look for a catapult left behind more than twenty years ago?

An old man is coming down the path through the litchi trees. He is not a major general but a poor street vendor. He carries a small tin trunk on his head, and walks very slowly. When he sees me, he stops and asks me if I will buy something. I can think of nothing I need, but the old man looks so tired, so very old, that I am afraid he will collapse if he moves any further along the path without resting. So I ask him to show me his wares. He cannot get the box off his head by himself, but together we manage to set it down in the shade, and the old man insists on spreading its entire contents on the grass; bangles, combs, shoelaces, safety pins, cheap stationery, buttons, pomades, elastic and scores of other household necessities.

When I refuse buttons because there is no one to sew them on for me, he piles me with safety pins. I say no; but as he moves from one article to another, his querulous, persuasive voice slowly wears down my resistance, and I end up buying envelopes, a letter pad (pink roses on bright blue paper), a one-rupee fountain pen guaranteed to leak and several yards of elastic. I have no idea what I will do with the elastic, but the old man convinces me that I cannot live without it.

Exhausted by the effort of selling me a lot of things I obviously do not want, he closes his eyes and leans back against the trunk of a litchi tree. For a moment I feel rather nervous. Is he going to die sitting here beside me? He sinks to his haunches and puts his chin on his hands. He only wants to talk.

'I am very tired, huzoor,' he says. 'Please do not mind if I sit here for a while.'

'Rest for as long as you like,' I say. 'That's a heavy load you've been carrying.'

He comes to life at the chance of a conversation and says, 'When I was a young man, it was nothing. I could carry my box up from Rajpur to Mussoorie by the bridle path—seven steep miles! But now I find it difficult to cover the distance from the station to Dilaram Bazaar.'

'Naturally. You are quite old.'

'I am seventy, sahib.'

'You look very fit for your age.' I say this to please him; he looks frail and brittle. 'Isn't there someone to help you?' I ask.

'I had a servant boy last month, but he stole my earnings and ran off to Delhi. I wish my son was alive—he would not have permitted me to work like a mule for a living—but he was killed in the riots in 1947.'

'Have you no other relatives?'

'I have outlived them all. That is the curse of a healthy life. Your friends, your loved ones, all go before you, and in the end you are left alone. But I must go too, before long. The road to the bazaar seems to grow longer every day. The stones are harder. The sun is hotter in the summer, and the wind much colder in the winter. Even some of the trees that were there in my youth have grown old and have died. I have outlived the trees.'

He has outlived the trees. He is like an old tree himself, gnarled and twisted. I have the feeling that if he falls asleep in the orchard, he will strike root here, sending out crooked branches. I can imagine a small bent tree wearing a black waistcoat; a living scarecrow.

He closes his eyes again, but goes on talking.

'The English memsahibs would buy great quantities of elastic. Today it is ribbons and bangles for the girls, and combs for the boys. But I do not make much money. Not because I cannot walk very far. How many houses do I reach in a day? Ten, fifteen. But twenty years ago I could visit more than fifty houses. That makes a difference.'

'Have you always been here?'

'Most of my life, huzoor. I was here before they built the motor road to Mussoorie. I was here when the sahibs had their own carriages and ponies and the memsahibs their own rickshaws. I was here before there were any cinemas. I was here when the Prince of Wales came to Dehra Dun... Oh, I have been here a long time, huzoor. I was here when that house was built,' he says pointing with his chin towards my grandfather's house. 'Fifty, sixty years ago it must have been. I cannot remember exactly. What is ten years when you have lived seventy? But it was a tall, red-bearded sahib who built that house. He kept many creatures as pets. A kachwa (turtle) was one of them. And there was a python, which crawled into my box one day and gave me a terrible fright. The sahib used to keep it hanging from his shoulders, like a garland. His wife, the burra mem, always bought a lot from me—lots of elastic. And there were sons, one a teacher, another in the air force, and there were always children in the house. Beautiful children. But they went away many years ago. Everyone has gone away.'

I do not tell him that I am one of the 'beautiful children'. I doubt if he will believe me. His memories are of another age, another place, and for him there are no strong bridges into the present.

'But others have come,' I say.

'True, and that is as it should be. That is not my complaint. My complaint—should God be listening—is that I have been left behind.'

He gets slowly to his feet and stands over his shabby tin box, gazing down at it with a mix of disdain and affection. I help him to lift and balance it on the flattened cloth on his head. He does not have the energy to turn and make a salutation of any kind; but, setting his sights on the distant hills, he walks down the path with steps that are shaky and slow but still wonderfully straight.

I wonder how much longer he will live. Perhaps a year or two, perhaps a week, perhaps an hour. It will be an end of living, but it will not be death. He is too old for death; he can only sleep; he can only fall gently, like an old, crumpled brown leaf.

I leave the orchard. The bend in the road hides my grandfather's house. I reach the canal again. It emerges from under a small culvert, where ferns and maidenhair grow in the shade. The water, coming from a stream in the foothills, rushes along with a familiar sound; it does not lose its momentum until the canal has left the gently sloping streets of the town.

There are new buildings on this road, but the small police station is housed in the same old lime-washed bungalow. A couple of off-duty policemen, partly uniformed but with their pyjamas on, stroll about.

I cannot forget this little police station. Nothing very exciting ever happened in its vicinity until, in 1947, communal riots broke out in Dehra. Then, bodies were regularly fished out of the canal and dumped on a growing pile in the station compound. I was only a boy, but when I looked over the wall at that pile of corpses, there was no one who paid any attention to me. They were too busy to send me away. At the same time they knew that I was perfectly safe; while Hindus and Muslims were at each other's throats, a white boy could walk the streets in safety. No one was any longer interested in the Europeans.

The people of Dehra are not violent by nature, and the town has no history of communal discord. But when refugees from the partitioned Punjab poured into Dehra in thousands, the atmosphere became charged with tension. These refugees, many of them Sikhs, had lost their homes and livelihoods; many had seen their loved ones butchered. They were in a fierce and vengeful frame of mind. The calm, sleepy atmosphere of Dehra was shattered during two months of looting and murder. The Muslims who could get away, fled. The poorer members of the community remained in a refugee camp until the holocaust was over; then they returned to their former occupations, frightened and deeply mistrustful. The old boxman was one of them.

I cross the canal and take the road that will lead me to the riverbed. This was one of my father's favourite walks. He, too, was a walking man. Often, when he was home on leave, he would say, 'Ruskin, let's go for a walk,' and we would slip off together and walk down to the riverbed or into the sugarcane fields or across the railway lines and into the jungle.

On one of those walks (this was before Independence), I remember him saying, 'After the war is over, we'll be going to England. Would you like that?'

'I don't know,' I said. 'Can't we stay in India?'

'It won't be ours any more.'

'Has it always been ours?' I asked.

'For a long time,' he said, 'over two hundred years. But we have to give it back now.'

'Give it back to whom?' I asked. I was only nine.

'To the Indians,' said my father.

The only Indians I had known till then were my ayah and the cook and the gardener and their children, and I could not imagine them wanting to be rid of us. The only other Indian who came to the house was Dr Ghose, and it was frequently said of him that he was more English than the English. I could understand my father better when he said, 'After the war, there'll be a job for me in England. There'll be nothing for me here.'

The war had at first been a distant event; but somehow it kept coming closer. My aunt, who lived in London with her two children, was killed with them during an air raid; then my father's younger brother died of dysentery on the long walk out from Burma. Both these tragic events depressed my father. Never in good health (he had been prone to attacks of malaria), he looked more worn and wasted every time he came home. His personal life was far from being happy, as he and my mother had separated, she to marry again. I think he looked forward a great deal to the days he spent with me; far more than I could have realized at the time. I was someone to come back to; someone for whom things could be planned; someone who could learn from him.

Dehra suited him. He was always happy when he was among trees, and this happiness communicated itself to me. I felt like drawing close to him. I remember sitting beside him on the verandah steps when I noticed the tendril of a creeping vine that was trailing near my feet. As we sat there, doing nothing in particular—in the best gardens, time has no meaning—I found that the tendril was moving almost imperceptibly away from me and towards my father. Twenty minutes later it had crossed the verandah steps and was touching his feet. This, in India, is the sweetest of salutations.

There is probably a scientific explanation for the plant's behaviour—something to do with the light and warmth on the verandah steps—but I like to think that its movements were motivated simply by an affection for my father. Sometimes, when I sat alone beneath a tree, I felt a little lonely or lost. As soon as my father rejoined me, the atmosphere lightened, the tree itself became more friendly.

Most of the fruit trees round the house were planted by father; but he was not content with planting trees in the garden. On rainy days we would walk beyond the riverbed, armed with cuttings and saplings, and then we would amble through the jungle, planting flowering shrubs between the sal and shisham trees.

'But no one ever comes here,' I protested the first time. 'Who is going to see them?'

'Some day,' he said, 'someone may come this way… If people keep cutting trees, instead of planting them, there'll soon be no forests left at all, and the world will be just one vast desert.' The prospect of a world without trees became a sort of nightmare for me (and one reason why I shall never want to live on the treeless moon), and I assisted my father in his tree planting with great enthusiasm.

'One day the trees will move again,' he said. 'They've been standing still for thousands of years. There was a time when they could walk about like people, but someone cast a spell on them and rooted them to one place. But they're always trying to move—see how they reach out with their arms!'

We found an island, a small rocky island in the middle of a dry riverbed. It was one of those riverbeds, so common in the foothills, which are completely dry in the summer but flooded during the monsoon rains. The rains had just begun, and the stream could still be crossed on foot, when we set out with a number of tamarind, laburnum and coral tree saplings and cuttings. We spent the day planting them on the island, then ate our lunch there, in the shelter of a wild plum.

My father went away soon after that tree planting. Three

months later, in Calcutta, he died.

I was sent to boarding school. My grandparents sold the house and left Dehra. After school, I went to England. The years passed, my grandparents died, and when I returned to India I was the only member of the family in the country.

And now I am in Dehra again, on the road to the riverbed. The houses with their trim gardens are soon behind me, and I am walking through fields of flowering mustard, which make a carpet of yellow blossom stretching away towards the jungle and the foothills.

The riverbed is dry at this time of the year. A herd of skinny cattle graze on the short brown grass at the edge of the jungle. The sal trees have been thinned out. Could our trees have survived? Will our island be there, or has some flash flood during a heavy monsoon washed it away completely?

As I look across the dry watercourse, my eye is caught by the spectacular red plumes of the coral blossom. In contrast with the dry, rocky riverbed, the little island is a green oasis. I walk across to the trees and notice that a number of parrots have come to live in them. A koel challenges me with a rising *who-are-you, who-are you.*

But the trees seem to know me. They whisper among themselves and beckon me nearer. And looking around, I find that other trees and wild plants and grasses have sprung up under the protection of the trees we planted.

They have multiplied. They are moving. In this small forgotten corner of the world, my father's dreams are coming true, and the trees are moving again.

THE WALKERS' CLUB

Though their numbers have diminished over the years, there are still a few compulsive daily walkers around: the odd ones, the strange ones, who will walk all day, here, there and everywhere, not in order to get somewhere, but to escape from their homes, their lonely rooms, their mirrors, themselves...

Those of us who must work for a living and would love to be able to walk a little more don't often get the chance. There are offices to attend, deadlines to be met, trains or planes to be caught, deals to be struck, people to deal with. It's the rat race for most people, whether they like it or not. So who are these lucky ones, a small minority it has to be said, who find time to walk all over this hill station from morn to night?

Some are fitness freaks, I suppose; but several are just unhappy souls who find some release, some meaning, in covering miles and miles of highway without so much as a nod in the direction of others on the road. They are not looking at anything as they walk, not even at a violet in a mossy stone.

Here comes Miss Romola. She's been at it for years. A retired schoolmistress who never married. No friends. Lonely as hell. Not even a visit from a former pupil. She could not have been very popular.

She has money in the bank. She owns her own flat. But

she doesn't spend much time in it. I see her from my window, tramping up the road to Lal Tibba. She strides around the mountain like the character in the old song 'She'll be coming round the mountain', only she doesn't wear pink pyjamas; she dresses in slacks and a shirt. She doesn't stop to talk to anyone. It's quick march to the top of the mountain, and then down again, home again, jiggety-jig. When she has to go down to Dehradun (too long a walk even for her), she stops a car and catches a lift. No taxis for her; not even the bus.

Miss Romola's chief pleasure in life comes from conserving her money. There are people like that. They view the rest of the world with suspicion. An overture of friendship will be construed as taking an undue interest in her assets. We are all part of an international conspiracy to relieve her of her material possessions! She has no servants, no friends; even her relatives are kept at a safe distance.

A similar sort of character but even more eccentric is Mr Sen, who used to live in the US and walks from the Happy Valley to Landour (five miles) and back every day, in all seasons, year in and year out. Once or twice every week he will stop at the Community Hospital to have his blood pressure checked or undergo a blood or urine test. With all that walking he should have no health problems, but he is a hypochondriac and is convinced that he is dying of something or the other.

He came to see me once. Unlike Miss Romola, he seemed to want a friend, but his neurotic nature turned people away. He was convinced that he was surrounded by individual and collective hostility. People were always staring at him, he told me. I couldn't help wondering why, because he looked fairly nondescript. He wore conventional Western clothes, perfectly acceptable in urban India, and looked respectable enough except for a constant nervous turning of the head, looking to the left, right, or behind, as though to check on anyone who might be following him. He was convinced that he was being followed at all times.

'By whom?' I asked.

'Agents of the government,' he said.

'But why should they follow you?'

'I look different,' he said. 'They see me as an outsider. They think I work for the CIA.'

'And do you?'

'No, no!' He shied nervously away from me. 'Why did you say that?'

'Only because you brought the subject up. I haven't noticed anyone following you.'

'They're very clever about it. Perhaps you're following me too.'

'I'm afraid I can't walk as fast or as far as you,' I said with a laugh,' but he wasn't amused. He never smiled, never laughed. He did not feel safe in India, he confided. The saffron brigade was after him!

'But why?' I asked. 'They're not after me. And you're a Hindu with a Hindu name.'

'Ah yes, but I don't look like one!'

'Well, I don't look like a Taoist monk, but that's what I am,' I said, adding, in a more jocular manner: 'I know how to become invisible, and you wouldn't know I'm around. That's why no one follows me! I have this wonderful cloak, you see, and when I wear it I become invisible!'

'Can you lend it to me?' he asked eagerly.

'I'd love to,' I said, 'but it's at the cleaners right now. Maybe next week.'

'Crazy,' he muttered. 'Quite mad.' And he hurried on.

A few weeks later he returned to New York and safety. Then

I heard he'd been mugged in Central Park. He's recovering, but doesn't do much walking now.

Neurotics do not walk for pleasure, they walk out of compulsion. They are not looking at the trees or the flowers or the mountains; they are not looking at other people (except in apprehension); they are usually walking away from something— unhappiness or disarray in their lives. They tire themselves out, physically and mentally, and that brings them some relief.

Like the journalist who came to see me last year. He'd escaped from Delhi, he told me. He had taken a room in Landour Bazaar and was going to spend a year on his own, away from family, friends, colleagues, the entire rat race. He was full of noble resolutions. He was planning to write an epic poem or a great Indian novel or a philosophical treatise. Every fortnight I meet someone who is planning to write one or the other of these things, and I do not like to discourage them, just in case they turn violent!

In effect he did nothing but walk up and down the mountain, growing shabbier by the day. Sometimes he recognized me. At other times there was a blank look on his face, as though he were on some drug, and he would walk past me without a sign of recognition. He discarded his slippers and began walking about barefoot, even on the stony paths. He did not change or wash his clothes. Then he disappeared; that is, I no longer saw him around.

I did not really notice his absence until I saw an ad in one of the national papers, asking for information about his whereabouts.

His family was anxious to locate him. The ad carried a picture of the gentleman, taken in happier, healthier times; but it was definitely my acquaintance of that summer.

I was sitting in the bank manager's office, up in the

cantonment, when a woman came in, making inquiries about her husband. It was the missing journalist's wife. Yes, said Mr Ohri, the friendly bank manager, he'd opened an account with them; not a very large sum, but there were a few hundred rupees lying to his credit. And no, they hadn't seen him in the bank for at least three months.

He couldn't be found. Several months passed, and it was presumed that he had moved on to some other town; or that he'd lost his mind or his memory. Then some milkmen from Kolti Gaon discovered bones and remnants of clothing at the bottom of a cliff.

In the pocket of the ragged shirt was the journalist's press card.

How he'd fallen to his death remains a mystery. It's easy to miss your footing and take a fatal plunge on the steep slopes of this range. He may have been high on something or he may simply have been trying out an unfamiliar path. Walking can be dangerous in the hills if you don't know the way or if you take one chance too many.

And here's a tale to illustrate that old chestnut that truth is often stranger than fiction.

Colonel Parshottam had just retired and was determined to pass the evening of his life doing the things he enjoyed most: taking early morning and late evening walks, afternoon siestas, a drop of whisky before dinner, and a good book on his bedside table.

A few streets away, on the fourth floor of a block of flats, lived Mrs L, a stout, neglected woman of forty, who'd had enough of life and was determined to do away with herself.

Along came the Colonel on the road below, a song on his lips, strolling along with a jaunty air; in love with life and wanting more of it.

Quite unaware of anyone else around, Mrs L chose that moment to throw herself out of her fourth-floor window. Seconds later she landed with a thud on the Colonel. If this was a Ruskin Bond story, it would have been love at first flight. But the grim reality was that he was crushed beneath her and did not recover from the impact. Mrs L, on the other hand, survived the fall and lived on into a miserable old age.

There is no moral to the story, any more than there is a moral to life. We cannot foresee when a bolt from the blue will put an end to the best-laid plans of mice and men.

WHO KISSED ME IN THE DARK?

This chapter, or story, could not have been written but for a phone call I received last week. I'll come to the caller later. Suffice to say that it triggered off memories of a hilarious fortnight in the autumn of that year (can't remember which one) when India and Pakistan went to war with each other. It did not last long, but there was plenty of excitement in our small town, set off by a rumour that enemy parachutists were landing in force in the ravine below Pari Tibba.

The road to this ravine led past my dwelling, and one afternoon I was amazed to see the town's constabulary, followed by hundreds of concerned citizens (armed mostly with hockey sticks) taking the trail down to the little stream where I usually went bird-watching. The parachutes turned out to be bedsheets from a nearby school, spread out to dry by the dhobis who lived on the opposite hill. After days of incessant rain the sun had come out, and the dhobis had finally got a chance to dry the school bedsheets on the verdant hillside. From afar they did look a bit like open parachutes. In times of crisis, it's wonderful what the imagination will do.

There were also black-outs. It's hard for a hill station to black itself out, but we did our best. Two or three respectable people were arrested for using their torches to find their way home in the dark. And of course, nothing could be done about the lights on the next mountain, as the people there did not even know there was a war on. They did not have radio or television or even electricity. They used kerosene lamps or lit bonfires!

We had a smart young set in Mussoorie in those days, mostly college students who had also been to convent schools and some of them decided it would be a good idea to put on a show—or old-fashioned theatrical extravaganza—to raise funds for the war effort. And they thought it would be a good idea to rope me in, as I was the only writer living in Mussoorie in those innocent times. I was thirty-one and I had never been a college student but they felt I was the right person to direct a one-act play in English. This was to be the centrepiece of the show.

I forget the name of the play. It was one of those drawing-room situation comedies popular from the 1920s, inspired by such successes as *Charley' Aunt* and *Tons of Money*. Anyway, we went into morning rehearsals at Hakman's, one of the older hotels, where there was a proper stage and a hall large enough to seat at least two hundred spectators.

The participants were full of enthusiasm, and rehearsals went along quite smoothly. They were an engaging bunch of young people—Guttoo, the intellectual among them; Ravi, a schoolteacher; Gita, a tiny ball of fire; Neena, a heavy-footed Bharatnatyam exponent; Nellie, daughter of a nurse; Chameli, who was in charge of make-up (she worked in a local beauty saloon); Rajiv, who served in the bar and was also our prompter; and a host of others, some of whom would sing and dance before and after our one-act play.

The performance was well attended, Ravi having rounded up a number of students from the local schools; and the lights were working, although we had to cover all doors, windows and exits with blankets to maintain the regulatory black-out. But the stage was old and rickety and things began to go wrong during Neena's dance number when, after a dazzling pirouette, she began stamping her feet and promptly went through the floorboards. Well, to be precise, her lower half went through, while the rest of her remained above board and visible to the audience.

The schoolboys cheered, the curtain came down and we rescued Neena, who had to be sent to the civil hospital with a sprained ankle, Mussoorie's only civilian war casualty.

There was a hold-up, but before the audience could get too restless the curtain went up on our play, a tea-party scene, which opened with Guttoo pouring tea for everyone. Unfortunately, our stage manager had forgotten to put any tea in the pot and poor Guttoo looked terribly put out as he went from cup to cup, pouring invisible tea. 'Damn. What happened to the tea?' muttered Guttoo, a line, which was not in the script. 'Never mind,' said Gita, playing opposite him and keeping her cool. 'I prefer my milk without tea,' and proceeded to pour herself a cup of milk.

After this, everyone began to fluff their lines and our prompter had a busy time. Unfortunately, he'd helped himself to a couple of rums at the bar, so that, whenever one of the actors faltered, he'd call out the correct words in a stentorian voice which could be heard all over the hall. Soon there was more prompting than acting and the audience began joining in with dialogue of their own.

Finally, to my great relief, the curtain came down—to thunderous applause. It went up again, and the cast stepped forward to take a bow. Our prompter, who was also the curtain-puller, released the ropes prematurely and the curtain came down with a rush, one of the sandbags hitting poor Guttoo on the head. He has never fully recovered from the blow.

The lights, which had been behaving all evening, now failed us, and we had a real black-out. In the midst of this confusion, someone—it must have been a girl, judging from the overpowering scent of jasmine that clung to her—put her arms around me and kissed me.

When the light came on again, she had vanished.

Who had kissed me in the dark?

As no one came forward to admit to the deed, I could only make wild guesses. But it had been a very sweet kiss, and I would have been only too happy to return it had I known its ownership. I could hardly go up to each of the girls and kiss them in the hope of reciprocation. After all, it might even have been someone from the audience.

Anyway, our concert did raise a few hundred rupees for the war effort. By the time we sent the money to the right authorities, the war was over. Hopefully they saw to it that the money was put to good use.

We went our various ways and although the kiss lingered in my mind, it gradually became a distant, fading memory and as the years passed it went out of my head altogether. Until the other day, almost forty years later...

'Phone for you,' announced Gautam, my seven-year-old secretary.

'Boy or girl? Man or woman?'

'Don't know. Deep voice like my teacher but it says you know her.'

'Ask her name.'

Gautam asked.

'She's Nellie, and she's speaking from Bareilly.'

'Nellie from Bareilly?' I was intrigued. I took the phone. 'Hello,' I said. 'I'm Bonda from Golconda.'

'Then you must be wealthy now.' Her voice was certainly husky. 'But don't you remember me? Nellie? I acted in that play of yours, up in Mussoorie a long time ago.'

'Of course, I remember now,' I was remembering. 'You had a small part, the maidservant I think. You were very pretty. You had dark, sultry eyes. But what made you ring me after all these years?'

'Well, I was thinking of you. I've often thought about you. You were much older than me, but I liked you. After that show, when the lights went out, I came up to you and kissed you. And then I ran away.'

'So it was you! I've often wondered. But why did you run away? I would have returned the kiss. More than once.'

'I was very nervous. I thought you'd be angry.'

'Well, I suppose it's too late now. You must be happily married with lots of children.'

'Husband left me. Children grew up, went away.'

'It must be lonely for you.'

'I have lots of dogs.'

'How many?'

'About thirty.'

'Thirty dogs! Do you run a kennel club?'

'No, they are all strays. I run a dog shelter.'

'Well, that's very good of you. Very humane.'

'You must come and see it sometime. Come to Bareilly. Stay with me. You like dogs, don't you?'

'Er-yes, of course. Man's best friend, the dog. But thirty is a lot of dogs to have about the house.'

'I have lots of space.'

'I'm sure... Well, Nellie, if ever I'm in Bareilly, I'll come to see you. And I'm glad you phoned and cleared up the mystery. It was a lovely kiss and I'll always remember it.'

We said our goodbyes and I promised to visit her some day. A trip to Bareilly to return a kiss might seem a bit far-fetched, but I've done sillier things in my life. It's those dogs that worry me. I can imagine them snapping at my heels as I attempt to approach their mistress. Dogs can be very possessive.

'Who was that on the phone?' asked Gautam, breaking in on my reverie.

'Just an old friend!'

'Dada's old girlfriend. Are you going to see her?'

'I'll think about it.'

And I'm still thinking about it and about those dogs. But bliss it was to be in Mussoorie forty years ago, when Nellie kissed me in the dark.

Some memories are best left untouched.

THE ROAD TO BADRINATH

If you travel up the Mandakini valley, and then cross over into the valley of the Alaknanda, you are immediately struck by the contrast. The Mandakini is gentler, richer in vegetation, almost pastoral in places; the Alaknanda is awesome, precipitous, threatening—and seemingly inhospitable to those who must live, and earn a livelihood, in its confines.

Even as we left Chamoli and began the steady, winding climb to Badrinath, the nature of the terrain underwent a dramatic change. No longer did green fields slope gently down to the riverbed. Here they clung precariously to rocky slopes and ledges that grew steeper and narrower, while the river below, impatient to reach its confluence with the Bhagirathi at Deoprayag, thundered along the narrow gorge.

Badrinath is one of the four dhams, or four most holy places in India. (The other three are Rameshwaram, Dwarka and Jagannath Puri.) For the pilgrim travelling to this holiest of holies, the journey is exciting, possibly even uplifting; but for those who live permanently on these crags and ridges, life is harsh, a struggle from one day to the next. No wonder so many young men from Garhwal find their way into the army. Little grows on these rocky promontories; and what does, is at the mercy of the weather. For most of the year the fields lie fallow. Rivers, unfortunately, run downhill and not uphill.

The harshness of this life, typical of much of Garhwal, was brought home to me at Pipalkoti, where we stopped for the night. Pilgrims stop here by the coachload, for the Garhwal Mandal Vikas Nigam's rest house is fairly capacious, and small hotels and dharamshalas abound. Just off the busy road is a tiny hospital, and here, late in the evening, we came across a woman keeping vigil over the dead body of her husband. The body had been laid out on a bench in the courtyard. A few feet away the road was crowded with pilgrims in festival mood; no one glanced over the low wall to notice this tragic scene.

The woman came from a village near Helong. Earlier that day, finding her consumptive husband in a critical condition she had decided to bring him to the nearest town for treatment. As he was frail and emaciated, she was able to carry him on her back for several miles, until she reached the motor road. Then, at some expense, she engaged a passing taxi and brought him to Pipalkoti. But he was already dead when she reached the small hospital. There was no morgue; so she sat beside the body in the courtyard, waiting for dawn and the arrival of others from the village. A few men arrived next morning and we saw them wending their way down to the cremation ground. We did not see the woman again. Her children were hungry and she had to hurry home to look after them.

Pipalkoti is hot (and peepul trees are conspicuous by their absence), but Joshimath, the winter resort of the Badrinath temple establishment, is about 6,000 feet above sea level and has an equable climate. It is now a fairly large town, and although the surrounding hills are rather bare, it does have one great tree that has survived the ravages of time. This is an ancient mulberry, known as the Kalpa Vriksha (Immortal Wishing Tree), beneath which the great Sankaracharya meditated, a few centuries ago. It is reputedly over 2,000 years old, and is certainly larger than my modest four-roomed flat in Mussoorie. Sixty pilgrims holding hands might just about encircle its trunk.

I have seen some big trees, but this is certainly the oldest and broadest of them. I am glad the Sankaracharya meditated beneath it and thus ensured its preservation. Otherwise it might well have gone the way of other great trees and forests that once flourished in this area.

A small boy reminds me that it is a Wishing Tree, so I make my wish. I wish that other trees might prosper like this one.

'Have you made a wish?' I ask the boy.

'I wish that you will give me one rupee,' he says. His wish comes true with immediate effect. Mine lies in the uncertain future. But he has given me a lesson in wishing.

Joshimath has to be a fairly large place, because most of Badrinath arrives here in November, when the shrine is snowbound for six months. Army and PWD structures also dot the landscape. This is no carefree hill resort, but it has all the amenities for making a short stay quite pleasant and interesting. Perched on the steep mountainside above the junction of the Alaknanda and Dhauli Rivers, it is now vastly different from what it was when Frank Smythe visited it fifty years ago and described it as 'an ugly little place...straggling unbeautifully over the hillside. Primitive little shops line the main street, which is roughly paved in places and in others has been deeply channelled by the monsoon rains. The pilgrims spend the night in single-storeyed rest-houses, not unlike the hovels provided for the Kentish hop-pickers of former days, some of which are situated in narrow passages running off the main street and are filthy and evil-smelling.'

Those were Joshimath's former days. It is a different place today, with small hotels, modern shops, a cinema; and its growth and comparative modernity date from the early sixties, when the old pilgrim footpath gave way to the motor road which takes the traveller all the way to Badrinath. No longer does the weary, footsore pilgrim sink gratefully down in the shade of the Kalpa Vriksha. He alights from his bus or luxury coach and drinks a cola or a Thums-up at one of the many small restaurants on the roadside.

Contrast this comfortable journey with the pilgrimage fifty years ago. Frank Smythe again: 'So they venture on their pilgrimage... Some borne magnificently by coolies, some toiling along in rags, some almost crawling, preyed on by disease and distorted by dreadful deformities...Europeans who have read and travelled cannot conceive what goes on in the minds of these simple folk, many of them from the agricultural parts of India, wonderment and fear must be the prime ingredients. So the pilgrimage becomes an adventure. Unknown dangers threaten the broad, well-made path, at any moment the gods, who hold the rocks in leash, may unloose their wrath upon the hapless passer-by. To the European it is a walk to Badrinath, to the Hindu pilgrim it is far, far more,'

Above Vishnuprayag, Smythe left the Alaknanda and entered the Bhyundar valley, a botanist's paradise, which he called the Valley of Flowers. He fell in love with the lush meadows of this high valley, and made it known to the world. It continues to attract the botanist and trekker. Primulas of subtle shades, wild geraniums, saxifrages clinging to the rocks, yellow and red potentillas, snow-white anemones, delphiniums, violets, wild roses, all these and many more flourish there, capturing the mind and heart of the flower lover.

'Impossible to take a step without crushing a flower.' This may not be true any more, for many footsteps have trodden the Bhyundar in recent years. There are other areas in Garhwal where the hills are rich in flora—the Har-ki-doon, Harsil, Tungnath, and the Khiraun valley where the balsam grows to a height of eight feet—but the Bhyundar has both a variety and a concentration of wild flowers, especially towards the end of the monsoon. It would be no exaggeration to call it one of the most beautiful valleys in the world. The Bhyundar is a digression for lovers of mountain scenery; but the pilgrim keeps his eyes fixed on the ultimate goal—Badrinath, where the gods dwelt and where salvation is to be found.

There are still a few who do it the hard way—mostly those who have taken sanyas and renounced the world. Here is one hardy soul doing penance. He stretches himself out on the ground, draws himself up to a standing position, then flattens himself out again. In this manner he will proceed from Badrinath to Rishikesh, oblivious of the sun and rain, the dust from passing buses, the sharp gravel of the footpath.

Others are not so hardy. One saffron-robed scholar, speaking fair English, asks us for a lift to Badrinath, and we find a space for him. He rewards us with a long and involved commentary on the Vedas, which lasts through the remainder of the journey. His special field of study, he informs us, is the part played by aeronautics in Vedic literature.

'And what,' I ask him, 'is the connection between the two?'

He looks at me pityingly.

'It is what I am trying to find out,' he replies.

The road drops to Pandukeshwar and rises again, and all the time I am scanning the horizon for the forests of the Badrinath region I had read about many years ago in James B. Fraser's *The Himalaya Mountains*! Walnuts growing up to 9,000 feet, deodars and 'bilka' up to 9,500 feet, and 'amesh' and 'kiusu' fir up a similar height—but, apart from strands of long-leaved excelsia pine, I do not see much, certainly no deodars. What has happened to them, I wonder. An endless variety of trees delighted us all the way from Dugalbeta to Mandal, a well-protected area, but here on the high ridges above the Alaknanda, little seems to grow; or, if ever they did, have long since been bespoiled or swept away.

Finally we reach the wind-swept, barren valley which harbours Badrinath—a growing township, thriving, lively, but somewhat dwarfed by the snow-capped peaks that tower above it. As at Joshimath, there is no dearth of hostelries and dharamshalas. Even so, every hotel or rest house is filled to overflowing. It is the height of the pilgrim season, and pilgrims, tourists and mendicants of every description throng the riverfront.

Just as Kedar is the most sacred of the Shiva temples in the Himalayas, so Badrinath is the supreme place of worship for the Vaishnav sects.

According to legend, when Sankaracharya in his digvijaya travels visited the Mana valley he arrived at the Narada Kund and found fifty different images lying in its waters. These he rescued, and when he had done so, a voice from Heaven said, 'These are the images for the Kaliyug, establish them here.' Sankaracharya accordingly placed them beneath a mighty tree which grew there and whose shade extended from Badrinath to Nandprayag, a distance of over eighty miles. Close to it was the hermitage of Nar-Narayana (or Arjuna and Krishna), and in course of time temples were built in honour of these and other manifestations of Vishnu. It was here that Vishnu appeared to his followers in person, as the four-armed, crested and adorned with pearls and garlands.' The faithful, it is said, can still see him on the peak of Nilkantha, on the great Kumbha day. It is, in fact, the Nilkantha peak that dominates this crater-like valley where a few hardy thistles and nettles manage to survive. Like cacti in the desert, the pricklier forms of life seem best equipped to live in a hostile environment.

Nilkantha means blue-necked, an allusion to the god Shiva's swallowing of a poison meant to destroy the world. The poison remained in his throat, which was rendered blue thereafter. It is a majestic and awe-inspiring peak, soaring to a height of 21,640 feet. As its summit is only five miles from Badrinath, it is justly held in reverence. From its ice-clad pinnacle three great ridges sweep down, of which the southern one terminates in the Alaknanda valley.

On the evening of our arrival we could not see the peak, as it was hidden in clouds. Badrinath itself was shrouded in mist. But we made our way to the temple, a gaily decorated building about 50-feet high, with a gilded roof. The image of Vishnu, carved in black stone, stands in the centre of the sanctum, opposite the door, in a dhyana posture. An endless stream of people passes through the temple to pay homage and emerge the better for their proximity to the divine.

From the temple, flights of steps lead down to the rushing river and to the hot springs which emerge just above it. Another road leads through a long but tidy bazaar where pilgrims may buy mementos of their visit—from sacred amulets to pictures of the gods in vibrant technicolour. Here at last I am free to indulge my passion for cheap rings, with none to laugh at my foible. There are all kinds, from rings designed like a coiled serpent (my favourite) to twisted bands of copper and iron and others containing the pictures of gods, gurus and godmen. They do not cost more that two or three rupees each, and so I am able to fill my pockets. I never wear these rings. I simply hoard them away. My friends are convinced that in a previous existence I was a jackdaw, seizing upon and hiding away any kind of bright and shiny object. So be it...

Even those who have renounced the world appear to be cheerful—like the young woman from Gujarat who had taken sanyas and who met me on the steps below the temple. She gave me a dazzling smile and passed me an exercise book. She had taken a vow of silence; but being, I think, of an extrovert nature, she seemed eager to remain in close communication with the rest of humanity, and did so by means of written questions and answers. Hence, the exercise book.

Although at Badrinath I missed the sound of birds and the presence of trees, it was good to be part of the happy throng at its colourful little temple, and to see the sacred river close to its source. And early next morning I was rewarded with the liveliest experience of all.

Opening the window of my room, and glancing out, I saw the rising sun touch the snow-clad summit of Nilkantha. At first the snows were pink; then they turned to orange and gold. All sleep vanished as I gazed up in wonder at that magnificent pinnacle in the sky. And had Lord Vishnu appeared just then on the summit I would not have been in the least surprised.

ONCE UPON A MOUNTAIN TIME

*My solitude is not my own, for I see now how much it belongs
to them—and that I have a responsibility for it in their regard,
not just in my own. It is because I am one with them that I
owe it to them to be alone, and when I am alone they are not
'they' but my own self. There are no strangers!*

—Thomas Merton, *Conjectures of a Guilty Bystander*

The trees stand watching over my day-to-day life. They are
the guardians of my conscience. I have no one else to
answer to, so I live and work under the generous but highly
principled supervision of the trees—especially the deodars, who
stand on guard, unbending, on the slope above the cottage.
The oak and maples are a little more tolerant, they have had
to put up with a great deal, their branches continually lopped
for fuel and fodder. 'What would *they* think?' I ask myself on
many an occasion. 'What would they like me to do?' And I do
what I think they would approve of most!

Well, it's nice to have someone to turn to...

The leaves are a fresh pale green in the spring rain. I can
look at the trees from my window—look down on them almost,
because the window is on the first floor of the cottage, and the

hillside runs away at a sharp angle into the ravine. The trees and I know each other quite intimately, and we have much to say to each other from time to time.

I do nearly all my writing at this window seat. The trees watch over me as I write. Whenever I look up, they remind me that they are there. They are my best critics. As long as I am aware of their presence, I can try to avoid the trivial and the banal.

Ramesh, the son of the municipal cleaner, looms darkly in the doorway. He is a stunted boy with a large head, but has wide gentle eyes. His orange-coloured trousers brighten up the surrounding gloom.

'What do you want, Ramesh?'

'Newspapers.'

'To sell to the kabari?'

'No. For wrapping my schoolbooks.'

'Well, take a few.' I give him half a dozen old newspapers, the headlines already look meaningless. 'Sit down and wait for it to stop raining.'

He sits awkwardly on a mora.

'And what is your cousin Vinod doing these days?' (Vinod is a good-looking ne'er-do-well who seldom does anything apart from hanging around cinema halls.)

'Nothing.'

'Doesn't he go to school?'

'He has stopped going to school. He got a job at fifty rupees a month, but he left after a week. He says he will join the army in September.'

The rain stops and Ramesh departs. The clouds begin to break up, the sun strikes the steep hill on my left. A woman is chopping up sticks. I hear the tinkle of cowbells. Water drips from a leaking drainpipe. And suddenly, clear and pure, the song of the whistling thrush emerges like a dark sweet secret from the depths of the ravine.

◆

Bijju is back from school and is taking his parents' cattle out to graze. He sees me at the window and waves, then grabs his favourite cow Neelu by the tail and tells her to hurry up.

Bijju is twelve, a fair, good-looking Garhwali boy. His younger sister and brother are very pretty children. The father, an electrician, is a rather self-effacing man. The mother is a strong, hard woman. I have watched her on the hillside cutting grass. She has the muscular calves of a man, solid feet and heavy hands; but she is a handsome woman. They live in a rented outhouse further up the hill.

Bijju doesn't visit me very often. He is rather shy. But one day I looked out of the window and there he was in the branches of the oak tree, smiling at me rather hesitantly. We spoke to each other across the three or four yards that separate house from oak tree.

'If I jump, I can land in your tree,' I said.

'And if I jump I will be in your house,' said Bijju.

'Come on then, jump!'

But he shook his head. He was afraid of me. The tree was safe. He put his arms round the thickest branch and held himself close to it. He looked very right in the tree, as though he belonged there, a boy of the woods, a tree spirit peeping out from a house of glossy new leaves.

'Come on, jump!'

'*You* jump,' he said.

In the evening his sister brings the cows home. I meet her on the path above the house. She is only a year younger than Bijju, a very bonny girl who is going to be ravishingly beautiful when she grows up, if they don't marry her off too soon. She too has the same timid smile. But if these children are timid of humans, they are not afraid in the forest, and often wander far afield with Neelu the blue cow and others. (And S, who is eighteen and educated at an English-medium private school, wouldn't go alone into the forest if you paid him!) But the trees know their own. They will cherish the wild spirits and frighten the daylights out of the tame.

◆

The whistling thrush is here, bathing in the rainwater puddle beneath the window. He loves this spot. So now, when there is no rain, I fill the puddle with water, just so that my favourite bird keeps coming.

His bath finished, he perches on a branch of the walnut tree. His glossy blue-black wings glitter in the sunshine. At any moment he will start singing.

Here he goes! He tries out the tune, whistling to himself, and then, confident of the notes, sends his thrilling full-throated voice far over the forest. The song dies down, trembling, lingering in the air; starts again, joyfully, and then suddenly stops, as though the singer had forgotten the words or the tune.

◆

Vinod, the ne'er-do-well, turns up with a friend, asking me to give them some work. They want to go to the pictures but have no money.

'You can dig up this slope below the house,' I tell them. 'The soil is good for growing vegetables.'

This sounds too much like hard work for Vinod, who says, 'We'll come and do it tomorrow.'

'No, we'll do it now,' says his more enterprising friend, and to my surprise they set to work.

Now and then I look out of the window. They are digging away with fair enthusiasm.

After about half an hour, Vinod keeps sitting down for short rests, to the increasing irritation of his partner. They are soon snapping at each other. Vinod looks very funny when he sulks, because he has a snub nose, and somehow a snub nose and a ferocious expression only reminds me of Richmal Crompton's William. But the work gets done by evening and they are quite pleased with their earnings.

◆

Bijju is right at the top of a big oak. The branches sway to his movements. He grins down at me and waves. The higher he is in the tree, the more confident he becomes. It is only when he is down on the ground that he becomes shy and speechless.

He has allowed the cows to wander, and presently his mother's deep voice can be heard calling, 'Neelu, Neelu!' (The other cows don't have names.) And then: 'Where is that wretched boy?'

◆

Sir Edmund Gibson has come up. He spends the summer in the big house just down the road. He is wheezing a lot and says he has water in his lungs—and who wouldn't, at the age of eighty-six?

'Ruskin, my advice to you,' he says, 'is never to live beyond the age of eighty.'

'Well, once ought to be enough, sir.'

He is a big man, but not as red in the face as he used to be. His Gurkha manservant, Tirlok, has to push him up the steep slope to my gate.

Sir Edmund was once the British Resident in the Kathiawar

states. He knew my parents in Jamnagar, when I was just five or six. He is a bachelor and is looked after by his servants.

His farm at Ramgarh doesn't make any money and he will probably give it to his retainers.

When Sir Edmund was Resident, he was once shot at from close range by a terrorist. The man took four shots and missed every time. He must have been a terrible shot, or perhaps the pistol was faulty, because Sir E presents a very large target.

He also treasures two letters from Mahatma Gandhi, which were written from prison.

'I liked Gandhi,' says Sir E. 'He had a sense of humour. No politician today has a sense of humour. They all take themselves far too seriously. But not Gandhi. He took his work seriously, but not himself. When I went to see him in prison, I asked him if he was comfortable, and he smiled and said, "Even if I was, I wouldn't admit it!"'

Sir E's servant brings tea, but there isn't any milk. I think I have exhausted Bijju's supply.

Now it's dusk and the trees are very still, very quiet. Far away I can hear the *chuk-chuk-chuk* of a nightjar. The lights on Landour hill come on, one by one. Prem is singing in the kitchen. There is a whirr of wings as the king crows fly into the trees to roost for the night. A rustling in the dry leaves below the window. A snake? Field rats? Porcupines? It is now too dark to find out. The day has ended, and the trees move closer together in the dark.

◆

We are treated to one of those spectacular electric storms which are fairly frequent at this time of the year, late spring or early summer. The clouds grow very dark, then send bolts of lightning sizzling across the sky, lighting up the entire range of mountains.

When the storm is directly overhead, there is hardly a pause in the frequency of the lightning; it is like a bright light being switched on and off with barely a second's interruption.

John Lang, writing in Dickens's magazine *Household Words* in 1853, over 120 years ago, had this to say about one of our storms:

> I have seen a storm on the heights of Jura—such a storm as Lord Byron describes. I have seen lightning, and heard thunder in Australia; I have, off Tierra del Fuego, the Cape of Good Hope, and the coast of Java, kept watch in thunderstorms which have drowned in their roaring the human voice, and made everyone deaf and stupefied; but these storms are not to be compared with a thunderstorm at Mussoorie or Landour.

Forgotten today, Lang was a popular writer in the mid-nineteenth century. He was also a successful barrister, who represented the Rani of Jhansi in her litigation with the East India Company. He spent his last years in Mussoorie and was buried in the Camel's Back cemetery. His grave proved to be almost as elusive as his books and I found it with some difficulty, overgrown with moss and periwinkle. Prem and I cleaned it up until the inscription stood out quite clearly.

Prem won't come home on a stormy night like this. He is afraid of the dark, but more than that, he is afraid of thunderstorms. It is as though the gods are ganging up against him. So he will spend the night in the school quarters, where he is visiting his mother who is staying there with relatives.

◆

In the morning he turns up with a sheepish grin, saying it got very late and he didn't want to wake me in the middle of the night. I try to feign anger, but it is a gloriously fresh and spirited morning; impossible to feel angry. A strong breeze is driving the clouds away, and the sun keeps breaking through The birds are particularly active. The king crows (who weren't here last year) seem to have taken up residence in the oaks. I don't know why they are called crows. They are slim, elegant black birds, with long forked tails, and their call, far from being a caw, is quite musical, though slightly metallic. The mynahs are very busy, very noisy, looking for a nesting site in the roof. The babblers are raking over fallen leaves, snapping up absent-minded grasshoppers. Now and then, the whistling thrush bursts into song, and then all other bird sounds pale into insignificance. Bijju has taken his cows to pasture and now scrambles up the hill, heading for home; he is late for school, and that is why he is in a hurry. He waves to me.

Both he and Prem have the high cheekbones and the deep-set eyes of the hill people. Prem, of course, is tall and dark. Bijju is small and fair; but he will grow into a sturdy young fellow.

The rain has driven the scorpions out of their rocks and crevices. I found one sitting on a loaf of bread. Up came his sting when we disturbed him. Prem tipped him out on the verandah steps and he scurried off into the bushes. I do not kill insects and other small creatures if I can help it, but there is a limit to my hospitality. I spared a centipede yesterday even though, last year, I was bitten by one which had occupied the seat of my pyjamas. Our hill scorpions and centipedes are not as dangerous as those found in the plains, and probably the same can be said for the people.

Prem tells me that his uncle is immune to scorpion stings, and allows himself to be stung in order to demonstrate his immunity. Apparently his mother was stung by a scorpion shortly before his birth!

◆

Azure butterflies flit about the garden like flakes of sky.

Learnt two new words: bosky = wooded, bushy (bosky shadows); girding = jesting, jeering (girding schoolboys, girding monkeys).

◆

Poor old Sir E is in a bad way. He has diarrhoea, and little or no control over the muscles that play a part in controlling the bowels. The Gurkha servant called me, and I went over with some tablets. Sir E looked quite exhausted and was panting from the exertion of walking from his bed to the toilet. The Gurkha is very good—gives Sir E his bath, dresses him, helps him on with his pyjamas.

Grateful for my alacrity in coming over with some medicine, Sir E offers me a whisky-and-soda (the first time he has ever done this), and pours himself a stiff brandy. He dozes off now and then, but the laboured breathing won't stop. He is a tough old tree, but I think he is beginning to find his massive frame something of a burden.

I make an attempt at conversation. 'Were you at Oxford or Cambridge?'

'Oxford. I joined Oxford in 1905 and left in 1909. Came out to India in 1910.'

He has an excellent memory, unlike Mr Biggs (a retired headmaster) who is ten years younger but will repeat the same story thrice in ten minutes.

'And when were you knighted?' I ask.

'1939 or 1940.'

He is too tired to do much talking. I let him doze off, and give my attention to the whisky. The log fire burns well, the flames cast their glow on Sir E's white hair and hanging jowls. The stertorous breathing grows in volume. He wakes up suddenly, complains that the fire is too hot; Tirlok opens the window. I finish the whisky; he doesn't offer another. It is his supper time, anyway, and I suggest soup and toast. 'Call me in the night if you have any trouble,' I say. He looks very grateful. The loneliness must press upon him a great deal.

I go out into the night. The trees are bending to a strong wind. From the foliage comes a deep sigh, the voice of leagues of trees sleeping and half-disturbed in their sleep. The sky is clear, tremendous with stars.

◆

For the first time this year I hear the barbet, a sure sign the summer is upon us. Its importunate cry carries far across the hills. It can keep this up for hours, like a beggar. Indeed, its plaint—*un-neow, un-neow!*—has been likened in the hills to that of the spirit of the village moneylender who has died before he can collect his dues. ('*Un-neow!*' is a cry for justice!)

It is difficult to spot the barbet. It is a fat green bird (no bigger than a mynah, but fatter), and it usually perches at the very top of a deodar or cypress.

The whistling thrush comes to bathe in the rainwater puddle. Sir E is much better and is sitting outside in the shade of an old oak. They are probably about the same age. What a rugged constitution this man must have; first, to survive, as a young man, all those diseases such as cholera, typhoid, dysentery, malaria, even the plague, which carried off so many Europeans in India (including my father); and now, an old man, to live and battle with congested lungs, a bad heart, weak eyes, bad teeth, recalcitrant bowels, and god knows what else, and still be able to derive some pleasure from living. His old Hillman car is equally indestructible. But, like Sir E, it can't get up the hill any more; he uses it only in Dehradun.

I think his longevity is due simply to the fact that he refuses to go to bed when he is unwell. No amount of diarrhoea, or water in his lungs, will prevent him from getting up, dressing, writing letters, or getting on with the latest Wodehouse (a contemporary of his) or *Blackwood's Magazine*, to which he has been subscribing for the last fifty years! He was pleased to find that some of my own essays were appearing in *Blackwood's*. Nothing will keep him from his four o'clock tea or his evening whisky-and-soda. He is determined, I am sure, to die in his chair, with all his clothes on. The thought of being taken unawares while still in his pyjamas must be something of a nightmare to him. (His favourite film, he once told me, was *They Died With Their Boots On*.)

◆

The cicadas are tuning up for their first summer concert. Even Mrs Biggs, who is hard of hearing, can hear them. Yesterday I met her on the road above the cottage and exchanged pleasantries. Up at Wynberg the girls' choir was hard at practice.

'The girls are in good voice today,' I remarked.

'Oh yes, Mr Bond,' she said, presuming I meant the cicadas. 'They do it with their legs, don't they?'

A week in Delhi. It is still only early summer, but the heat almost knocks one over. Slept on a roof, along with thousands of mosquitoes. It cools off in the early hours, but only briefly, before the sun comes shouting over the rooftops. The dust lies thick on floors, leaves, books, people. May's golden dust!

Now, back in the hills, I am struck first of all by the silence. The house, too, makes itself felt. It has been here too long not to have acquired a personality of its own. It is not a cheerful-looking place, nor is it exactly gloomy. My bedroom is rather dark (because it faces the abrupt slope of the hillside), but there is a wild cherry growing just outside the window—a cherry tree which I nurtured ever since it was a tiny seedling, five or six years ago, and which has now grown so tall that the branches tap against the roof whenever there is a breeze. It is a funny sort of cherry because it flowers in November instead of in the spring like other fruit trees. Small birds and small boys willingly eat the berries, which are too acidic for adult palates.

The sitting room, with its two big windows looking out on the forest, is a bright room. Most of the wall space is taken up by my books. The rugs are worn and tattered—they have been with the house right from the beginning, I think—and I can't afford new ones.

> On books and friends I spend my money;
> For stones and bricks I haven't any.

Sir E, quite recovered from his recent illness, has gone down to Dehra again to attend to his farm and the demands of his farm workers. He should be back at the end of the month.

The brilliant blue-black of the whistling thrush shows up best when the sun is glinting off its back, but this seldom happens, because the bird likes to keep to the shade where it is almost black. Hopping about, it reminds me of Fred Astaire dancing in tophat and tails.

Now that it's getting hot, my small pool attracts a number of afternoon visitors—the mynahs, babblers, a bulbul, a magpie. After their dip they perch in the cherry tree to dry themselves and I can watch them without getting up from my bed, where I take an afternoon siesta. I reserve the afternoons for doing nothing. 'Silence and non-action are the root of all things,' says Tao. Especially on a drowsy afternoon.

But I haven't seen the whistling thrush for several days. Perhaps he is offended at having to share the pool which he was the first to discover. I haven't heard his song either, which probably means that he has moved down to the stream where it is cooler and shadier.

◆

Prem's mother and younger sister come for a few days. His mother is a very quiet woman and doesn't say much even to her son. She is quite handsome, although she looks rather worn and tired, due probably to her recent illness.

His little sister, about four, is a friendly little gazelle; not in the least pretty, but lively and intelligent. She will have to stay here for at least six months to be properly treated for her incipient tuberculosis. There is no treatment to be had in their village.

While I am resting, still exhausted from an attack of hill dysentery (who called this a health resort?), Sir E blows in, red-faced, as distressed as a stranded whale. His Gurkha servant has walked out, after quarrelling with his wife and mother-in-law, and has taken with him his twin sons (aged one and a half). I calm Sir E, tell him Tirlok will be back in a day or two—he is probably trying to show how indispensable he is!

Sir E takes out a cigarette and strikes a match, and the entire matchbox flares up, burning a finger. Definitely not his day. I apply Burnol.

'It's all that damned girl's fault,' he says. 'She has a vile temper, just like her mother. We were very wise not to marry, Ruskin.'

Wise or not, I seem to have acquired a family all the same.

◆

Hundreds of white butterflies are flitting through the forest.

When Prem told his mother that I kept a human skull in my sitting room (given to me by Anil, a medical student, and *not* pinched from the cemetery as some suppose), she told him not to spend too much time near it. If he did, he would be possessed by the spirit of the woman who had originally inhabited the skull.

But Prem, at the present time, is immune to spirits, having succumbed to the charms of his young wife who stays downstairs with his mother. They have only been married a few months. He leans over the balcony, chatting with her; advises her on how to keep the courtyard clean; then makes her a small broom from the twigs of a wild honeysuckle bush. She enjoys all the attention she is getting.

The sky is overcast this morning. Dust from the plains has formed a thick haze which hides the valley and the mountains. We are badly in need of rain. Down in the plains, over two hundred people have died of heatstroke.

I haven't seen Bijju for some days, but this morning his sister, Binya, was out with the cows. What a sturdy little girl she is; and pretty, too. I will write a story about her.*

◆

'We'll take you to the pictures one day, Sir Edmund.'

'Yes, I must see one more picture before I die.'

So there comes a time when we start thinking in terms of the last picture, the last book, the last visit, the last party. But Sir E's remark is matter of fact. He is given to boredom but not to melancholy.

And he has a timeless quality. I have noticed this in other old people; they look more permanent than the young.

He sums it all up by saying, 'I don't mind being dead, but I shall miss being alive.'

A number of small birds are here to bathe and drink in the

---

*This story was called 'The Blue Umbrella'.

little pool beneath the cherry tree: hunting parties of tits—grey tits, red-headed tits and green-backed tits—and two delicate little willow warblers. They take turns in the pool. While the green-backs are taking a plunge, the red-heads wait patiently on the moss-covered rocks, coming down later to sip daintily at the edge of the pool; they don't like getting their feet wet! Finally, when they have all gone away, the whistling thrush arrives and indulges in an orgy of bathing, as he now has the entire pool to himself.

The babblers are adept at snapping up the little garden skinks that scuttle about in the leaves and grass. The skinks are quite brittle and are easily broken to pieces with a few hard raps of the beak. Then down they go! Babblers are also good at sifting through dead leaves and seizing upon various insects.

The honeybees push their way through the pursed lips of the antirrhinum and disappear completely. A few minutes later they stagger out again, bottoms first.

◆

1 June

The dry spell continues. It is only before sunrise that there is any freshness in the air.

At dawn I said, 'Day, you will not begin without me.' I was up with the whistling thrush at five. The cicadas were tuning up, the crickets were already in full cry, and the whistling thrush was calling most sweetly. As none of these songsters could be seen, it was as though the forest itself was singing.

Feeling the dawn wind stir, I was happy that I had met the day at its very beginning.

When the sun came up, the day became sultry and oppressive. I had to walk two miles to Ban Suman and back. There was no shade anywhere along the road. But we are equipped with legs for the purpose of walking. As more and more people grow dependent on their cars, a new species of humans will evolve. Around the turn of the twenty-second century, I can see legless humans being born. By then, of course, there will be flying wheelchairs.

A pall of dust hangs over the mountain.

Someone asked Sir E if he could shoot a bird on his land at Ramgarh. The man wanted the bird for dissection in a biology lab. Sir E refused.

'It's in the interests of science,' protested the man. 'Do you think a bird is better than a human?'

'Infinitely,' said Sir E. 'Infinitely better.'

He goes down today to pay his farm-hands. He will return in a few days unless it gets cooler in Dehra. He complains of being very bored up here, for he can't get about, and in Dehra he has his Hillman. 'I'm *rotting* with boredom,' he says.

Vinod, I hear, is laid low with a fever—the result of a day's hard work. He is now in retirement for the rest of the season.

◆

Walked five miles down the Tehri road to Suakholi, where I rested in a small tea shop, a loose stone structure with a tin roof held down by stones. It serves the bus passengers, mule drivers, milkmen and others who use this road.

I find a couple of mules tethered to a pine tree. The mule drivers, handsome men in tattered clothes, sit on a bench in the shade of the tree, drinking tea from brass tumblers. The shopkeeper, a man of indeterminate age—the cold dry winds from the mountain passes having crinkled his face like a walnut—greets me enthusiastically, as he always does. He even produces a chair, which looks like a survivor from the Savoy's 1890 ballroom. Fortunately the Mussoorie antique dealers haven't seen it, or it would have been carried away long ago. In any case, the stuffing has come out of the seat. The shopkeeper apologizes for its condition: 'The rats were nesting in it.' And then, to reassure me: 'But they have gone now.'

Unlike the shopkeeper, the mule drivers have somewhere to go and something to deliver: sacks of potatoes. From Jaunpur to Jaunsar, the potato is probably the crop best suited to these stony, terraced fields. Oddly enough, it was introduced to the Himalayas by two Irishmen, Captain Young of Dehra and Mussoorie and Captain Kennedy of Simla, in the 1820s. The slopes of Young's house, Mullingar, were known as his Potato Farm. Looking up old books, I was surprised to learn that the potato wasn't known in India before the nineteenth century, and now it's an essential part of our diet in most parts of the country.

As the mule drivers lead their pack animals away, along the dusty road to Landour bazaar, I follow at a distance, singing 'Mule Train' in my best Nelson Eddy manner.[*]

◆

A thunderstorm, followed by strong winds, brought down the temperature. That was yesterday. And today, June, it is cloudy, cool, drizzling a little, almost monsoon weather; but it is still too early for the real monsoon.

The birds are enjoying the cool weather. The green-backed tits cool their bottoms in the rainwater pool. A king crow flashes past, winging through the air like an arrow. On the wing, it snaps up a hovering dragonfly. The mynahs fetch crow feathers to line their nest in the eaves of the house. I am lying so still on the window seat that a tit alights on the sill within a few inches

---

[*]Not Nelson's song originally, but he sang it better than anyone else.

of my head. It snaps up a small dead moth before flying away.

Sir E is back. He found it too hot in the valley. Even up here he has given up wearing a necktie. I'll have him wearing a kurta and pyjamas before long; the only sensible dress in summer.

At dusk I sit at the window and watch the trees and listen to the wind as it makes light conversation in the leafy tops of the maples. A large bat flits in and out of the trees. The sky is just light enough to enable me to see the bat and the outlines of the taller trees. Up on Landour hill, the lights are just beginning to come on. It is deliciously cool, eight o'clock, a perfect summer's evening. Prem is singing to himself in the kitchen. His wife and sister are chattering beneath the walnut tree. Down the hill, a kakar is barking, alarmed perhaps by the presence of a leopard. All the birds have gone to sleep for the night. Even the cicadas are strangely silent. The wind grows stronger and the tall maples bow before it: the maple moves its slender branches slowly from side to side, the oak moves its branches up and down. It is darker now; more lights on Landour. The cry of the barking deer has grown fainter, more distant, and now I hear a cricket singing in the bushes. The stars are out, the wind grows chilly, it is time to close the window.

◆

Bijju is very much an outdoor boy, even when he isn't grazing cows. He isn't very strong in the chest, but his legs are sturdy; he was having no difficulty in scaling the high retaining wall. He grinned down at me. He is rather like the whistling thrush— absent for days, then unexpectedly reappearing in the forest or on the hillside. Bijju sings too, although his voice is more vigorous than melodic.

And that reminds me of the story of the whistling thrush. The bird was once a village boy who tried very hard to play the flute in the same style as the god Krishna. When the god heard his favourite melody being plagiarized, he was furious and turned the unfortunate boy into a bird. The whistling thrush still tries to copy the divine melody, but somehow it always breaks off right in the middle of a stanza. There ought to be a moral here, especially in a land full of plagiarists. Or to be fair, I should say film-land...

◆

The Whistler. This is my name for the youth who labours part-time in the school. He is something of a character—scatterbrained, carefree, easy-going. He is always whistling—loudly and quite tunefully (this time a bird turned into a boy?)—so that you know when he's coming round a bend or through the trees, and even when it's dark you know who it is. He's usually out quite late, because he spends all his money at the pictures. He has three sisters, and they and the mother are all working as maids or ayahs, and as they are quite indulgent to him (the only brother) he doesn't have to work too hard. His shoes are always torn, even though his clothes look new.

He has a reputation for being a waster, but he returned the few rupees he borrowed from me last month. I suppose a youth who is always singing and whistling on the roads gives everyone the impression that he has nothing to do from morn till night, unlike that jolly miller of Dee who worked *and* sang the whole day through. (I know one man who forbids his children from singing in the home.)

But back to the Whistler, he is really quite enterprising. The other day he asked me for one of my books, and as I knew he hadn't squandered too many years in school, I gave him an easy Hindi translation of one of my children's books. But it was the paper he valued, not the words. He flogged it to the bania's small son, who took it apart and converted the large pages into envelopes, which were then used for selling gram and peanuts. In India it doesn't take long for anything to be recycled. On the way home, I saw a couple of customers throwing their empty packets away, and these were promptly consumed by a stray cow. There went my beautiful story!

Is there a lesson to be learnt from this? Yes. Don't give away complimentaries.

◆

It rained all night, and the morning is cool and fresh. Parrots are on the wing. I feel like tap-dancing like Gene Kelly, but you can't tap dance on a hillside, you'd break an ankle. Only the roads (and not all of them) are suitable for a song-and-dance act, and no doubt the Whistler will oblige before long. At forty, I must refrain from being too frisky and boyish. But I'll do a reel in the garden when no one is looking.

◆

24 June

The first day of monsoon mist. And it's strange how all the birds fall silent as the mist comes climbing up the hill. Perhaps that's what makes the mist so melancholy; not only does it conceal the hills, it blankets them in silence too. Only an hour ago the trees were ringing with birdsong. And now the forest is deathly still, as though it were midnight.

Through the mist Bijju is calling to his sister. I can hear him running about on the hillside but I cannot see him.

Feeling sorry for Sir E (or maybe for myself), I walked over to see him. The door was closed, so I looked in at the French window (nothing could be more *English* than a French window, and no Agatha Christie mystery would be complete without one), I saw him sleeping in his chair with his chin on his chest. There was no dagger sticking out of his back, only a bit of stuffing from his old coat. My footsteps on the gravel woke him, and he got up and opened the door for me. He said he felt a bit tipsy; had taken his usual peg, but thought the quality of whisky varied from bottle to bottle, and wished he could lay his hands on a bottle of Scotch or even Irish. He could only offer me an Uttar Pradesh brand. I said I'd given up drinking, and this pleased him because in truth he hates anyone drinking his whisky; said he might give it up himself, it 'cost too damn much'! I told him it would be unwise to give up drinking at this stage of his life. As he had reached the age of eighty-six on two pegs a day, he was obviously thriving on it. Giving it up now would only play havoc with the orderly working of his system. I'd given it up in order to help an alcoholic friend abstain, and also because I wanted to give up *something*, and strong drink seemed the easiest thing to do without.

◆

A cicada starts up in the tree nearest my window seat. What has he been doing all these weeks, and why does he choose this particular moment and this particular evening to play the fiddle so loudly? The cicadas are late this year, the monsoon has been late. But soon the forest will be ringing with the sound of the cicadas—an orchestra constantly tuning up but never quite getting into tune—and the sound of the birds will be pushed into the background.

Outside the front door I found an elegant young praying mantis reclining on a leaf of the honeysuckle creeper. I say young because he hadn't grown to his full size, and was that very tender pale green which is the colour of a young mantis. They are light brown to begin with, like dry twigs, but as they grow older and the monsoon foliage becomes greener, they too change, and by mid-August they are dark green.

◆

As though to make up for lost time, the monsoon rains are now here with a vengeance. It has been pouring all day, and already the roof is leaking. But nothing dampens Prem's spirits. He is still singing love songs in the kitchen.

Kailash, whom I have known for a couple of weeks, asks me for twenty-five rupees.

'What do you need it for?' I ask.

'It's for my Sanskrit teacher,' he says. 'I have failed in Sanskrit but if I give the teacher twenty-five rupees he'll alter my marks. You see, I've passed in all the other subjects, but if I fail in Sanskrit I'll fail the entire exam and remain a pre-Inter student for another year.'

I took a little time to digest this information and ponder on the pitfalls of the examination system.

'He must be failing a lot of boys,' I said. 'Twenty-five rupees each! Are there many others?'

'Some. But he dare not fail the good ones. They can ask for a recheck. It's the borderline cases like me who give him a chance to make money.'

This placed me in a quandary. Should I yield to the evils of the examination system and provide the money for pass-marks? Or should I adopt a high moral stance and allow the boy to fail?

Whatever the evils of the exam system, they are not the fault of the student. And either way he isn't going to turn into a great Sanskrit scholar. So why be a hypocrite? I gave him the money.

Kailash slogs in his uncle's orchard all morning, gets a midday meal (no breakfast), and hasn't any shoes. And yet his uncle, a member of one of Garhwal's well-known upper-caste families, is a wealthy man.

Kailash tells me he will return to his village once he knows his result. According to him his uncle is such a miser that at mealtimes he pauses before each mouthful, wondering: 'Ought I to eat it? Or should I keep it for tomorrow?'

◆

I am visited by another kind of student, a small girl from one of the private schools. Her mother has brought her to me for my autograph.

'She studies your book in class six,' I was informed.

'And what book is that?' I asked the little girl.

'*Tom Sawyer*,' she replied promptly. So I signed for Mark Twain. When a small storeroom collapsed during the last heavy rains, I was forced to rescue a couple of old packing cases that had been left there for three or four years—since my arrival here, in fact. The contents were well soaked and most of it had to be thrown away—old manuscripts that had been obliterated, negatives that had got stuck together, gramophone records that had taken on strange shapes (dear 'Ink Spots', how will I ever listen to you again?*)... Unlike most writers, I have no compunction about throwing away work that hasn't quite come off, and I am sure there are a few critics who would prefer that I throw away the lot! Sentimental rubbish, no doubt. Well, we can't please everyone; and we can't preserve everything either. Time and the elements will take their toll.

But a couple of old diaries, kept in exercise books almost twenty years ago, had managed to survive the rain, and I put them out in the sun to dry, and then, almost unwillingly, started

---

*This was before the advent of audiotapes.

browsing through them. It was instructive, and sometimes a little disconcerting, to discover the sort of person I had been in my twenties. In some ways, no different from what I am today. In other ways, radically different. A diary is a useful tool for self-examination, particularly if both diary and diarist are still around after some years.

One particular entry caught my eye, and I reproduce it here without any alteration, because it represented my credo as a young writer, and it set me wondering if I had lived up to my own expectations. (Nobody else had any expectations of me!)

The entry was made on 19 January 1958, when I was living on my own in Dehradun:

> The things I do best are those things I do on my own, alone, of my own accord, without the advice or approval of others. Once I start doing what other people tell me to do, both my character and creativity take a dip. It is when I strike out on my own that I succeed best.
>
> There was a time when I was much younger and poorer than I am now. I had been over a year in Jersey, in the Channel Islands; I was unhappy, and the atmosphere in which I was writing was one of discouragement and disapproval. And that was why I wrote so well—because I was defiant! That was why I finished the only book I have finished so far. I had to prove to myself that I could do it.
>
> One night I was walking alone along the beach. There was a strong wind blowing, dashing the salt spray in my face, and the sea was crashing against the St Helier rocks. I told myself: I will go to London; I will take up a job; I will finish my book; I will find a publisher; I will save money and I will return to India, because I can be happier there than here.

And that was just what I did.

I had guts then.

What's more, I had an end in view.

The writing itself is not enough for me. Success and money are not enough. I had a little of both recently,[*] but they did not help me to do anything wonderful. I must have something to write for, just as I must have something to live for. And that's something I have yet to find.

There was more in that vein, but I give this excerpt as an example of a young man's determination to be a writer in what were then adverse circumstances. Thirty-five years later, I'm still trying.

◆

27 June

The rains have heralded the arrival of some seasonal visitors—a leopard; and several thousand leeches.

Yesterday afternoon the leopard lifted a dog from near the servants' quarters below the school. In the evening it attacked one of Bijju's cows but fled at the approach of Bijju's mother, who came screaming imprecations.

As for the leeches, I shall soon get used to a little bloodletting every day. Bijju's mother sat down in the shrubbery to relieve herself, and later discovered two fat black leeches feeding on her fair round bottom. I told her she could use one of the spare bathrooms downstairs. But she prefers the wide open spaces.

Other new arrivals are the scarlet minivets (the females are yellow), flitting silently among the leaves like brilliant jewels. No matter how leafy the trees, these brightly coloured birds cannot conceal themselves, although, by remaining absolutely silent,

---

[*]When *The Room on the Roof* was published (1956).

they sometimes contrive to go unnoticed. Along come a pair of drongos, unnecessarily aggressive, chasing the minivets away.

A tree creeper moves rapidly up the trunk of the oak tree, snapping up insects all the way. Now that the rains are here, there is no dearth of food for the insectivorous birds.

In spite of there being water in several places, the whistling thrush still comes to my pool. He, at least, is a permanent resident.

◆

Kailash has a round, cheerful face, only slightly marred by a swivel eye. His hair comes down over his forehead, hiding a deep scar. He is short, but quite compact and energetic. He chatters a good deal but in a general sort of way, and a response isn't obligatory.

It's quite possible that he will go away as soon as he gets his exam results. He's fed up with being the Cinderella of his uncle's house. He tells of how his miserly uncle went to see a rather permissive film, and was very shocked and wanted to walk out, but couldn't bear the thought of losing his ticket money; so he sat through the film with his eyes closed.

◆

Sir E departed for Dehra with his large retinue of servants and their dependants, all of whom would have done justice to an eighteenth-century nabob. 'I am at the mercy of my servants,' he told me the other day.

But he had placed himself at their mercy long ago, by setting himself up as a country squire surrounded by 'faithful retainers'—all of whom received generous salaries but did little or no work. If he sold his white elephant of a farm, he'd be quite comfortable with one servant.

'I'll probably come up in September, after the rains,' he said. 'If I live that long... I'm just living from day to day.'

'So am I,' I told him. 'It's the best way to live.'

◆

A couple of days passed before Kailash came to see me. I was beginning to wonder if he'd come again. Apparently the teacher had at first proved elusive; but the deed was done, and Kailash passed with the marks he needed. Ironically, his uncle was so impressed that he is now urging the boy to remain with him and complete the Intermediate exam.

'I must write a story about your uncle,' I remark.

'Don't give him a story', says Kailash. 'A short note will do.'

Now that Prem is preoccupied with his wife, and the house is at the mercy of uninvited visitors, I stay out most of the time, and these days Kailash is my only companion. Yesterday we took Camel's Back Road, past the cemetery. He chatters away, and I can listen if I want to, or think of other things if I don't want to listen; apparently it makes no difference to him. He is a cheerful soul, with an infectious laugh. He walks with a slight swagger, or roll. He says he doesn't mind staying here now that he has me for a friend; that he can put up with two sour uncles as long as he knows I'm around. I suspect he's quite capable of pulling a fast one on his uncle; but all the same, I find myself liking him.

◆

Moody. And when I'm moody I'm bad.

Prem says: 'It is easier to please God than it is to please you.'

'But God is easily pleased,' I respond. 'God makes absolutely no demands on us. We just imagine them.'

The eyes.

Prem's eyes have great gentleness in them.

His wife's eyes are round and mischievous and suggestive...

Suggestive enough to invite the attention of a mischievous or malignant spirit.

At about two in the morning I am awakened by Prem's shouts, muffled by rain. Shouting back that I am on my way, for it is obviously an emergency, I leap out of bed, grab an umbrella, dash outside and then down the stairs to his room. His wife is sobbing in bed. Whatever had possessed her has now gone away, and the crying is due more to Prem's ministrations—he exorcizes the ghost by thumping her on the head—than to the 'possession' itself. But there is no doubt that she is subject to hallucinatory or subconscious actions. It is not simply a hysterical fit. She walks in her sleep, moves restlessly from door to window, holds conversations with an invisible presence, and resists all efforts to bring her back to reality. When she comes out of the trance, she is quite normal.

This sort of thing is apparently quite common in the hills, where people believe it to be a ghost taking temporary possession of a human mind. It's happened to Prem's wife before, and it also happens to her brother, so it seems to run in families. It never happens to Prem, who deeply resents the interruption to his sleep.

I calm the girl and then make them bring their bedding upstairs. I give her a sleeping tablet and she is soon fast asleep.

During a lull in the rain, I hear a most hideous sound coming from the forest—a maniacal shrieking, followed by a mournful hooting. But Prem and his wife sleep through it all. The rain starts again, and the shrieking stops. Perhaps it's a hyena. Perhaps something else.

◆

A morning of bright sunshine, and the whistling thrush welcomes it with a burst of song. Where do the birds shelter when it rains? How does that frail butterfly survive the battering of strong winds and heavy raindrops? How do the snakes manage in their flooded holes?

I saw a bright green snake sunning itself on some rocks; no doubt waiting for its hole to dry out.

◆

In my vagrant days, ten to fifteen years ago (long before the hippies made vagrancy a commonplace), I was a great frequenter of tea shops, those dingy little shacks with a table and three chairs, a grimy tea kettle, and a cracked gramophone. Tea shops haven't changed much, and once again I find myself lingering in them, sometimes in company with Kailash, who, although he doesn't eat much, drinks a lot of tea.

One can sit all day in a tea shop and watch the world go by. Amazing the number of people who actually do this! And not all of them unemployed. The tea shop near the clock tower is ideal for this purpose. It is a busy part of the bazaar but the tea shop, though small, is gloomy within, and one can loll about unseen, observing everyone who passes by a few feet away in the sunlit (or rain-spattered) street. The tea itself is indifferent, the buns are stale, the boiled eggs have been peppered too liberally. Kailash is unusually quiet; there is no one else in the shop. People who would stop me in the road pass by without glancing into the murky interior. This is the ideal place; not as noble as my window opening into the trees, but familiar, reminiscent of days gone by in Dehra, when cares sat lightly upon me simply because I did not care at all. And now perhaps I have begun to care too much.

I gave Bijju a cake. He licked all the icing off it, only then did he eat the rest.

◆

It was a dark windy corner in Landour bazaar, but I always found the old man there, hunched up over the charcoal fire on which he roasted his peanuts. He'd been there for as long as I could remember, and he could be seen at almost any hour of the day or night. Summer or winter, he stayed close to his fire.

He was probably quite tall, but we never saw him standing up. One judged his height from his long, loose limbs. He was very thin, and the high cheekbones added to the tautness of his tightly stretched skin.

His peanuts were always fresh, crisp and hot. They were popular with the small boys who had a few paise to spend on their way to and from school, and with the patrons of the cinemas, many of whom made straight for the windy corner during intervals or when the show was over. On cold winter evenings, or misty monsoon days, there was always a demand for the old man's peanuts.

No one knew his name. No one had ever thought of asking him for it. One just took him for granted. He was as fixed a landmark as the clock tower or the old cherry tree that grew crookedly from the hillside. The tree was always being lopped; the clock often stopped. The peanut vendor seemed less perishable than the tree, more dependable than the clock.

He had no family, but in a way all the world was his family, because he was in continuous contact with people. And yet he was a remote sort of being; always polite, even to children, but never familiar. There is a distinction to be made between aloneness and loneliness. The peanut vendor was seldom alone; but he must have been lonely.

Summer nights he rolled himself up in a thin blanket and

slept on the ground, beside the dying embers of his fire. During the winter, he waited until the last show was over, before retiring to the rickshaw-coolies' shed where there was some protection from the biting wind.

Did he enjoy being alive? I wonder now. He was not a joyful person; but then, neither was he miserable. I should think he was a genuine stoic, one of those who do not attach overmuch importance to themselves, who are emotionally uninvolved, content with their limitations, their dark corners. I wanted to get to know the old man better, to sound him out on the immense questions involved in roasting peanuts all his life; but it's too late now. The last time I visited the bazaar the dark corner was deserted; the old man had vanished; the coolies had carried him down to the cremation ground.

'He died in his sleep,' said the tea-shop owner. 'He was very old.'

Very old. Sufficient reason to die.

But that corner is very empty, very dark, and whenever I pass it I am haunted by visions of the old peanut vendor, troubled by the questions I failed to ask; and I wonder if he was really as indifferent to life as he appeared to be.

◆

Prem brought his wife some of her favourite mangoes. This afternoon he took her into my room so that she could listen to the radio. They both fell asleep at opposite ends of the bed; are still asleep as I write this in the next room, at my window. If I curled up a little, I could fall asleep here on the window seat. Nothing would induce me to disturb those innocents; they look far too blissful in their slumbers.

◆

Kailash and I are caught in a storm and it's by far the worst storm of the year. To make matters worse, there is absolutely no shelter for a mile along the main road from the town. It was fierce, lashing rain, quite cold, whipping along on the wind from all angles. The road was soon a torrent of muddy water, as earth and stones came rushing down the hillsides. Our one umbrella was useless and was very nearly blown away. The cardboard carton in which we were carrying vegetables was soon reduced to pulp. We broke into a run, although we could hardly see our way. There were blinding flashes of lightning—is an umbrella a good or a bad conductor of electricity? Kailash sees humour in these situations and was in peals of laughter all the way home, even when we slid into a ditch.

He takes my hand and holds it between his hands. He is happy. He has got his self-confidence back, and can now deal with his uncles and Sanskrit teachers.

◆

In the morning I work on a story. There is a dove cooing in the garden. Now it is very quiet, the only sound is the distant tapping of a woodpecker. The trees are muffled in ferns and creepers. It is mid-monsoon.

Kailash, his hair falling in an untidy mop across his forehead, drags me out of the house and over the wet green grass on the hillside. I protest that I do not like leeches, so we make for the high rocks. He laughs, talks, chuckles, and when he grins his large front teeth make him look like a 1940s' Mickey Rooney. When he looks sullen (this happens when he talks about his uncle), he looks Brando-ish. He has the gift of being able to convey his effervescence to me. Am I, at thirty-eight, too old to be gambolling about on the hill slopes like a young colt? (Am I, sobering thought, going to be a character of enforced youthfulness like the man on the boat in *Death in Venice?* Well, better that than the Gissing hero of *New Grub Street* who's old at forty.) If I am fit enough to gambol, then I must gambol. If I can still climb a tree, then I must climb trees, instead of just watching them from my window. I was in such high spirits yesterday that I kept playing the clown, and I haven't done this in years. To walk in the rain was fun, and to get wet was fun, and to fall down was fun, and to get hurt was fun.

'Will it last?' asks Kailash.

'This feeling of love between us?'

'*This* won't last. Not in this way. But if something *like* it lasts, we should be happy.'

◆

Prem is happy, laughing, giggling all the time. Sometimes it is a little annoying for me, because he is obviously unaware of what is happening around him—such as the fact that part of the roof blew away in the storm—but I am a good Taoist, I say nothing, I wait for the right moment! Besides, it's a crime to interfere with anyone's happiness.

◆

Prem notices the roof is missing and scolds his wife for seeing too many pictures. 'She's seen ten pictures in two months. More than she'd seen in her whole life, before coming here.' She pulls a face. Says Prem: 'My grandfather will be here any day to take her home.'

'Then she can see pictures with your grandfather,' I venture. 'While we repair the roof.'

'I wouldn't go anywhere with that old man,' she says.

'Don't speak like that of my grandfather. Do you want a beating? Look at Binya'—we all look at Binya, who is perched very prettily on the wall—'she hasn't seen more than two pictures in her life!'

'I'll take her to the pictures,' I offer.

Binya gives me a radiant smile. She'd love to go to the pictures, but her mother won't allow it.

Prem relents and takes his wife to the pictures.

Binya's mother has a bad attack of hiccups. Serves her right, for stealing my walnuts and not letting me take Binya to the pictures.

In the evening I find Prem teaching his wife the alphabet, using the kitchen door as a blackboard. It is covered with chalk marks. Love is teaching your wife to read and write!

◆

These entries were made in 1973, twenty years ago.

The following year I did not keep a journal, but these are some of the things that happened:

Sir E had a stroke and, like a stranded whale, finally heaved his last breath. According to his wishes, he was cremated on his farm near Dehra.

To Prem and Chandra was born a son, Rakesh, who immediately stole my heart—and gave me many a sleepless night, for as a baby he cried lustily.

Kailash went into the army and disappeared from my life, as well as from his uncle's.

Bijju and Binya were to remain a part of the hillside for several years.